Rushing to Die

A Sorority Sisters Mystery

LINDSAY EMORY

WITNESS
IMPULSE

An Imprint of HarperCollinsPublishers

RUSHING TO DIE. Copyright © 2015 by Lindsay Emory. All rights reserved under International and Pan-American Copyright Conventions. By payment of the required fees, you have been granted the nonexclusive, nontransferable right to access and read the text of this e-book on screen. No part of this text may be reproduced, transmitted, downloaded, decompiled, reverse-engineered, or stored in or introduced into any information storage and retrieval system, in any form or by any means, whether electronic or mechanical, now known or hereafter invented, without the express written permission of HarperCollins e-books.

EPub Edition DECEMBER 2015 ISBN: 9780062418432

Print Edition ISBN: 9780062418425

10 9 8 7 6 5 4 3 2 1

This book is dedicated to Sonic Route 44's,
Taco Cabana queso and Spanx.
I couldn't have survived rush without you.

Acknowledgments

THIS BOOK COULD not have been written without the support of my agent, Cassie Hanjian, and my editor, Trish Daly. Much appreciation to Sara Schwager for her infinite patience and attention to detail that I do not possess, to Emily Homonoff, Angela Craft, and the rest of the HarperCollins team. Your enthusiasm for books and for Margot are truly a rush for this author (see what I did there?).

As always, a big cookie to my Ladies who Lunch, Alexandra Haughton and Ophelia London, without whom this book would have been ten thousand words shorter because I was tired and wanted to stop, and they scowled at me so I had to finish the last bit.

A million kisses to my family, my husband, and children, who love me when I'm writing and a little less when I'm editing.

Thanks to everyone who welcomed Margot Blythe and the Delta Betas into their hearts.

Margot is written with love and laughter, and thanks for sharing the love and laughs with me.

Disclaimer

All rush-related events, pranks, and shenanigans described in this book have been fictionalized. And the statute of limitations has run out as well.

Rushing to Die

Chapter One

SORORITY WOMEN ARE exceptional in many respects. Our average GPA is generally higher than that of non-Greek women. We are leaders on campus and, quite frankly, the world (just ask Madeleine Albright, Hillary Clinton, and Shonda Rhimes)[1]. We're trendsetters in fashion and social events, and we have unbelievable motor skills.

Exhibit A: the bounce and snap.

A classic staple of rush, this move consists of an entire chapter's bouncing and snapping in perfect synchronization, inspiring all who see it to be better people. Sorority women invented this choreography, along with the Ponytail Shake©, the Clap–n–Slide©, and the Weeble Wobble (Patent Pending).

All week long, the Sutton College chapter of Delta Beta had been practicing the bounce and snap along with their rendition of "Doncha Woncha Delta Beta," the stirring anthem that Delta Beta sorority rushees everywhere would have rattling in their pretty little highlighted heads.

But today, something was off.

1. Not sorority women themselves, but I'm sure they'd agree with me.

Okay. If I were being honest, something had been off for the past week. Even after all the rehearsals, the chapter still wasn't able to snap and bounce to the beat of the ditty (which, let's be real, was off tune). But I hadn't been able to inspire them to achieve bouncing greatness, let alone reliable snapping proficiency, because I was too busy doing what chapter advisors needed to do before sorority rush: i.e., everything.

The chapter had just started the song from the top (for the forty-fifth time), when there was a high-pitched squeal behind me. "Are you kidding me? Really? Are you freaking kidding me?" The squeal was bad enough. Coming out of a megaphone, it made dogs' ears perk up all the way in Charlotte. "You call that a bounce and snap? Mary Gerald Callahan would be ashamed of all of you!" The harsh words came from Ginnifer Martinelli, the Delta Beta sisterhood mentor assigned to help the chapter during rush. Bringing up Mary Gerald, the esteemed founder of our sorority, was tough talk, sure to make the ladies stop and think hard about their bouncing technique.

Three months ago, that would have been me, Margot Blythe, screaming through the megaphone. Well, no. I never used a megaphone while training sorority women; it's my opinion that whistles are far more effective at catching young women's attention.

"Margot!" Ginnifer screamed at me, and I could understand perfectly why the chapter was calling her "the Gineral" behind her back. Of course, I didn't think that was appropriate. "The Martinet" was my nickname of choice for her.

But in front of the chapter, the sisterhood mentor and the chapter advisor had to keep a united front, and Delta Beta headquarters had assured me that Ginnifer had the most impressive record at helping struggling chapters succeed at rush. As a collegian, she had served as rush chair three years in a row at the University of Alabama, and by all accounts had brought in the highest-ranked pledge classes each year—documented on several fraternity message boards, with pictures featuring a lot of swimwear.

While I was appreciative of the fact that Ginnifer took the job seriously, organizing rush was nothing compared to what I had to go through when I had returned to Sutton College as a sisterhood mentor. On my first night, the chapter advisor died right before our eyes, and this house was changed forever. We had done everything in our power to distance ourselves from that horrible memory. We had a chapter retreat, completely reworked our Web site, and had a lot of late-night bonding sessions over *Supernatural* marathons. But some things were harder to get over than others.

Not that the Sutton College Delta Beta chapter was struggling. Of course not. The Delta Beta national president had appointed me chapter advisor pro tem, and I wasn't going to let my sisterhood down. The fall GPAs were higher than they'd been in years, our table manners were unparalleled, and our local philanthropy was positively swamped in more hand-knotted fleece blankets than rescue cats could ever use.

I had devoted myself to ensuring that Sutton College Delta Betas were the smartest, classiest, cutest, best women on campus, all with an eye to one thing—RUSH. Delta Beta was always at the top of the Panhellenic pile, but this year we couldn't leave anything to chance. Not since the murders.

"Do it again!" The Gineral—I mean Ginnifer—yelled through her megaphone. "And this time, act like you know what you're doing!"

The sorority women filed out of the chapter room, their heads hanging low. There was some muttering, maybe a wet cheek or two, but I couldn't show mercy, not now. Rush started in three days; this was not the time to give someone a hug or an encouraging smile. This was life or death. Metaphorically speaking, of course.

We'd had enough of death here at Sutton College ever since two Delta Beta sisters had been murdered three months ago. But some people couldn't let it go. Like the press. Even though my best friend and public-relations genius Casey Kenner had tried to put a lid on the story, it had spread like an outbreak of mono after spring break. Then Nick Holden, the supertan former network morning-show host, used the story to get ratings for his struggling cable-news program.

The special report, titled THE REAL SCREAM QUEENS OF SUTTON COLLEGE had brought not only the continued attention of the press on us, but parents and administrators breathing down our necks to make sure the sorority environment was healthy, and their daughters were safe. Now the Delta Beta national president, Mabel Donahue, had even whispered that Nick Holden might have another special in the works.

Basically, this rush had to be perfect. We had to overcome our recent history and show the world that bids to Delta Beta didn't come on a toe tag.

"Can you believe them?" Ginnifer had sidled up next to me in the back of the chapter room. "They act like they haven't been practicing this since third grade."

"It'll come together." I tried to sound positive, but the Gineral had a point, as much as I hated to admit it. The chapter's snapping left a lot to be desired.

Ginnifer's mouth settled into a determined little line. "It will, or they'll deserve what's coming to them."

"That sounds a little harsh." I laughed a little even as my stomach felt like it was going to expel the contents of my three-shot three-Equal latte that I'd had for lunch. And the one I'd had for breakfast. And the two I'd had at last night's dinner.

She made a tsking sound. "You've grown soft since you've settled down here, Margot. You know as well as I do what this rush means. It's a brutal world out there. If the Sutton Debs can't make quota, they're as good as gone."

Maybe I had gotten closer to this group of women than any of the hundreds of other groups I'd worked with in six years of serving as a Delta Beta sisterhood mentor (longer than any other sister had ever served, I'd point out to Ms. Martinet if it didn't sound a little braggy.) But I could still be tough as nails and whip this chapter into prime snapping and perky bouncing and pitch-tastic singing shape.

"Gimme that," I muttered, as I yanked the megaphone out of the Gineral's hand. I'd show her the Generalissimo of Rush.

We heard the pitch pipe at the front door, and the chapter immediately launched into a three-part a cappella harmony. "We the girls of Delta Beta."

Then a nearly perfect cutoff. I couldn't see it from the chapter room, but I imagined the music chair's hand slicing through her throat before holding up one, two, three fingers and cueing the chapter to—

STOMP

STOMP

STOMP.

I lifted an eyebrow at Ginnifer. Their stomps had gotten as fierce as the finals of Ru Paul's Drag Race.

"WE ARE THE GIRLS."

A loud cry rose from the front door, the women half singing, half cheering at the top of their lungs. It was enough to convince any right-minded college-aged woman to sign up for an unbreakable bond of lifelong sisterhood.

"THE GIRLS OF DELTA BEE."

"WHO ARE THE GIRLS?" asked one-half of the chapter.

"WE ARE THE GIRLS—THE GIRLS OF DELTA BEE."

The sound roared down the hallway toward the chapter room, and, in an instant, I was an undergrad again, exhausted and spent, yelling my last ounce of voice in the general direction of fifty rushees, forcing all my love and devotion into the timeless classic.

The chapter filed in, filling the stage in the chapter room. I held my breath as the crucial part of the song began.

Snap. Snap. Snap.

"DONCHA WONCHA BE A DELTA BEE, TOO?"

Bounce snap.

"YOU KNOW YOU WANNA BE DONCHA WANNA BE . . ."

Bounce snap.

I watched the ladies carefully, willing them to be the best, the most perfect, the women that Mary Gerald Callahan and Leticia Baumgardner would be proud of, and I was happy . . . then.

Bounce.

No snap.

My face fell. My stomach churned. A group of three sophomores had dropped their snaps. Yes, their faces were red from screaming their little Deb hearts out. Yes, their bounces were sufficiently springy.

But.

We had no room for error. Not this rush. I picked up the megaphone. "Christopher! Berger! Prejean!"

Their faces paled. They knew they were in trouble when I used their surnames. "TAKE A LAP AROUND THE HOUSE AND THINK ABOUT WHAT YOU'RE DOING HERE."

I ignored the shame on their sweet red faces as they hurried outside. I handed the megaphone back to Ginnifer and ignored the conflicting emotions rising inside me. The panic was real. So was the compassion.

No. I loved this chapter too much. I had to do what was necessary to overcome the events of three months ago. WE had to do what was necessary.

My mind was in a better place as I retired to the chapter advisor's office to review, for the hundredth time, the Panhellenic rush manual. Everything was fine, I told myself. Even if we were a little tough on each other, a good rush would make everything better. No. It would make everything perfect.

I was in that happy place for about five minutes before three panicked sophomores rushed through my office door.

It was Berger who spoke first, flying through her words so fast, I couldn't process them for a moment. But then, they became horribly clear.

"Dead Deb," she huffed through strangled sobs. "Backyard."

Then everything fell apart. Again.

Chapter Two

THREE MONTHS' EXPERIENCE as a chapter advisor, combined with my deep and abiding love for my sisterhood, had prepared me, yet again, for this nightmare of a situation. The girls hadn't been over-reacting. There was a corpse in the middle of the frozen Delta Beta backyard, one with straight blond hair splayed in the dead grass, matted with dried brown blood. She was facedown, and even though I was normally a curious person, I was not touching the body to see if it was anyone I knew. I just couldn't face it. Not yet.

I made the dreaded call to 911. Delegating the chapter's care to Ginnifer, I hugged Christopher, Berger, and Prejean tightly and handed them off to Callie Campbell, the chapter standards and morals director, for hot chocolate. Then I went to wait at the street for the first responders.

The nightmare continued when two fire trucks, an ambulance, and two squad cars came blaring down sorority row, lights flashing. Could there be anything worse? Even if the dead woman was a hundred-year-old nun who died in the process of running a triathlon benefiting Ethiopian orphans, this was not a good look for our chapter. But I couldn't think about public relations or rush rumors or how the heck I was going to explain this to the Panhellenic Council, much less Deb HQ, just yet. Not until I after I dealt with the tall police officer crossing the street to talk to me with a grim, hard look on his face.

"Lieutenant Hatfield."

"You rang." He was not amused despite his sort of cute greeting. I burst into tears.

He let me cry for almost a full minute before he asked, "Where is the body?"

I wiped my nose. "Is that all you can think about? At a time like this?"

Hatfield leveled me with his no-nonsense blue stare. Okay, it came out wrong. But still. Even on *Law & Order*, they'd show a little compassion to the overwrought chapter advisor who had sent sisters outside for light punishment, only to have them stumble on a dead body.

I resolved to handle this like the professional I was. I knew the drill from experience, so I pointed out the location of the deceased and got out of the way while the police and EMTs did their thing.

After the initial photos and observations, Ty Hatfield knelt in front of me with his little pad of paper, just like Olivia Benson used. "What was her name?"

"Whose?"

Hatfield blinked slowly.

"Oh." I closed my eyes and recalled the body I'd looked at earlier, briefly. "I don't know."

Hatfield didn't believe me. "I couldn't see her face!" The woman had been facedown, in a sky-blue T-shirt and jeans. I ran my hands over the sleeves of my cardigan, thinking I should probably feel colder, sitting out in the parking lot on a January evening.

Ty frowned, then took a small digital camera out of his back pants pocket. He selected a photo and showed me the face of the woman I'd only seen from her lifeless back side. "Do you know her?"

The dead woman's eyes were wide open, frozen in shock, her complexion gray and waxy. I shivered, finally feeling the bite of the North Carolina winter wind. "No. Who is she?"

Not accepting that answer, Ty kept his arm outstretched, the camera still shining that frozen face in mine. "Are you sure?"

"Yes." I couldn't look anymore. I shifted my gaze back to the slightly-less-dangerous eyes of the handsome police lieutenant who had avoided me for the past three months.

This just wasn't fair. All of the chapter's hard work, all of our toil and strife, and it was all going to be for nothing because someone had to die a bloody and probably tragic death in our yard.

I pushed myself up off the ground and stood tall for my chapter. "I want a transfer!"

Ty followed me with a quizzical look. "What? Where are you going?"

"Not me! You!" I waved my finger around the rest of the Sutton town public-safety workers still hanging around the crime scene.

"You want *my* transfer? Why?"

"You're biased!" I knew my voice was raised, and I didn't care. It felt good. Positive, if slightly unprofessional. "And the rest of the town! I want new people out here. Who haven't already investigated a crime scene here."

"The town's not that big."

"This is not a laughing matter!" I gestured toward the sheet-covered gurney being wheeled by us.

"Of course it's not. What the hell do you take me for?"

I crossed my arms and thought briefly about how to put this. "What do you have?"

"Huh?"

"In the pool."

"Margot, I really don't know—"

"The 911 operator told me about the pool down at the station."

Now the police officer was the one getting caught out. Lieutenant Hatfield paused, awareness on his distractingly handsome face.

"It was probably not the best idea—"

I threw my hands up. "Probably? How do you think it makes me feel when I call 911 and the operator asks me if I could just wait another week to report a crime so he'd win fifty bucks?"

A muscle worked in Ty's hard jaw. "I'll definitely have a talk with someone . . ."

But I kept going, my voice rising hysterically. "It makes me feel bad, that's how it makes me feel. It makes me feel like no one in the community supports me or thinks that I can do my job—"

Ty's hand clamped around my shoulder and gave it a small shake. "Get a grip, Blythe. You've got an audience."

Filing out the side door was a bunch of girls, holding each other, blankets wrapped around their shoulders. Ty leaned over and spoke in a low voice. "You're right about one thing. I am biased. No one believes you can handle this more than I. But there's another dead body, and you're going to have to get it together, or else no one is going to be able to help you."

Out of the small crowd of Debs, a small, determined figure

marched toward us. Ginnifer was holding her megaphone, and from the fierce glint in her eye, I feared she'd use it to issue orders to the police—not always the best idea, in my experience.

"Have we got this straightened out yet?" she asked, skewering both of us with her stare.

Ty's face was back to his usual professionally blank expression. "Miss?"

Ginnifer thrust her hand toward him. "Miss Ginnifer Claire Martinelli. I'm the designated sisterhood mentor to the Sutton College Delta Beta chapter for the next ten days."

Ty shook her hand and glanced toward me. "Another one?"

"Margot is just the chapter advisor now. I'm the representative of headquarters," Ginnifer informed him. "Now. Can we go? We have work to do."

It took a lot to rattle Lieutenant Cool Hand Luke, but Ty looked taken aback.

"Take the girls inside, have them work on decorations," I said. Ginnifer looked like she was going to argue but gave a sharp nod and returned to round up the sisters. Hopefully, an hour or two of crafting and stringing tulle and twinkle lights would be sufficiently distracting from a fresh murder investigation.

I should have known it wouldn't be that easy.

"She was wearing a Deb shirt."

I had automatically gone into chapter-advisor and rush-preparation mode in my mind, running through the checklist of decorations that needed to be completed that night. "It's required for sisterhood mentors," I explained.

"No." His voice was low, almost gentle. "The DOA. She was wearing a Delta Beta T-shirt."

Because I was a *Law & Order* megafan, I understood the acro-

nym and who Ty was talking about. I didn't understand the rest
of it until he showed me another picture on his digital camera,
this one from farther away—showing that the DOA was indeed
wearing a sky-blue T-shirt imprinted with hot-pink Greek letters:
delta and beta.

And I still had no idea who she was.

"We'll have to ask the members then—"

"No!" I think I might have stomped my foot. These girls were
young, innocent, and identifying dead bodies was traumatizing.
Not only that, but they had a lot of twinkle lights to hang.

As usual, Ty Hatfield would not be moved by my arguments for
the best interest of the Delta Beta sisterhood.

"I'll give them a day or two," he relented. "But if we can't ID
her, we're going to need to bring some people in."

I nodded and thanked him for understanding. A day or two
wasn't much, but during rush, it was a lifetime.

Chapter Three

AN EIGHT O'CLOCK meeting on a Saturday is just inhumane—not only terribly unrealistic but a travesty of justice. I hurried into the Panhellenic offices of the Commons, the student center, on the Sutton College campus to find that of the eleven people invited to attend the meeting, ten people were already in the room.

Eight o'clock. A.M., people. Who does that?

Still, I lifted my chin, squared my shoulders, and smiled brightly at the other four Sutton College sorority chapter advisors, the new campus Panhellenic advisor, and the five women of the Sutton College Panhellenic Rush Council. "Long line at the coffee shop," I said by way of explanation, holding up my huge coffee tumbler emblazoned with the Delta Beta letters. (When you get a dozen extra-large triple-shot lattes a week, it's much kinder to the environment to use a personal cup.)

"Thank you for joining us, Margot. We were worried something had happened . . ." Louella Jackson's voice trailed off, leaving a thread of innuendo hanging in the air. I didn't bite. I knew what they wanted, and they weren't getting it from me. Not yet, anyway.

"Just needed coffee!" I said with a chipper air that I wasn't feeling yet. "You know how it is during work week."

Despite their lust for gossip, the other ten sorority women nodded in agreement. We might have been competing, but we could still commiserate. Work week required coffee. Lots of it.

"Let's get started then. We have a lot to go over," said the new Panhellenic advisor, Maya Rodman. She had been hired over the winter break, and no one knew much about her yet besides the basics: She had been a Kappa at Tulane, majored in international studies followed by a master's in educational counseling, and moved to New York. Also that she had a four-year-old daughter and a suspicious scar on her right eyebrow that some gossips believed was the remnant of an unwise piercing. I wasn't one to judge her for that, of course, but let's just say there are some very traditional sorority women at Sutton College, and the phrase "unfit to be a role model" might have been whispered over a glass of Chardonnay at the annual prerush advisor girls' night out.

Maya went over an agenda, and I had to admit, I was very impressed with her ability to read, let alone prepare an agenda, at this hour of the day. I silently sipped my coffee, waiting for the caffeine to do its heavenly magic. As the ladies droned on about quotas and late registrations, I slowly became more alert. There were a whole bunch of new rules this year about rush, and some of the other advisors were not happy with it. For my part, it didn't matter—the Debs were going to follow the rules, no matter what, or die trying. My million-item task list started zooming through my brain, and I itched to pick up a pen and make notes. But to do so here would be a bad idea.

Sorority rush is the single most cutthroat, competitive event in the world today. When sorority women heard about Tonya

Harding's arranging Nancy Kerrigan's knee injury with a lead pipe, they laughed and called her an amateur. Dance moms? They've got nothing on sorority moms, angling for their precious legacies to secure a bid. When Hillary Clinton talks about right-wing conspiracy, sorority women roll their eyes. They invented vast conspiracies to take down the powerful, the bold, and the beautiful. A sorority woman during rush is more vicious than a Taylor Swift breakup song, and just as pretty in red lipstick.

So me, writing down my rush to-do list here in a roomful of my competition? Well, it would just be admitting weakness—and inviting them to accidentally spill my coffee in my lap so they could get a look at my notes. And I was not willing to sacrifice my coffee. Not today.

Finally, Maya gave the floor over to the Rush Council. I knew most of them from my days as a collegiate member at Sutton College. Fifty years ago, there had been some sort of scandal during rush involving the not-at-all-impartial Panhellenic counselor giving the Epsilon Chis an extra five hundred dollars in their budget to fly the Beach Boys in for bid day. Since then, Sutton College rush has been presided over by a council of five women, an alumna of each of the houses. They were like the United Nations Security Council except way more powerful.

The five elderly women sat at a long table in front like oracles from on high, their wisdom and experience still clear in their eyes, in fine lines that, at eighty, even a great dermatologist couldn't erase. We defer to their every ruling, seek their approval in all things, and avoid their wrath like a chipped manicure. Behind their backs, we call them the Mafia because they rule sorority rush like Tony Soprano ruled trash pickup in the Garden State. We can do nothing without their say-so.

Patty Huntington, the Epsilon Chi member of the cabal, spoke first like a kindly grandmother. "Is everyone ready for Monday?"

The room's response was unanimous. We nodded and smiled with the appropriate blend of polite enthusiasm.

Clara-Jane Booth raised an eyebrow toward the Beta Gam chapter advisor. "We've been hearing some chatter about some interesting behavior."

Lucy, the Beta Gam advisor, ducked her head. Wuss. She should just own the fact that her chapter went out on the town last night. We all saw the shots on Instagram.

"I don't think anyone has to remind you of the standards that we expect from all the chapters here at Sutton," said Louella Jackson, the Delta Beta representative. She avoided looking my way. We have a complicated relationship going back to my sophomore year, because of my strong stand on free speech—specifically the chapter's right to include a Black Eyed Peas song in a rush skit. Suffice it say, she is not the biggest Fergie Ferg fan.

The four other members of the Mafia shook their heads gravely, then, as if on cue, they all did what Louella wouldn't. They stared pointedly at my end of the table.

This wasn't going to be good.

Alexandria Von Douton sniffed conspicuously. She hadn't changed at all in the past ten years, thanks to regular trips to a spa in the Swiss Alps, religious application of platinum dye to her classic French twist, and her (rumored) string of young Latin dance tutors. That was a Tri Mu for you. "With all the attention placed on Sutton College Panhellenic this year, we must all be doing our utmost to ensure everyone does her part to ensure that the media has no more fodder for its reprehensible programming. The administration is also going to be keeping a close eye on further misconduct. With that in mind, we will have a zero-tolerance policy on any and all rush infractions."

I tried to keep my face blank, as if I didn't know she was obliquely referring to my chapter and Nick Holden's special report. I firmly believe in the wise adage of, if you can't say anything true, don't say anything at all. My brief time in the Sutton city jail drove that message home.

The Tri Mu advisor, however, couldn't resist the chance to pile on.

"I so agree with everything you've all said." Sarah smiled at the Mafia. *Kiss ass.* "I want you to know that the Tri Mu chapter is absolutely, one hundred percent committed to having a classy, coordinated and, most importantly, crime-free rush."

Oh, Sarah McLane and I were going to have it out one of these days. I could see that trashy Tri Mu setting me up, but I would not—could not—let her goad me to public action. Private retaliation was another story.

Sarah continued, "Which is why we've arranged for Sheila De-Grasse to assist our chapter with rush this year."

My stomach dropped. No. It couldn't be.

The other advisors were having similar reactions given their sudden sharp gasps and nervous shifting in their seats. Even the Mafia looked discomfited at this bombshell dropping right in the middle of their meeting. Well, all of them except for Alexandria Von Douton. She had probably arranged the whole darn thing.

"Sheila DeGrasse?" Maya repeated the question in a slightly confused way, bless her heart. "Isn't she a rush consultant?"

"Yes," Lucy replied, looking mournful.

"She's very good at what she does." Sarah looked triumphant, and why not? She had Sheila DeGrasse on the Tri Mu side.

"She's legendary," Alexandria assured the room, as if we all (minus poor, clueless Maya) didn't know the international reputation of Sheila DeGrasse. She was the rush consultant with a flawless record for not only hitting quota with each pledge class but also filling each with girls as beautiful, rich, and mercenary as an entire clan of Kardashians.

"Thank you for the update," said Sue Barton, the Lambda leg of the Mafia, seemingly anxious to move on from the discussion of how Tri Mu had rush in the bag. "Anyone else have something they'd like to talk about?"

Sarah raised her hand. Hadn't she done enough? "I'd like to ask Margot about the presence of emergency vehicles at the Delta Beta house last night."

It was a fair question, but I resolved right then and there that Sheila DeGrasse or not, Sarah McLane and the rest of her Tri Mus were going down.

Chapter Four

"SHUT THE DOOR," I instructed the last person to enter the chapter advisor's office, now converted into the Rush Dungeon.

I stood behind the desk, piled with papers and pictures and miscellaneous peacock feathers (I didn't even know what for), and took a deep breath. These were my core team, the ones I had to trust if Delta Beta was going to pledge anyone this year.

Aubrey St. John, Callie Campbell, and Zoe were not at their personal best. Aubrey's perfect blond hair hadn't seen a curling iron in a week, Callie's mascara had rubbed off hours ago, and Zoe's T-shirt was rumpled and might have been slept in. But I knew these imperfections were because these three young women were devoting twenty-one hours a day to skit practice, decorations, and conversation development.

Yes. Conversation development. Where would we be as a society without a preplanned and approved list of riveting yet insightful conversation topics between nineteen-year-olds?

"Margot?" Aubrey's eyes were filled with concern. "What happened?"

"You're shaking," Callie pointed out.

"More like vibrating," Zoe said.

I held up a hand. Maybe there was a slight tremor there. But that was probably normal for someone who had gone through what I had in the past twenty-four hours.

"Where's the Martinet?" I asked.

"Who?" Callie asked.

"She means the Gineral," Aubrey explained. "And she's on the third floor, sewing the drapes for the skit."

"I thought Melissa was going to do that?" I asked, reaching for the massive to-do list in my rush binder.

"She was, but the Gineral said her seams weren't straight enough," Zoe answered with a tone that said exactly what she thought about Ginnifer's critique.

Notwithstanding the validity of Ginnifer's straight-seam judgment, this worked in our favor. I did not want Ginnifer in this meeting.

I gave a quick update to the girls about the Panhellenic meeting that morning. Aubrey covered her mouth. Zoe's hand went to her forehead as if she wanted to claw her frontal lobe out. Callie stayed ice-cold.

"Does this mean what I think it means?" Callie asked. As a fifth generation Delta Beta and direct descendant of one of our founders, Mary Gerald Callahan, Callie had grown up with Deb blood running through her veins. She understood the way the sorority world worked.

I nodded grimly.

"All because of this Sheila DeGrasse person? She's working for Tri Mu. We're really afraid of her?"

Zoe had a point. See, sororities were supposed to be supportive of each other, encourage the entire Greek community, blah-blah. Generally, Delta Beta was a prime example of this Panhellenic spirit except when it came to the sorority officially known as Mu Mu Mu. Or Tri Mu. Or their more appropriate nickname, the Moos. Tri Mu was our archenemy, for good reason. Namely, they were kind of trashy.

So, no. Generally, a Delta Beta woman is not intimidated by the Moos. It's like comparing a unicorn to a My Little Pony doll. Just because they both have four legs and a tail doesn't mean they're in the same class.

But this was Sheila DeGrasse we were talking about. I decided to lay it on the line, so that the ladies would understand. "Four years ago, I was visiting Immaculate Conception University during rush, in my official capacity as sisterhood mentor. Sheila DeGrasse was hired by the Lambda chapter, which then had twelve members, three of whom were pregnant and one of whom was facing a federal indictment. At the end of rush week, the Lambdas had grown to three hundred sisters, and the Miss Universe pageant director had asked for head shots of the pledge class."

"That's great for them and all, but—"

I cut Zoe off. "That's not all. During that rush, the entire Epsilon Chi chapter was hospitalized for food poisoning. The Tri Mus lost their hot water during rush week. And the Deb house got bedbugs."

Aubrey gasped and clenched at her shirt. I held up a calming hand. "We took care of them fairly quickly. There was a lot of hair spray used. And a sister's lighter."

Zoe shook her head. "So Sheila DeGrasse did all of that?"

I shrugged. "It could have been a coincidence. But do we want to find out what it's like not to have hot water?"

Three heads shook solemnly before me.

"I'm going to need your help, ladies. We had a hard enough challenge in front of us just trying to overcome the murders three months ago."

"But now we have another one," said Aubrey. Smart as a whip, that one.

"We don't know for sure."

"You said there was blood."

I lifted my hands. "Who knows how that happened?"

Zoe scratched her chin. "Are you saying it was an accident?"

"Anything's possible?"

"A stranger, dressed in a Delta Beta shirt, spontaneously dies of a head wound in our yard?" And sometimes Aubrey made too much sense for me.

"Look. I'm just saying, I'm not ready to give up. Now is not the time to think negatively. We need to be focusing on the positives." I tapped the papers in front of me. "Like all of these things that we haven't done yet."

The girls nodded, like I knew they would. They were dependable, hardworking Debs, and right now we needed to work our little hearts out if we wanted to have any advantage over the other chapters—especially Sheila DeGrasse and the Moos. I picked up the list and was about to start dividing tasks when I was interrupted by Callie.

"What about Plan B?"

"Callie, I don't think—"

"We came up with Plan B for a reason. And if Sheila DeGrasse isn't a good reason, I don't know what is."

I dropped the to-do list and considered what Callie was saying. Over the holiday break, Callie's family had graciously invited me and the rush team to their Richmond, Virginia, home. There, surrounded by Delta Beta historical memorabilia, Callie's mother and grandmother helped Callie, Aubrey, Zoe, and me formulate Plan B. It was top secret and very, very illegal. Well, illegal in a sorority sense. No actual laws of the state of North Carolina would be broken.

Aubrey looked doubtful, and Zoe seemed on the fence as well. Their expressions mirrored my own, I was sure. Things looked challenging but not quite devastating. "It's not time for Plan B."

"But we can't waste time—"

"We're not wasting time. We've worked hard, harder than any other house on Greek Row. We have Panhellenic, the Mafia, our alumnae, headquarters, everyone watching every step we take." I lowered my voice. "We have a sisterhood mentor in this house right now who, if you haven't noticed, is a little obsessed with following the rules. We will not break the rules, not until we absolutely have to."

"But—"

I cut Callie off again. She had to realize that I was the chapter advisor, albeit cute honorary older sister. I was calling the shots. "No. We're not talking about it anymore. We can still do this."

"Do what?" Ginnifer was standing in the doorway.

The girls leaped to attention, and I might have peed my pants a little. "This," I said quickly, picking up my to-do list and wondering how much Ginnifer had heard. If she knew what the girls and I had planned, she would go straight to headquarters, and President Mabel Donahue would have my pin, for sure.

Ginnifer nodded approvingly at the papers in my hand before barking, "Campbell, St. John, Witherspoon! You're dismissed!"

The three women could hardly argue with the authority in

the Gineral's orders, and I wondered if they'd ever listened to me with such respect and jump-to-it-ness. It seemed like I was always trying to "reason" with people or "explain" my actions. Maybe I could stand to incorporate a little of the Gineral's dictatorial style.

"Good job learning their names," I said, trying to give credit where credit was due. "When I visited chapters, I always had trouble learning so many names right away."

"It's easy for me." Ginnifer sniffed as she closed the office door. "How did the Panhellenic meeting go?"

I sank into my desk chair and briefly relayed all the updates again; the lower-than-usual registration numbers, the rule changes, the Sheila DeGrasse news.

Unlike everyone else in Sutton, the Gineral was not impressed with that last bit of news.

"Sheila DeGrasse," I repeated, more loudly this time, just in case Ginnifer's hearing had been damaged from the constant megaphone use.

Ginnifer shrugged. "She's a cheat. Everyone knows that."

"But she's a ruthless, malicious, bloodthirsty cheat."

"The way to beat her is to follow the rules." Ginnifer's eyes glinted dangerously. "We document every violation, every toe they put over the line, and if keep our hands clean, we won't have anything to worry about."

In my experience at Immaculate Conception University, following Panhellenic's rules hadn't saved the other houses, but it wasn't a point I was going to argue with Ginnifer.

"You're right." I nodded, sitting up in my chair. "We're going to rock this rush."

"Recruitment."

"What?"

"Recruitment. That's the appropriate terminology, approved by National Panhellenic in Volume 6, register 4.2 of the revised rules and regulations."

I was a bit put out. Of course I knew that, but, "No one calls it that, even the rushees—"

"Potential new members," chirped Ginnifer. "Please, if we don't use the right vocabulary . . ." Her words hung there, chiding me.

"Well, it's not like the rush police are going to come get us." I laughed, trying to make a joke. Really. Every real sorority woman used the traditional vocabulary, like "rush" and "rushee" and "pledge," and darned if we were going to let Panhellenic try to change us. We were sororities, for Leticia's sake. We were all about traditions.

Ginnifer sighed. "Recruitment, Margot. This is what I'm talking about. We can't let ourselves slip, not even for a moment. Don't you care about rescuing this chapter? After what happened three months ago, I'd think that you of all people would be trying to do what's right."

I hated being corrected by a twenty-two-year-old. Even more, I hated that she was probably right. I knew that the murders three months ago weren't my fault, but I still felt responsible, in some dysfunctional way that my high-school therapist would probably have a field day with. It probably had to do with my mother. Her guilt trips could be written up in scholarly journals and used as examples of how not to parent on the *Dr. Phil Show*.

"Have you heard anything?"

I shook my head, like I was trying to shake Mother's voice out of my ears. "About what?"

"About the . . . body." She whispered it, like there was a possibility our conversation was being recorded. Which, given the history of this office, wasn't the craziest fear.

"No," I replied. "It's been less than twelve hours." Hopefully, the county medical examiner had determined that the girl had a rare condition that caused her head to explode. I'm sure I've heard of those on TLC shows. Unfortunately, the event had happened in our backyard, while she was wearing a Delta Beta T-shirt . . .

Ginnifer must have seen the look on my face. "Are you worried? You're worried. You can't be worried."

Something about the way those three phrases came out made me look closer at the heretofore unflappable, stern martinet. A little more flappy, a little less stern, Ginnifer's breath had quickened, and she was waiting for my response, as if I were about to tell her my secret to a poreless complexion.

I wasn't ready to admit I was worried. Not to Callie, Zoe, and Aubrey, and certainly not to the Gineral. She might be an alumna sisterhood mentor, but she was only twenty-two, and I had to set a good example for her.

"Of course I'm not worried."

Ginnifer's shoulders relaxed a little when I said that. "No. Of course you're not. We're not," she added. "We have to be a team, Margot." Ginnifer's voice was stern yet filled with sincerity. Even though she was tougher, meaner, and scarier than I, I knew it was coming from a good place. Down in her heart, she loved Delta Beta just as I did. "You and I, together. We cannot let this chapter down."

"Of course we won't," I promised her. Letting Delta Beta down was never an option. Not for me.

Chapter Five

THERE WAS A short knock on the doorframe. Ginnifer spun around and gasped in horror. "Excuse me!" Ginnifer's voice was shrill. "There are no men allowed in this part of the Deb house."

I looked around her and had to agree with the horror. Brice Concannon, the fraternity-council advisor, stood there looking as cute and preppy as ever. Too bad he was a misogynist weirdo who didn't think there was anything wrong with slipping sorority girls roofies, or so he'd told me a few months ago while he was trying to get me to go out with him. To his surprise, my answer was no.

"Margot," he said with a superwhite smile. "I was hoping I'd catch you."

"You need to leave," Ginnifer said. "Or didn't you hear me?"

"You must not know me. I'm Brice Concannon. I'm with President Desper's office."

Ugh. He was so gross. "He's actually the Interfraternity Council advisor," I told Ginnifer. "And I'm assuming he's here on official business?"

"Of course."

Darn. If he were here on personal business, I'd have happily let Ginnifer employ her Alabama kung fu and throw him out.

"He can stay," I told Ginnifer. "But leave the door open."

After Ginnifer left, Brice came in the office without an invitation. I crossed my arms. "What can I help you with?"

"I just came from the president's office."

"How exciting for you."

"We had a special guest." Brice paused, waiting for me to ask, but he couldn't help himself from explaining. "Nick Holden. From ITV."

Crap. I shut the door behind me. This was not what the women inside needed to hear tonight. "What did Nick Holden want?" I asked. One never knew. Maybe the reporter was doing an investigative report on the theater department's groundbreaking production of *Guys and Dolls*, starring guys as dolls and dolls as guys. Those theater nerds could really make you think about social issues in a new way.

Brice looked downright regretful. "He's doing a follow-up, prime-time special. This time, the college is participating."

My cheeks got hot in the chilly air. "What for?"

"There's been another death, and during sorority recruitment, too," Brice responded solemnly. "The college has to take this seriously. The special was already in the works and he was already in town conducting interviews with students and staff. When the president found out about the chick kicking the bucket he invited Nick—and me—in to talk."

Brice patted my arm. Somehow he'd slid closer to me without my gagging. "Don't worry, Margot. I'm here for you."

Ew.

"Am I interrupting something?" Thank God. I jumped back

from Brice's cologne-scented personal space and nearly bumped into Lieutenant Hatfield.

"Brice was just leaving," I said hurriedly. To Brice, I said, "Police stuff. It's privileged," and tried to ignore the amused crinkle of Ty's eyes when I added that.

"Lieutenant Hatfield," Brice greeted Ty. "I've left five messages for you. President Desper has appointed me again to keep him updated on the police investigation. As a liaison, if you will." Gah. The man pronounced liaison like he was in a French movie.

"Then I'll be sure to give you an update when I have one."

That took the wind out of Brice's sails. Since he couldn't force Ty to update him, he focused back on me. "Nick wants to meet you."

That was not going to happen. "I'm really busy this week," I said.

"It's rush week," Ty added.

I did a double take at Ty. Brice said to me, "He's interviewing someone named Sheila DeGrasse first—"

"I'll be there," I said.

"I'll send you the details," Brice said with a smarmy grin, and made his exit, leaving me with a suspicious cop.

"Who's Nick?"

"Nick is Nick Holden, the former host of *Have A Super Day USA*. The one who did the special on us."

Ty looked annoyed. "He misquoted me."

"He's awful," I agreed. "And apparently he's back and doing another special. Just our luck that someone had to go and die."

Ty looked troubled; I knew national-media attention on his investigation was a major pain in his rear. So I thought I'd cheer him up.

"You look nice today," I said. And he did—nice and cozy, wearing a black parka with the Sutton Police Department logo.

"That's not what the guard dog down the hall said to me."

It was an easy guess. Ginnifer. "She's trying to keep us in line."

"Now why would she think we need a chaperone?"

Something fluttered in my chest. "Not us. I mean, she's trying to keep the chapter in line."

Ty scratched below his ear, but it didn't hide the interested light in his eyes. "Sure it's not because she's afraid for your virtue?"

I rolled my eyes. "Please don't egg her on. She's doing a great job for Delta Beta."

"I would never tease an official Delta Beta representative. I've learned that one the hard way."

His delivery was so dry, I didn't know what to make of the comment, so I decided to let it go. After all, it would be nice if sorority officials finally got the equal treatment we deserve from local law enforcement. It is our civil right not to be discriminated against based on the Greek letters on our chest.

Speaking of which, I pulled back my shoulders and tried to look as professional as I could while dressed in a monogrammed North Face fleece and Lululemon yoga pants. It was T minus two days to rush; I couldn't be expected to be fashion-blog-worthy at this stage of the game.

But, of course, Ty Hatfield noticed everything. "What happened to your hair, by the way?"

A self-conscious hand went to the side of my head. "Highlights. For rush." I dropped my hand and changed the subject, second-guessing my new blond streaks all of a sudden. "Is there something we needed to discuss?"

Ty stared at my hair for another half second before shaking

his head a little. "We haven't been able to identify the DOA from yesterday."

"Why?"

"She didn't have identification on her. Just a set of car keys and these." Ty reached into his pocket and withdrew a plastic baggie with a pair of eyeglasses in it.

"Did you get any prints?" I asked, completely familiar with the lingo after being involved in the last two murder investigations involving this sorority house.

"Just hers. And she hasn't come up in any searches."

Don't say it, don't say it. I prayed and kept my face blank and my mouth zipped. I was not going to make this easy for him.

There was a pause, like he was waiting for me, but I was not walking into this one. "So, if you're available this afternoon . . ."

"Excuse me?"

"Since it's Saturday, I thought you could come down to the station and—"

"Oh. Since it's Saturday, and I *obviously* don't have anything better to do, is that what you're saying?"

"Well, this is a murder investigation, Margot. I'm trying to be respectful here."

I threw up my hands. "Rush starts in two days! *Two* days!" I knew I was coming close to making a very unladylike screeching sound, but I was beyond reason. "What do you think I'm doing with my time? Spending a relaxing Saturday afternoon watching *Law & Order* reruns and Internet shopping?" He opened his mouth, and I held a finger out. "Do NOT answer that."

"We're going to need to see if anyone recognizes her."

"You want to call my chapter members down? Do you have any idea how much needs to be done?" I picked up the four-inch-thick rush binder and let it fall to the desk in a loud smack. "DO YOU?"

"Margot." Ty's voice was low and authoritative; and then he was in front of me, taking me by the shoulders. "Breathe."

But I found that breathing was difficult, and the air I was taking in wasn't filling my lungs completely.

"You're shaking. Vibrating." Ty's hand went to the back of my head and forced me to look into his eyes. "When was the last time you ate."

"I had a latte this morning," I managed to say.

"Okay, but when did you eat last?"

This man had no clue. I didn't have time for chewing. Or breathing, for that matter.

"You have to take care of yourself," he said. Ty Hatfield was never going to understand me or my work. I was not here on this planet to take care of me.

"I have a job to do," I muttered shakily.

He pulled back and studied me. "So do I. Which is why you and the members of this chapter are coming down to the station at four this afternoon to identify the body."

"But—"

Ty cut off my protest. "I'm compromising, and this is all you're going to get. You can schedule an hour out of your day so that that girl's family can know where she is."

Of course, he was right. Just because I didn't know this person didn't mean somebody else didn't love her and want her at home. Feeling suddenly exhausted and ashamed, I nodded, keeping my face low to hide my embarrassment. Taking an hour out of rush prep wasn't the end of the world. Maybe we could even bring some work with us; after all, Delta Betas had invented multitasking. It was in our Wikipedia entry.

"What if none of us recognizes her?"

Ty looked grim. "We'll figure something out." His grip tightened on the plastic bag in his hand.

"You have car keys," I pointed out. He didn't seem to understand what I was saying. "Was there a fob? What kind of car is it?"

"Why?" he asked, a sudden suspicion in his eyes.

I shrugged. "Maybe it's a stupid idea. It's not like you could go around town pointing a key chain at every Toyota or Chevrolet to see which car alarm goes off."

"Do you know what goes into being a cop? You think I have time to go around town clicking at random cars?" He looked down at the plastic bag with the glasses, then back up at me. "I hope one of your girls knows who she is."

After Ty had gone, I wondered. Was it in the chapter's best interest to identify this mystery woman? At the thought, a rush of shame washed over me again. In everything I did, I tried to exemplify the standards that our esteemed founders, Leticia Baumgardner and Mary Gerald Callahan, had established for the sisters of Delta Beta. Two days before rush, I just wasn't sure whether they'd want me to help the police investigate a murder that could totally derail our chapter—or support my sisters in kicking some serious Tri Mu butt.

Chapter Six

SUTTON COLLEGE RUSH was at the beginning of the spring semester, right at the end of winter break—timing that had been a source of despair and dismay for many sorority alumnae for years. The common name for this practice is "deferred rush" and is generally only something that Greek systems do when they don't take themselves seriously and want freshmen to focus on things like "getting used to college" and "grades." Which, I mean, come on.

As an undergraduate at Sutton, I had heard stories of the glory days: when rush took place in the heat of early September, rushees would spend all summer planning their outfits, carefully cultivating their tans, and pass out from lack of hydration while standing in line outside the houses on Greek Row. But sometime during the 1970s, some do-gooder feminist decided that this system turned women into "commodities." The Sutton College Panhellenic moved rush to winter, so that sorority women would get to know the freshmen on campus and around town, and when rush came around, they would be choosing sisters based on their personalities and not their sartorial choices.

Well, that happened sometimes.

Of course, it sounds like a great idea. I am a proponent of making friends and choosing sisters based on substance, not style. But deferred rush brings its own set of unique challenges—winter in North Carolina, for one. It can be extremely difficult to find cute Lilly Pulitzer shift dresses that also have thinsulate in them. And no one wants to wear tights with their peep-toe Tory Burch wedges. It ruins the whole look.

Deferred rush also makes the fall semester much more stressful for the rushees. Instead of enjoying their first semester of college joyfully embraced by their new sisterhood, bonding over fun hazing and illegal keg parties, they're watching every step they take in their shiny new Hunter boots, worried they will accidentally ruin their chances at pledging a new house in January.

That's why I invested so much of my personal energy into rush. It wasn't just about making my chapter stronger. It was about giving all these young, hopeful women their futures so bright in their Ray-Ban shades, the time of their lives. Rush is a pivotal moment for every sorority-woman-to-be: the last week of their sad, sister-free lives, their chance to fully consider their options and learn just where they fit into the societal structure of Sutton College Greek life. Were they Delta Beta material? Or did they want to follow in their unfortunate older sister's footsteps to Lambda—or even worse, Tri Mu?

These were life-changing times for the rushees. And it was just as important on the inside of the sorority house. This week was the chapter's chance to show its best, most stylish, most rhythmic, most cheerful sides. This week we had the opportunity to select the women we would be pledging ourselves to for a lifetime. If that didn't deserve two weeks of sleepless self-destruction, what did?

All of the rush events would take place on the grand, elegant first floor of the house, with a huge, curved staircase into the front hall. Each day, a different banner would be hung from the stairwell, welcoming the rushees with an eye-catching yet classy slogan and hand-painted artwork. They would be ushered into the house to the sound of foot stomping, clapping, and screaming— instantly making each woman feel at home. Then they would be "picked up" by a sister wearing an outfit that coordinated with the group, with chapter-approved hair, makeup, and nails, and led away to quietly discuss prescribed conversation topics. This was a finely tuned, highly specific process that really showed how unique we were opposed to chapters.

So here we were, a mere twenty-two hours before the first set of potential new sisters walked through our front door, and the Delta Beta house was in organized yet frantic chaos. There was a crew of sisters in the dining room painting signs and banners, a cadre of girls singing around the baby grand piano, another squad practicing dance moves on the chapter-room stage. I had to give it to Ginnifer, she was a real help. My four-inch-thick rush binder in my arms felt a little lighter at the sights around me, and I started to see the light at the end of tunnel. Maybe we were going to pull this off, after all. Sometimes, college students just needed some verbal abuse in order to produce their best efforts.

I was helping the decorations committee with a three-foot pile of tissue paper that needed to be crafted into massive, glitter-encrusted chrysanthemums, my hands full with about sixty sheets of black-and-gold tissue, when Asha, the social director, called my name. "There's someone to see you."

When I heard who it was, the sheets were quickly thrown to the floor.

"You didn't let her in, did you?" I asked Asha under my breath. Asha, like the wise and experienced senior she was, shook her head fervently.

"No! She's in the atrium."

The atrium was our fancy word for the huge tent we had set up directly off our front porch. Years ago, our chapter advisor had the brilliant idea to provide the rushees with warmth and shelter from the January weather while waiting at our house.

That was my senior year, and we kept the plan hush-hush. The first day of rush, it was sleeting and thirty-eight degrees; when our tent went up, complete with space heaters and cozy blankets provided in the Delta Beta signature colors of black and gold, let's just say we were the most popular house on the block—with the rushees. The other houses ranted and raved about unfair advantage as they scrambled to rent tents. Unfortunately for them, we had a very generous alumna who had put deposits on every large party tent in a fifty-mile radius; and there were no Panhellenic rules specifically proscribing chapters from providing rushees heat and shelter.

The next year, Panhellenic rules changed to require tents at all houses.

This was the name of the game. Every time you thought you had an advantage, someone tried to knock it out of your hand or create an even playing field. So we played smarter, quicker. Some played dirtier.

Like the woman standing in the atrium waiting for me. Sheila DeGrasse.

In the years since I'd last seen her, she hadn't changed much. She was like a Barbie doll, if Barbie had a six-foot-tall wicked stepsister with double Ds and killer Manolo Blahniks. And even though I knew she was evil incarnate, I still felt self-conscious in my fleece and yoga pants next to her sharp black pantsuit, with a pale pink and orange silk scarf knotted precisely at her neck.

"Hello. Miss . . . ?" It was petty, but pretending I didn't know who she was gave me that little dash of confidence.

She pursed her demon-red lips in amusement. "Sheila De-Grasse," she said, dripping smugness. She extended her hand. "I asked for the chapter advisor. I had no idea I'd find *you*."

I ignored her hand. Looked like we weren't going to pretend to be civil, after all. "Yes. I'm the chapter advisor. How can I help you?"

"I thought I'd heard you were the mentor for Delta Beta headquarters, traveling the country. And now you're babysitting a bunch of schoolgirls who can't seem to keep their collective nose out of trouble. Is this a . . . demotion?"

I had to laugh. There was no such thing as a demotion in my world. Margot Blythe didn't get demoted, she was only asked to showcase alternative talents. "Assisting Delta Betas in any capacity is better than selling myself to the highest bidder—with the lowest standards."

Sheila smacked a hand against her chest, but that Joker-like grin widened across her too-tan-for-January complexion. "Oh, Margot, you were always so cute. With your standards and your loyalty and your . . . original nose."

I resisted the impulse to check my crooked Blythe nose. "Did you come here for something, or did you just miss being in the presence of greatness?" I spread my arms to gesture at the tent, wishing we'd hung our cute banner with our Greek letters and our sorority flower, the yellow rose.

Sheila crinkled her nose at me, her smile as perky and hard as her boobs. "I'm going around the block introducing myself. I thought everyone should be able to put a face with the legend."

This time I couldn't help but roll my eyes. Sweet Leticia, help me. Before I could come back with a sassy comeback about what, exactly, kinds of legends I'd heard about her, she continued. "I kept you for last, you know. I wasn't sure about how to deal with the crime-scene tape and all."

A chill raced through my North Face jacket, as if it wasn't the finest recycled plastic money could buy. Sheila smelled blood in the water.

I spread my arms again. "As you can see, we're open for business."

"What about the—"

"It's a police matter. Confidential. I'm sure you understand."

For the first time, Sheila DeGrasse flinched. Her smile was glossy and as red as ever. Confidence oozed like slick La Mer hand cream. But there was a flicker of something in her eyes, a momentary glitch in the Matrix, that chilled me to the bone.

She recovered so quickly, nodding knowledgeably, that I couldn't be sure what I'd seen. "The police. Of course. Well, I guess you're used to that, with the murderous rampages your sisters like to go on from time to time."

I could handle Sheila's making snide remarks about me and my nose, but talking trash about my sisters brought out the inner Hope Solo in me. I made an obvious show of checking my Michael Kors watch. "Oh, look at that. My allotted time for sellouts talking smack is all up. I hope you understand."

Sheila crossed her arms as the smile melted off her face. "I thought we could be friends, Margot. I was here to offer support. We can be on the same side. We're kind of alike, you and I."

The nerve. I drew myself up, threw my shoulders back, and looked her up and down like I smelled something nasty. "No, we're not. I'm silicone-free and proud of it."

With that zinger, I twirled around on my sneakers like they were four-inch Manolos and marched straight back into my Delta Beta home.

The words of Sheila DeGrasse haunted me through the next hour. We were nothing alike. Sheila DeGrasse was a legend, yes, but only because she played dirty and sold herself out to whatever chapter paid her ridiculous rates during rush season. I didn't even know what sorority she was a member of, if she'd ever pledged at all. I couldn't imagine that any organization worthy of Panhellenic status would extend a bid to someone who mocked everything our sisterhoods stood for. Except maybe the Tri Mus she was helping—further proof that Sheila and I were as different as Blair and Serena.

Chapter Seven

SINCE I HAD some free time, I hunkered down in my small apartment, near the front door of the house, to try to get some financial reports for headquarters finished. Getting out of the Rush Dungeon had a positive effect on my productivity, and I was almost done with the triplicate Form 1872 when there was a knock at my door.

Usually, a knock at my door meant there was some kind of drama or emergency that required the diplomatic and leadership skills of a chapter advisor—but instead, I had received a delivery. I took one look at the large, beautifully presented gift basket and knew immediately who it was from. My best friend in the whole wide world, Casey Kenner.

"CASEY!" I squealed when he picked up. "You shouldn't have!"

"Girl, of course I should have. You totally deserve it."

Casey was not only my best friend, but also my best friend at Delta Beta headquarters. Yes, he's a man. But he's Delta Beta to his core, thanks to the proper instruction he received at a young age from his mama, his sisters, and his mama's mama. (His daddy's mama was a Tri Mu, but thankfully, she wasn't around much when he was a boy and couldn't lead him astray.) He serves the sisterhood as director of public relations—he got the interview because of his unisex name but got the job because he's the Delta Beta total package: classy, cheerful, and color-coordinated.

I started untying the gigantic yellow-and-black bow holding the cellophane wrapper. "It's not even my birthday," I said, unable to keep the smile off my face.

"It's just a little rush care package. You've done so much for that chapter, I thought you should have something for you."

I waved at my face a little. He was going to make me cry, and he wasn't even here. "Where are you, anyway?"

Casey's sigh was loud and clear. "I'm at the University of Texas chapter."

Wow. For Casey to leave headquarters in Atlanta and visit a chapter meant a huge crisis was in the making —like when he'd visited here three months ago because the chapter advisor was murdered. "What did they do?" I asked in a scandalized voice.

Now Casey lowered his voice. "A stupid idea for a date dash."

A date dash was a fun, impromptu social event where the ladies were given short notice to run out, grab a date, then meet up for a party at a club or for a fun activity, like bowling. In my mind, it was the pinnacle of the social calendar.

"How could anyone mess up a date dash?" I wondered aloud. It was inconceivable.

"They had a theme. They called it a Mexican roundup. They dressed up as immigration officers."

They didn't . . . Ugh. I felt sick to my stomach. "You sure it was Debs?" I asked, grasping at straws. Maybe someone had put them up to it.

From the hesitation in his voice, I could tell Casey didn't want to believe it either. "We're going to spin it as a social-awareness experiment."

"Oh. Well . . ." My voice trailed off as I tried to be encouraging. "At least you've got a plan!"

"Yeah." Casey was glum, then brightened. "But I have one chapter I don't have to worry about. I don't know if I've told you, but headquarters is so psyched about your being in charge there at Sutton. You've done such an amazing job, hardly anyone remembers the scandal."

Then I remembered the news that I hadn't told Casey . . . the part about the dead woman in our backyard. Alternately ignoring it and telling myself it didn't matter, I hadn't called headquarters to report it. Even during the last five minutes, caught up in the joy of talking to my best friend and savoring his presents, I hadn't spared a thought for the great black threat that hung over this chapter. Again.

Could I do it? Should I? Should I tell Casey and headquarters and send them all into hysterics again? And what if they lost their trust in me? There would be no more sweet care packages. No more encouraging phone calls and uplifting notes on stationary monogrammed with the Delta Beta crest.

This time, no one would count on Margot Blythe to save the Deb chapter. This time, they'd install a new sister. One who could avoid death and mayhem.

I flipped open the card that was signed, "DEB LOVE" and listened as Casey rattled on about the men in Austin. The combination of hipster beards and tight cowboy jeans was apparently exciting to some. Finally, I blurted out: "So someone might have died in the backyard."

Casey paused. "Might have?"

"Yeah, they pretty much died."

"Anyone we know?"

"No," I said definitively. I told Casey about the situation and the fact that I hadn't recognized the DOA.

Which seemed to relieve his worries until he asked, "You haven't heard from Nick Holden, have you?"

"No, not technically." I relayed my conversation with Brice about Holden's worming his way into Sutton to prepare for a follow-up news story.

Casey swore elegantly. "I have a friend in New York who mentioned something about the network's wanting another exposé on sororities. I can't believe they're doing it now."

I fingered the edge of the basket's cellophane wrapping. Another Nick Holden antisorority special report would undo everything we'd been working for. The Sutton College administration would have a fit, and the people who thought sororities were awful would have a truckload of ammo.

"Why did I agree to talk to him?" I moaned to Casey. "I have a trillion and one things to do. I don't have time to aid and abet the enemy."

"You did the right thing," Casey assured me. "You can't let his only contact with sorority life be a sit-down with Sheila DeGrasse. He'd think we were all insane!"

"True."

"And anyway . . ." Casey's voice turned thoughtfully sly. "Who said you had to help Nick Holden?"

"No one, but I said I would talk to him."

Casey chuckled. "Yes, but you don't have to give him what he wants. We've had this conversation before."

Yes, we had. It was Casey's favorite topic to discuss before any date I had, along with how to keep my skin dewy, not oily, under stress.

"Flip the script on him. Use it as an opportunity to promote Delta Beta, and when he asks a tricky question—"

"Give him a Miss America answer," I finished.

"You got this," Casey affirmed. "And get his number, so I can follow up with him."

As always, Casey was supersmart about all things. After being friends for so many years, why hadn't I remembered that he could solve basically all my problems with some good advice and a beautiful gift basket.

"I really love the basket," I told him again, wanting to move on from depressing talk about reporters who wanted to libel my chapter.

"I wanted to get you all the things you needed for rush. Do you love it?"

I pulled out a small envelope with the distinctive green mermaid logo on it. "You know I love my Starbucks." And it wasn't just a coffee-shop gift card. There were chocolate-covered coffee beans, several bottles of 5 Hour Energy, and a box of organic No Doz.

"It's herbal," Casey explained when I commented on the meds. "Nothing to worry about there."

There was a miniature measuring tape, a box of Band-Aids, a tin of extrastrong mints (handy after copious amounts of caffeine), an extra phone charger, three cute Delta-Beta-themed hair ties, and a mysterious black canister.

"Is this . . ." I paused. It wasn't hair spray. "Is this MACE?"

Casey sighed. "Pepper spray. I'm pretty sure Mace is illegal."

The canister felt heavier than it should have been in my palm. "Why did you get me pepper spray?"

"Just in case. You never know; remember what happened that year at Tulane?" A creepy old man had hidden in the bushes during the sorority parties and exposed himself, having his own little Mardi Gras celebration. But surely, deviants weren't around here, at Sutton College.

Or were they? I gently pressed a thumb on the trigger of the pepper spray. When the time came, I would be ready, for whatever happened.

Chapter Eight

GINNIFER SHOUTED A warning over the megaphone, and I glanced at my watch. It was time for our afternoon sisterhood-bonding session, as important as stringing twinkle lights and painting the giant wooden letters that would grace our front lawn during rush. The plan was a coffee break and catching up on the latest episode of *Grey's Anatomy*, but as I walked into the chapter room, I knew a change of plans was in order.

When everyone had coffee, I asked Ginnifer if I could use her megaphone and wheeled out the whiteboard we used for choreographing the dances for the skits. I wrote the numbers one through five. "Before we get to *Grey's Anatomy*, I have to go over these with you one more time."

The ladies might have groaned. Probably just from the satisfaction they were getting from hot, foamy milk and extra shots.

"Top five Panhellenic rush rules!" I shouted through the Gineral's megaphone, which brought the entire Deb chapter to attention. I could see the benefits to these gadgets.

I pointed at a junior with suspiciously unsmudged eyeliner. Apparently, someone had too much free time. "Tell us one."

She nodded solemnly. "No talking to other chapters."

"RIGHT!" My bark shot through the room as if on performance enhancers. I put down the megaphone. "Why do we have this rule?"

A curvy blond in the front row raised her hand. "Because they don't want us to gang up on each other."

I paused because that wasn't a bad idea. We could form an alliance with the Epsilon Chis, like on *Survivor* . . . I shook my head. *No, Margot.* "Not exactly," I said. "The purpose of this rule is to make sure each house makes its sisterhood decisions free from the influence of others." I looked around the room and was satisfied that everyone was nodding. "Anyone know the next one?"

Cheyenne, the pledge trainer, called out from the back of the room. "No dirty rushing!"

I nodded in the affirmative. "Why is that a rule?"

"Because every rushee"—Cheyenne flinched at Ginnifer's glare—"I mean, potential new member, should make her decisions without sisters in the houses lying and promising sh—stuff—they're not going to deliver."

"Exactly. Number three?"

Two more ladies held up their hands. I chose Katie, the cutie from Kansas City. "No social media?" This was one of the most unpopular rules. But, as I liked to remind the women, it wasn't that long ago that Delta Beta successfully rushed women without constant checking of Instagram, Twitter, and Snap Chat.

"Yes. No social media during rush. Again, this is because we don't want to make decisions about women based on 140 characters, or just a fun pic of their roommates goofing off on the weekend. And"—I held up a finger—"we don't want them to make a decision about us based on the same considerations."

Ginnifer stepped forward and grabbed the megaphone from my hand. "IF I SEE ANY OF YOU ON SOCIAL MEDIA THIS WEEK, THERE WILL BE SEVERE CONSEQUENCES."

I reached over and flipped the OFF switch on her megaphone. "Number four?" I asked loudly.

There was a moody silence after the social-media restriction, and the next rule was even more chafing. I put a hand up to my ear, but no one volunteered. "All chapters must abide by a mandatory curfew during rush week. Everyone will be in the chapters' houses between the hours of 7 P.M. and 7 A.M."

Dissatisfied rustling and murmuring spread through the room. "Come on, ladies," I said in my best empathetic but stern chapter-advisor voice. "You've been here twenty-four/seven this whole week, and it hasn't killed you. What's another week?"

There was a cough at the back of the room that sounded suspiciously like "Kill me now," but I had learned long ago to ignore the negative and focus on the positive. "The fraternity parties will still be there next weekend!" I said cheerily.

I tapped on the whiteboard and circled the number one on the list. "Speaking of, the most important Panhellenic rule is, of course, that no men will be involved in—"

Ginnifer cleared her throat obviously.

I'd give her this one. We were talking about rules and all. "No men will be involved in *recruitment*," I said, with a nod in her direction. She looked satisfied, and I was glad to appease her. I paused and looked out over the room, waiting for the inevitable sarcastic comment. When it didn't come, I had to ask. "No one has something to say about that one?"

The women looked around, and some of them shrugged. Callie half laughed, and said, "I don't think most of them want to be involved in rus—I mean, recruitment."

Asha nodded in agreement, as did several other women. "What would we even have them *do*?" Giggles at the absurd idea of having boys involved in rush spread throughout the room, and I breathed a sigh of relief. It was refreshing to finally have a group of women who weren't obsessed with the idea of men being included in every activity. Maybe the ideal of true sisterhood had finally become reality here at the Deb house.

Ginnifer turned down the lights and switched the TV on, and soon, the chapter settled into an enjoyable communal television experience. Thirty minutes into the show, a doctor was yelling at another doctor about another doctor (I wasn't quite sure, I wasn't a medical-drama-type girl, myself) when I first noticed the movements. There, in the back row, then, two on the side of the room. Then the whole front row moved to check their phones. Stifled gasps and giggles circled the room first, then whispers, then murmurs. I checked my cell, just in case there was some sort of national emergency in the making, but my phone was silent. I saw a few ladies' faces and the decision that had been made there. Just as I expected, the girls stretched their legs nonchalantly and moved as if they were taking a break. They got up as one, and the entire chapter watched them, waiting for something.

I threw my arm across the chapter-room door. "Where are you three going?"

They exchanged a nervous glance before Sarah Plaisance spoke. "We're just going to the bathroom."

Given the way half of the chapter were muttering over something on their phones, and the other half was watching the door, I doubted that everyone had suddenly received a helpful text reminding them their bladders were full.

"What's up?" I asked, no-nonsense style.

Apparently, the Gineral was a huge *Grey's* fan. She was glued to the television. "Shh!"

Sarah Plaisance couldn't stand it anymore. She leaned in and showed me her phone screen and the tweet she'd been looking at. "We have to go."

I clasped my hand over my mouth in horror, and Sarah, Kennedi, and Blair burst out of the room. The rest of the room jumped to their feet and stampeded out, and after I debated for a millisecond, I followed. This, I couldn't miss.

Most of the girls went straight for the front door, but not me. I stormed up the stairs, bypassed the second floor, and sprinted to the third floor. A few footsteps followed me, but I wasn't stopping to explain. The best view was going to be from the third-floor storage room. From this window, I could see the entire span of Greek Row to the west, and had the perfect vantage to look into the Epsilon Chi backyard and the drama unfurling there.

The tweets had come fast and furious, first from the Epsilon Chi sisters, then from the rest of the Greek system—about the real African lion that had somehow been released into their yard. And the cage of live chickens that the lion was trying to access.

"Carnage at the EX house!" the tweet had joyfully proclaimed. Even from the third floor next door, we could hear the screams of horror from the Epsilon Chi sisters as the lion successfully smashed through the lock on the chicken carrier, selected a victim, and settled down for an afternoon snack.

It was gruesome. And strangely satisfying. I hit a number on my cell phone.

"Nine-one-one, what's your emergency?"

"Yes, my name is Margot Blythe, and I'm calling to report a wild animal." I gave the address of the Epsilon Chi house.

"We're aware of it, and we'll have a crew there shortly." The operator seemed less than impressed.

But I wasn't done yet. "It's the Epsilon Chi house," I said.

"We have that information."

"Not the Delta Beta house."

The operator was silent. "Does this screw up the pool?" I asked.

"Let me check." I heard a flip of paper. "Actually, since you called, looks like Bob from animal control is going to get twenty bucks."

I gritted my teeth. "Really? The pool is whether *I'M* going to call 9–1–1? I thought it was just about an emergency at the Delta Beta house."

"Eh. More people wanted in, so we expanded the criteria."

It was kind of a compliment, in a way. I was almost a celebrity in Sutton emergency services.

"It's a lion," I said, watching the majestic king of the animals snack on a domestic fryer. "There's a lot of blood."

"Gross."

"Yeah, you should probably dispatch Bob from animal control."

The operator chuckled, and said, "Good idea" and I hung up. It wasn't the greatest revenge, but it was something.

The group around the window had grown, and we alternatively

gasped and laughed at a team of frantic Epsilon Chis sneaking around the backyard to open the gate and let the lion out. We watched, riveted, as, finished with the available prey, the lion noticed the opening and stalked out, headed toward the Tri Mu house. I looked behind me, and the rest of the women in the room all had their heads over their phones, tweeting and texting. I caught Callie's eye. "Let me guess. Are there chickens behind the Tri Mu house?"

Callie's beautiful blue eyes widened in innocence. "What if they're in their tent?"

I held up a hand. I didn't need to know the details. Then, as we watched the emergency vehicles descending on other sorority houses, I realized what time it was and picked up my phone to make yet another call to Sutton emergency services.

"You're late," growled the answering voice. Ty could be so testy when I didn't do what I'd agreed to do.

"I guess you haven't heard. The whole street is on lockdown."

"What did you do?"

I could honestly answer, "Nothing." And I resolved to keep it that way all throughout rush week.

Chapter Nine

THE DELTA BETA chapter awoke bright and early the next morning and caravanned to the Sutton police station. Normally, I would have expected sullen attitudes and furtively muttered curses, but the events of the night before had made everyone superalert. Or maybe they were just terrified of Ginnifer Martinelli, who was marching around the station like she was about to throw a sorority sister or two into a cell. I knew what the cells were like here. They were not homey at all.

Our most recent pledge class was responsible for picking up breakfast, and they came through the double glass doors bearing a dozen boxes of the finest donuts the town of Sutton had to offer. Yeasty, warm, and sugary, their scent filled the air, and for the first time in days, I was hungry. I helped myself to a glazed and watched Ty Hatfield enter the waiting area, turning nearly every female head in the room. Tall, good-looking, in a uniform; Ty was pretty easy on the eyes if he wasn't questioning you in a holding cell.

He crossed immediately to me and lowered his head. "You brought *all* of them?" he asked, glancing around the waiting room filled with sorority women. I tried seeing what he saw. Maybe he was intimidated by their beauty, poise, and professionally styled hair at 8 A.M. on a Sunday.

"I wanted to get it all out of the way before rush. Which starts tomorrow," I added.

Ty snatched the warm glazed donut out of my hand and speared me with that hard, no-nonsense, police-detective look. "I've heard."

I might not have liked being back in the police station, but that was my donut he had just illegally stolen. I plucked it out of his hand. "So let's get started."

Ty closed his eyes briefly. "I can't have sixty people strolling through the morgue identifying a dead body." He helped himself to my donut again and took a bite.

"It's almost like you've never seen one of those," I muttered.

"Cop donut joke. Almost like you've never heard one of those."

"Coals to Newcastle, I guess." I crossed my arms. Fine. I didn't want the donut now. It had cop cooties on it. "You could spread photos out on the conference table, and we could enter in groups of ten, to make it easier."

He stopped chewing. "That's a good idea."

A semicompliment from Ty Hatfield made my mouth drop open in a very unladylike way. Just went to show that chapter advisors had some very valuable and marketable skills that even police departments could learn from. I began to say just that when Ty pushed the remainder of the donut in my mouth. "Thanks," he said as he turned and got the attention of the room, leaving me with a bite of sugar-glazed heaven.

Fifteen minutes later, the room was set up, but thirty minutes later, it was clear that this educational excursion was going to be a bust. No one recognized the dead blond woman in the Delta Beta T-shirt. We had organized the chapter from newest pledge class to oldest, and as they filed through the room, I stayed in the back, ready to offer comfort, emotional support, or quasi-legal advice, but the women didn't seem too traumatized looking at pictures of a lifeless, bloody body. I didn't know whether to be proud of their poise or horrified that at the tender age of twentyish, they were immune to the violence that Delta Beta life had exposed them to.

Our seniors came in last, and I could see that they were trying to be strong leaders for the chapter. Callie, Cheyenne, Aubrey, Asha, Zoe, and the rest were taking this seriously. Another woman murdered in our yard was bad enough; if she was a Delta Beta, who in her right mind would pledge us?

The women looked closely at the photos, one by one. Sweet Asha's lip trembled. Cheyenne put a hand on her stomach, as if she were going to be sick. Each of them tried their hardest, then looked at Ty and gave the same answer. "I don't know who she is."

As the line dwindled, Ty grew tenser, his jaw clenching, his words growlier. I hoped no one took it personally. He was just kind of obsessed with solving crimes.

This last group of ladies were almost out the door when Zoe paused and put her hand on the table, staring at the two plastic bags of evidence that Ty had put out, almost as an afterthought.

She looked up at Ty, and asked hesitantly, "Can I see those?" She pointed to the plastic baggie with the glasses.

"Don't take them out of the bag, please."

I quickly looked around the room and saw the rest of the faces were almost as blank as mine. Zoe held the bag up closer to her face and nodded. Ty nearly jumped at the first affirmative sign of . . . something.

But Zoe looked more nervous after she put the bag down, and said, "Those are Witness glasses. Model XV-99. Top-of-the-line."

I was certainly proud of a Deb's knowing the obscure details of such an important fashion accessory, but I wasn't sure this information was something the Sutton Police Department needed to be concerned with. And neither, it seemed, was Lieutenant Hatfield.

With effort, he patiently asked, "Does that help us identify her?"

Once again, Zoe looked around the room nervously. "Maybe." She reached for the bag again. "These aren't sold everywhere. So I guess you might be able to track down who bought them. But . . ." She bit her lip before continuing. "Most people buy them anonymously."

I guessed that made sense; most people didn't brag about their glasses. Unless they were personally designed by Karl Lagerfeld or something.

Ty had picked up his pad of paper. "Model XV-99 . . ." he mumbled to himself.

Zoe tapped the plastic covering the lenses. "There could be something on the card, too."

Ty's head snapped up. "Card?"

"The card, in the earpiece. Here." Zoe put her finger over the long black part of the frame. "It's all integrated. That's why these are top-of-the-line."

My stomach rumbled as if it was still hungry after eating half a donut. But it was churning because I suddenly knew what Zoe was talking about. And why she looked so nervous.

Now attentive, Ty stared hard at the plastic bag in Zoe's hand, and she misinterpreted his silence for continued cluelessness. "They're spy-glasses." Her voice was a little shaky, and I wanted to give her a hug. She wasn't doing anything illegal, just something a little shady. "The camera is integrated into the frame and re-cords when someone presses . . ." She paused and looked through the baggie. "It's probably . . . okay. The button's here." She had her finger on the end of the earpiece, then she lifted her hand and tucked her hair behind her ear, demonstrating how a hypo-thetical spy would be able to turn the video-recording glasses on surreptitiously.

"Unless you're really familiar with the Witness series, it's hard to know what they are," Zoe explained, then paled a little under Ty's intense scrutiny.

I knew why Ty was pissed. Men are generally insecure when their lack of expertise is exposed. "It's okay," I said. "I wouldn't have been able to tell, either."

I could tell from his glare that didn't make him feel any better.

"The rest of you are excused. While Miss . . ." He consulted his notes again. "Witherspoon answers a few questions for me."

I raised my hand, and Ty didn't even look at me when he said, "Yes. You can stay. And no. I don't give a damn about rush."

Well. You win some, you lose some. At least my average was improving.

Ginnifer led the chapter out while I stayed behind with Zoe. At least he questioned her in his office, marginally better than the bare, imposing gray walls of the interrogation room. With a two-way mirror and everything, it was just like a real life *Law & Order* set.

Unfortunately, Lieutenant Hatfield's office had no mirrors at all. What if a visitor needed to check for donut crumbs around her mouth, or whether her hair was as greasy as it felt like? There was just a desk, piled high with reports and files and manuals. The computer looked outdated and grimy, and the bookcases held assorted police memorabilia, like nunchucks and what looked like an actual ball and chain. In a way, it wasn't so different from my chapter advisor's office; except my office had a Fresh-Linen-scented oil diffuser.

Because I didn't care what Ty Hatfield thought, I gave Zoe a big, squeezy hug and moved our chairs closer to hold her hand or comfort her as needed. Ty went through the basics with her. Her name, her address, did she recognize the woman in the pictures? (No.) How was she familiar with the Witness spy-glasses?

Zoe looked over at me with fear in her eyes for the first time. I put an arm around her shoulders as if I, just by my sheer presence, could give her courage. "It's okay. You can tell him."

Zoe nodded, and her chin wobbled at bit as she began to tell her story.

Thirty seconds later, Ty stopped taking notes. Thirty seconds after that, he leaned back in his chair as if he could no longer hold his spine at a perpendicular angle. A full two minutes into Zoe's tale, both hands went over his eyes as he scrubbed his forehead vigorously.

When she was finally done, red-faced and tired out from her dramatics, she leaned into my arms.

"Do you have what you needed?" I asked him, trying to keep a neutral face.

Ty set his jaw and tapped his pen against the desk. "I'll call you if I have any more questions."

Chapter Ten

I wasn't sure the coffee shop on campus was the best place to meet Nick Holden. After all, it was public, and there was a possibility that people would see us and gossip about the purpose of our meeting. But as soon as I stepped inside and felt my skin flush from the humid, espresso-scented air, all those concerns disappeared like steam off my paper cup. The only way I was going to keep my wits about me during this interview was to have an extra-grande four-shot caramel latte in my hand.

I had already selected a shadowy corner table when Holden arrived. He looked exactly as he did on TV except he was oranger, shorter, and had a much larger head.

"Miss Margot Blythe. We meet at last. May I call you Margot?"

What does one say to a question like that? As if I were going to answer, "No, call me Penelope." I bit my lip to keep myself from doing just that.

Holden pulled a small digital recorder out of his jacket pocket and put it on the table. "You don't mind if I record our conversation, do you?" He flipped the recorder on before I answered, either way.

"Are there hidden cameras, too?" I cast a look around the coffee shop for people wearing suspicious glasses or adjusting tacky handbags toward me.

Holden chuckled. "No, I like to get to know people before I put them on film. Make sure I know what they're going to say."

That . . . didn't seem right.

"Who do I have to screw to get coffee around here?" Holden muttered, screwing up his face toward the hardworking baristas.

"You have to order at the counter."

"Terrific. Half-caf drip with steamed soy. Thanks, Marg."

I didn't move. Maybe it was because he called me Marg. Maybe it was because we hadn't even started talking yet, and he wasn't listening to me. Maybe it was because I didn't trust someone who ordered "half-caf."

"I can only be here for thirty minutes," I said. "So what can I help you with?"

Holden blinked a few times, then said, "I've heard your chapter is once again experiencing a turbulent police investigation."

I remembered the chapter filing through the Sutton Police Department's conference room in an orderly fashion and enjoying a few donuts. Hardly a turbulent event. But if I said that, would it be misconstrued? Could it be seen as flippant? Like we didn't care? Like we were putting our breakfast in front of justice?

So I took a sip of coffee, and said, "Nobody likes tragedies."

"True." Holden nodded. "So true. Tell me about the deceased. What kind of person was she?"

Heck if I knew. "To protect the privacy of the families, I can't answer anything like that at this time."

"Good point." Holden nodded. "The investigation is ongoing."

Oh yeah. That was it. I smiled. "Exactly."

"So let's talk about a completed investigation. Of the murder that occurred in the Delta Beta house three months ago."

My stomach dropped. This was not how this was supposed to go. *Think fast, Margot. You can get him off that trail.* "By the way, your special on that was thorough and informative."

Holden pushed the recorder closer to me. "Really?"

"It was fair yet hard-hitting journalism. And so very comprehensive. I don't think I can bring anything else to the table, do you?"

Holden thought about that for a moment and realized that no, he couldn't very well ask for more information on the subject of his first news special. "With the rise in violence against college women across the country, do you feel unsafe being part of a sorority?"

This was a question I hadn't expected or prepared for. "Unsafe?" I echoed. "Why would I feel unsafe?"

"Because in the last four months, three women have died at the Sutton Delta Beta house," Holden replied, dropping his voice into a news-anchor "story-at-eleven" range. "Doesn't that indicate that women are unsafe there?"

When he put it that way, I would sound like an idiot if I said no. And if I said yes, I was opening myself up to all sorts of follow-ups that would necessarily involve thorny topics like "responsibility" and "liability" and "accountability."

So I asked myself that age-old question: *What would Miss America do?*

"That an excellent question, Nick—may I call you Nick?" Nick nodded, because how else was he going to answer? "The thing about sororities, in the case of Delta Beta especially, is that we are very old institutions. In 1879, Mary Gerald Callahan and Leticia Baumgardner founded Delta Beta, as a way for women to grow as individuals, to form lifelong bonds of sisterhood, and to contribute to the community as a large group would, for example, men."

"Men?"

"Men, who have long been encouraged by society to have this sort of organization. In that way, Mary Gerald Callahan and Leticia Baumgardner were pioneers. Heroines, in my book. And 1879 was such a long time ago, and many sisters have died in our metaphysical house, bonded by friendship. Therefore, the answer is, no. The Delta Beta sisterhood doesn't bring women down, it empowers women."

Nick Holden squinted at me. "I see." Then he seemed to have trouble forming his next question. "Are you saying that if the Delta Beta sorority were filled with men, then I wouldn't be asking these questions?"

"I would never call you sexist," I assured him.

He recovered quickly. "In this day and age, is there really a point to Greek life? I understand that in 1879, there was a good reason for women to empower themselves. But in the twenty-first century, don't incidents like the recent murders show us that there's no safety in secret societies that cloister women away from the world?"

I had lost control of something along the way. This was an entirely new direction that I wasn't expecting and one that my brain couldn't quite grasp. "Is there a *point* to being *Greek*?" I asked incredulously. Surely, that wasn't a real question.

"Isn't it time to stop walling off our colleges? Bring everyone together, regardless of color, class, culture?"

Despite the warm air of the coffee shop, I was suddenly chilled to the bone.

"Isn't that what Mary Callahan and Leticia Baumgardner would have wanted?"

Gerald, I wanted to add. It was Mary Gerald Callahan. But it was so beside the point. Nick Holden didn't pose a danger to Delta Beta. Quite clearly, I understood that his second cable-news special wasn't going to be about another murder at the Sutton Deb house.

"I can tell you're an intelligent, motivated woman," he was saying. "You're educated, accomplished, and a feminist. Surely you can see that the time for Greek systems has come and gone. They're antiquated bastions of misogyny, privilege, and pseudo-religion, and there's just no place for them in modern society."

"What . . . How . . ." I choked. No Miss America worth her crown could come up with an answer to the hate speech Nick Holden was spewing, and neither could I.

"I've been conducting interviews with various students and staff, and I'm hearing that more and more people are seeing what I'm seeing."

"You want to end the Greek system?" It was inconceivable. "All of it?"

Nick lifted his shoulders. "More like, just let it die off. Like a spider, trapped under a cup."

Which was an inaccurate analogy, if you asked me. Sorority women hated spiders.

I searched my soul and realized that the time for playing games with Nick Holden was over. It was all well and good for me to dissemble and act coy when he was trying to pin my chapter for being accomplices to murder. But he had gone a step too far by threatening our entire way of life. I couldn't in good conscience leave this coffee shop without speaking my truth. I leaned over the digital recorder, and, in a clear voice, said, "I disagree with you one hundred percent."

Nick was intrigued. "With which part?"

"All of it," I said. "You're wrong about everything." I felt the ghostly support of Mary Gerald and Leticia behind me, cheering me on as I stood up for their principles.

"Excellent." Nick reached out and turned off the recorder. "Will you say that on film?"

Suddenly, I wasn't sure if Nick had just slapped a plastic cup over a spider—and the spider was me.

I took a pen out of my purse and scribbled a number on my paper napkin. "Call my PR person." I pushed the napkin across the table. "Then we'll talk."

I wasn't sure whether Casey could make this situation any better, but I was pretty darn sure it wouldn't get any worse.

Chapter Eleven

THE SHED AT the back of the Delta Beta property line was creaky, dusty, and cramped. It housed spare lumber and paint cans for the giant wooden letters that graced the front yard during celebratory times of the year, along with the rakes and clippers and shovel that the yard crew used. It was the perfect place for a secret meeting of my most trusted sisters.

I had texted Callie, Aubrey, and Zoe to meet me there. First, Callie opened the door, followed by Aubrey and Zoe a few minutes later.

"We told Ginnifer there were extra twinkle lights out here," Aubrey explained.

"She's furious we don't have enough," Zoe said grimly.

"And every store in town is sold out," Aubrey finished.

"It's not like every house on Greek Row doesn't use them," Callie said. We all nodded. Twinkle lights were a rush-decor staple.

"She sent the Leonard twins up to their rooms as a punishment."

"What?" I gasped. I hadn't heard this. "What did they do?"

"They used the word 'rushee' instead of 'potential new member.'" Aubrey answered. "It threw the Gineral into a tailspin. Now she's on a rampage about 'rules' and 'terminology.'" Aubrey used air quotes around the words, and I could tell that they were all on edge.

"The lion thing didn't help." Even in the dim light of the storage shed, I saw an accusation in Aubrey's eyes directed at Callie and Zoe. Only three months ago, she and Callie had been near-mortal enemies; I hoped their new friendship wasn't in danger because of a stupid prank.

"It was a baby lion." Callie sniffed.

"Callie . . ." I said her name in a voice as full of gentle reproach as I could.

"What?" She slung her hands up. "It wasn't me."

"I hope not. We can't afford to get caught up in these silly pranks, not when we have real issues to work on."

"I'm sorry," Zoe said, wringing her hands. "I hope I didn't make it worse with the glasses."

This was going to be difficult, but we all had to be on the same page. "You lied to the police, Zoe."

"I didn't!"

"What did you say, Zoe." That was Aubrey's responsible big-sister tone.

"He wanted to know how I knew about the spy-glasses. I told him the truth, that I bought a pair when I suspected that John Schnaefel was cheating on me with the entire Epsilon Chi pledge class."

Callie nodded sagely. "He was such a Man Ho."

"Anyway," I prompted. "That's why Zoe knew so much about

the spy-glasses. She used them to catch her boyfriend doing the dirty with a bunch of trashy Epsilon Chis." The girls all looked at me with trepidation. "That's the truth, and that's what we're going with."

"It is the truth," Zoe agreed. "But what was the dead girl doing with Witness glasses in her pocket?"

The four of us had fairly active imaginations.

"She was a reporter for Nick Holden?"

"She was in the CIA?"

"She was dating John Schnaefel, too?"

I appreciated their abilities to consider all the alternatives, but the truth was staring us in the face.

"Ladies, I think she was sent here to spy on the Debs."

Aubrey covered her mouth and gasped.

Zoe's face showed me that she agreed. "After all, we had considered that possibility."

Callie nodded. "Page three of Plan B."

"Does that mean someone knows about Plan B?" Aubrey's perfectly shaped eyebrows drew together in concern.

"No. It means we're not alone in considering it," Callie said pointedly, but also with an implied question. I knew what she wanted to know.

"We're going for it." I said, ignoring the tightening in the pit of my stomach. Plan B was full of potentially illegal, definitely shady maneuvers—to ensure that Delta Beta rush had every chance of success.

Callie and Zoe high-fived each other. Even the most cautious of the group, Aubrey, looked pleased with my call. I wasn't sure how I felt yet. But as soon as Zoe had identified the Witness XV-99 glasses at the police station, I knew one thing—that other chapters were not experiencing scruples about the ethics of strategies like sending undercover sorority women with spy-glasses to other houses.

The other possibilities—that the dead woman was a reporter or a CIA agent—while possible, were not probable. For one, why would a CIA agent dress in a Delta Beta T-shirt? A trench coat and thigh-high stiletto boots seemed much more appropriate.

And could the dead woman be a reporter for Nick Holden? After meeting with him, I knew that wasn't possible. Nick Holden was ambitious, thirsty even. If one of his colleagues had died in the midst of gathering information for a story, he would have already organized a candlelight vigil and gone on every morning show vowing to catch the criminal. He would already have his front-page story instead of padding around Sutton looking for one. But the thought did spark something in my brain.

Callie, Zoe, and Aubrey knew just what they had to do—we had decided and rehearsed the next steps several times over winter break. And even though it wasn't necessary, I again stressed the need to keep Ginnifer Martinelli in the dark. No one could know what we were about to launch. Plan B made D-day look like a Black Friday shopping trip.

Over the course of the next few minutes, the girls plotted, then staggered their exits from the shed. They would be giving me regular updates, and we would meet only under the cover of night. Maybe with disguises. I hadn't decided yet.

I also hadn't decided how forthcoming I should be to aid in the murder investigation. Was I going to give Ty Hatfield any of the conclusions that I had come to after learning about the Witness XV-99 glasses? On the one hand, telling him my suspicions that the dead woman was a sorority spy would very likely confirm his beliefs that I was a little too intense about Delta Beta rush. On the other hand, it could help him identify the body faster, help the woman's family get closure, help catch a murderer.

But rush started tomorrow. And telling Ty would bring more scrutiny on the Deb house, attention that we did not need before hundreds of Sutton College freshmen were invited to get dressed up and listen to our chants and clapping.

Telling Ty might mean he would give the other chapters a heads-up that we were onto them, erasing any possible advantage we had.

He was probably looking at the Witness digital card right now, I told myself. There was very likely information on it that would identify the girl. It could even solve the crime in one stroke: Like if she happened to have the glasses on while talking to the murderer, and the murderer said something like, "You better do what I say, or I'm going to murder you tonight in the Delta Beta backyard. With no involvement from the Delta Beta chapter whatsoever."

Zoe had handed him all the evidence he needed to solve the case, really. He didn't need me to help him solve crimes—hadn't he told me that five or six times?

Really, I was doing Ty a favor by not interfering and benefiting my chapter at the same time. And good Delta Betas always put the interests of both their sisterhood and their community first.

Chapter Twelve

THANKS TO THE last week of boot-camp-like training, the Delta Beta house rose with the dawn, right on schedule—0800 hours: coffee orders delivered by four angelic sisters; 0900 hours: calisthenics in the chapter room; 1100–1400: hair, makeup, and light lunch. By 1500, we were lined up inside the house in a precise, tight formation. I inspected the troops—I mean chapter—from the front door and saw fifty of the finest young women the country had to offer, all dressed in identical JCrew chambray tops tucked into adorable black tartan pencil skirts over black tights and knee-high boots. Freshly tanned from the visiting spray tan salon last night, the ladies were a plucked, whitened, glossy show of ideal, postadolescent womanhood. They made me proud just looking at them.

At 1520, I checked my Michael Kors watch and synced it with my iPhone. I climbed the entry staircase and got the chapter's attention with the aid of my lucky whistle hung around my neck.

I put a hand over my heart, right where my Delta Beta pin was resting. "Ladies, tonight you will introduce yourselves to a new generation of sorority women. Whether they ultimately pledge our legendary sisterhood, the impression you make will stay with them for a lifetime, invoking their admiration, respect, and fear. Although our chapter has suffered loss and unimaginable pain, you will show not only the Sutton College Greek system, but the world, what Delta Beta women are made of!"

I blew my whistle again. "DO NOT CRY! Think of your mascara!" That brought a giggle out of everyone. I pointed toward the front door of the house. "Tonight, you will meet your new sisters!"

It was a battle cry worthy of *Spartacus*—the hot, modern version—and the chapter responded appropriately, with cheers and fist pumps and stomping on the floor.

It was an intoxicating feeling. I almost felt high off the energy pulsing through the house, and it wasn't just the organic herbal No Doz in my system. No, there was a palpable zing running through the air. I'd only felt this way on a few other occasions in my life, right before something magical occurred.

Fifteen minutes later, you could cut the knotted tension with a knife, and when the Panhellenic rush counselor knocked on the door, the chapter let out its collective breath.

It was showtime.

I held my hand up. From my position on the grand stairwell, everyone could see my fingers count down the seconds, three, two, one . . .

The door opened.

The ground shook with fifty determined women stomping the ground in their boot soles, fortified with lead plates. STOMP STOMP STOMP STOMPstompstompstompstompstomp.

"WE'RE FUN WE'RE CUTE WE'RE BACK IN BLACK" The Debs half sang/half screamed their welcome song. The first rushees in line looked terrified. Good. It meant we were intimidating and incredible. They'd never seen anything like a Delta Beta rush.

"YOU'RE FUN YOU'RE CUTE YOU'LL WANNA COME BACK"

Pickups started, like a high-tech German automotive assembly line. Debs moved forward, greeting the next rushee in line with an enthusiastic smile and a shouted name read from their name tags. It didn't matter that no one could hear over the din of the foyer.

"TO THE BEST HOUSE DEB HOUSE DELTA BETA IS THE BEST HOUSE!"

In seven minutes and six seconds, the front door was closed and all of the rushees accompanied to their designated places. This was the part where bonds were formed, friendships were forged, and lies were fabricated.

There's a lot to a successful rush. There's the glitz, the glamour; logistics and legalities; and the hard sell, the salesmanship. We wanted each and every one of these women, when they returned to Panhellenic that night, to rank Delta Beta as their number one choice. That didn't mean that we were choosing all of them. We had to rank them as well, and sometimes hard decisions had to be made, with impassioned pleas and arguments. Sometimes, this was made easier by the research we'd done before the rushees ever entered the house.

I'm not going to spill all the tricks up the figurative Delta Beta sleeve, but we routinely check [XXXXX] and order [XXXXXX] (redacted to protect Delta Beta trade secrets) before rush, to ensure that anyone we seriously consider offering a bid can comply with our high standards. But, ultimately, rushees made their own cases, providing their transcripts, resumes, and photos to Panhellenic, which helps match them up with sisters who would be a good fit.

For instance, on the southwest corner next to the marble bust of Leticia Baumgardner was McKayla Monroe, a junior biology major. Her hometown was Charleston, and she had been a cheerleader in high school. For this party, she was paired with a girl from Savannah, who had volunteered at a nursing home in high school and was a cheerleader in high school. They should have a lot to talk about; if not, there were conversation prompts that the ladies had memorized.

"How are you liking Sutton College?"

"What was your favorite class last semester?"

"Do you like to go to basketball games?"

All of these topics were thoughtfully worded and vetted through the conversation subcommittee to ensure maximum conversation success. As anyone who has ever been involved in a sorority recruitment process could tell you, it's the conversations that make you fall in love with a house. And their well-styled hair.

I checked the time on my phone. One minute until bumping. I watched the extra women start to nonchalantly make their way through the crowds, a smile here, a hand on a shoulder there. It looked like they were just mingling, casually strolling through a crowd of a hundred, very cute, very-pulled-together collegiate women, where half the people were dressed alike.

Five . . . four . . . three . . . two. . . . one. I hit a button on a remote hidden inside my skirt pocket, specifically added for just this accessory. The lights in the house dimmed ever so slightly. Only two or three rushees noticed, blinking for a second, before returning to their fascinating description on how freshman geology totally wasn't what she thought it was. Then there were bumps.

The bumpers politely inserted themselves into conversations as we'd practiced, over and over during the practices. "Hi! [insert name here] I couldn't wait to come talk to you!" With enough sincerity and cheer, the rushee would never notice that all over the room, sisters were introducing themselves in the exact same way. The first sister excused herself and went and found her second station and on and on. Like a Rube Goldberg machine that the mechanical-engineering nerds insisted on building every nice day in the George Klooney (with a K, not a C, unfortunately) Quad at the student center on campus, the bumping process was both technical and beautiful in its simple, effective choreography.

Delta Betas flowed through the room, going from rushee to rushee with an ease and graciousness that I was sure could not be matched at any other sorority house on Greek Row. I watched it all from the staircase, and when it was time to wind down the party, I dimmed the lights to give a five-minute warning, then again to give a two-minute warning. The women who were currently not holding conversations about the basketball record of the Sutton Saints lined up at the door and began to clap and sing.

"WE'RE FUN WE'RE CUTE WE'RE BACK IN BLACK—"

Soon, all the potential new members had been ushered through the front door, and the chapter as a whole finished singing Monday's signature ditty.

"YOU'RE FUN YOU'RE CUTE YOU'LL WANNA COME BACK—

TO THE BEST HOUSE THE DEB HOUSE DELTA BETA IS THE BEST HOUSE!"

The front door slammed, and a roar rose, shaking the house to its foundation. We had done it. First party done. Four more to go. In five ... four ... three ...

By NINE O'CLOCK that night, the door closed on the final party of the first day of rush. This time when the door closed, the resulting roar probably formed a seismic fault line deep in the crust under North Carolina. The chapter had, quite simply, kicked major ass.

Everything had gone off without a hitch. No emergencies had occurred, no wardrobe malfunctions, no lipstick on teeth, no one had gotten on the floor and pretended to be a cow (there was an incident my junior year—let's just say certain people were locked in their rooms for the rest of the week).

"We did it!" I hooted. I ran down the stairs into the celebrating throng, grabbed several sisters by the neck, and gave them huge bear hugs. I spun around and saw Ginnifer and raised my hand to give her a high five, which she ignored. Denied.

It was as if I heard a giant set of brakes squealing to a halt. "What's wrong?"

The Gineral was not celebrating. Women around me started to notice, alarmed by the steam coming out of her ears.

"THIS!" She smacked a piece of paper into her other palm. "The rush counselor just slid it under the door."

I reached for it and uncrinkled the single sheet. The message was short and to the point.

Again, it was probably a sign that I needed to get more than forty-five minutes of sleep that night that I started to laugh hysterically. This got the attention of the rest of the chapter, who hadn't sobered up, watching the Gineral snort fire.

I held up the paper. "LADIES!" I yelled, even though we were all pressed pretty close together in the entry way. "Panhellenic has issued a new regulation in response to recent events on Greek Row!"

Lowering the paper to my face, I read the pronouncement slowly and clearly. "From this point on, all Panhellenic sororities shall NOT employ, dispatch, detour, or otherwise engage live animals during recruitment."

Another roar rose through the house, this time of laughter. I didn't look at my inner circle, but I did see Ginnifer out of the corner of my eye and wondered why she was taking this so seriously. After all, there was no proof that Delta Beta had anything to do with a baby lion wandering through sorority row. None whatsoever.

Chapter Thirteen

A CHAPTER ADVISOR'S job is never done, and certainly not on the first day of rush. As the celebrations continued, I quickly changed gears. We had to do this over again tomorrow and the stakes were still high. Many a chapter has gotten overconfident after a successful first day and let its standards slip the next day, resulting in less-than-optimal return rates. That was so not going to happen with this chapter.

The doorbell rang with dinner delivery, and there were whoops heard around the first floor—no one had eaten since Ginnifer doled out bananas and protein bars that morning.

I went to the door to pay for the thin-crust, no-cheese, extra-veggie pizzas (the ladies had rush clothes to fit into; spanx could only do so much). When the pizza delivery boy left the porch, I saw who had been standing behind him.

A curse word escaped me that was inappropriate for a lady, much less a lady who aspired to Delta Beta ideals. I closed the front door behind me. No one needed to see that Lieutenant Ty

Hatfield had come to visit our house, not after we were all feeling so good about the day.

I quickly glanced around, to see if anyone was watching us from the shadows. "Come on," I said, grabbing his arm and leading him straight into the atrium. The space heaters were turned off after the last rushees had left, but it was still warmer than our front porch—and a whole lot more private. A horrible thought occurred to me. "You didn't drive a police car, did you?"

That was all I needed. A Sutton Police Department squad car parked outside of the Delta Beta house. We'd be dead in the water before we ever got a chance to show off our cute new bikini body.

"An unmarked one," Ty replied shortly, as if that were some kind of affront. I understood. Driving around in a cool police cruiser with all the lights and sirens must be a big perk of the job. "Here." He pushed a pizza box toward me that I hadn't noticed, with my concern for keeping him under the cloak of night.

I hadn't thought about food for hours. Now the smell of fresh dough and steamy toppings made my mouth water. I took the box, and the warm cardboard made me weak at the knees.

"For crap's sake . . ." Ty muttered, taking me by the elbow and steering me toward a folding chair. "What are you on?"

I sank into the chair, all of a sudden realizing that my legs hadn't bent at this angle for a very long time. But that was okay. It was called stamina. I was scarily good at standing for days at a time.

A light shone in my eyes. "OW!" I flinched away from the cop and his flashlight. "Are you serious?"

The beam flicked off. "Five-hour energy, okay?" I said it mainly to avoid another blinding flash.

"Your pupils are huge," he said as if he didn't believe me.

"Two bottles do that to me."

Ty looked up at the ceiling of the tent, frustrated at something.

"Did you come down here to yell at me?" I asked, still sounding as energetic as ever even though I was fairly certain this folding chair might be the most comfy thing ever.

"Maybe," Ty bit out. That was confusing. Even more confusing was when he flipped open the pizza box and told me to eat.

"But that's pepperoni. And sausage. And ham . . ." I protested. Something about the set of his jaw made me stop arguing. And also the smell. And the heat. And the massive rumbling in my stomach. One slice wouldn't hurt, I was sure.

Two bites in, I understood why he was feeding me. He wanted me discombobulated when he sprang the news on me.

"We've identified the body."

A sick feeling settled in my stomach. It could have been the re-introduction of solid calories; but it was more likely my intuition telling me this was bad, bad news.

"Her name is Shannon Bender."

The name meant nothing to me. "How did you figure it out?" I asked through a mouthful of hot cheese and assorted Italian meats.

"I assigned a rookie to travel around town with the car keys. The fob worked on a car parked at the Fountain Place Inn. We found enough personal effects to be able to make a positive ID."

Huh. I guessed my crazy ideas about the car keys hadn't been so crazy. I nodded, then realized that Ty wasn't saying something. I put the half-eaten slice of pizza back in the box and prepared myself. "Go ahead. I know the worst is still to come."

Ty's eyes narrowed. "Why do you say that?"

"Please. Shannon Bender was wearing a Delta Beta shirt, but she wasn't a Delta Beta. There's going to be more to this, and I'm sure I'm not going to like it."

"How did you know she wasn't a Delta Beta at another school?" He was still doing that squinty-eyed suspicious thing. Well, two of us could pull that off.

"How do you know she wasn't?"

"Now's the time to tell me what you know, Margot."

I matched his tough-guy stare. "That goes for both of us."

He threw up his hands. "I thought we were beyond this."

"Yeah, me, too. Until another body shows up at my house. Do you know how that affects me?"

Ty raised an eyebrow.

"What I mean is, that puts me in a difficult position. I have to protect my sisters, Ty."

"Here we go with the sisterhood talk again."

"I have an affirmative duty—" I was interrupted by his snort. "I took a vow—"

"So did I. Tell me what you know."

"That's a broad question. Ask me something specific."

"I did." His teeth ground together. "How did you know that Shannon Bender wasn't a Delta Beta?"

In the grand scheme of things, it was a fair question. But I wasn't sure he was going to like the answer. "I didn't—well, I wasn't sure. But her shirt . . ."

"Yes?" he prompted.

"It was blue, okay?"

"And?"

"It was blue with pink letters. Delta Beta's official colors are black and gold. I'm not saying that some sister, someplace, doesn't totally disregard our membership manual and wear our letters in other colors, but it's just not likely. So I had a hunch."

"A hunch." Ty sighed and rubbed a hand over his face. "Why didn't you tell me this before?"

I frowned down at the pizza box. "I didn't really think about it."

"You didn't think about it?"

"I have a lot of things on my mind, right now, okay? And I don't appreciate your insinuation."

"What am I insinuating."

"You know." I was tired of this, back-and-forth, he-said, she-said game. "Now it's your turn."

He just lifted his brows. I elaborated. "Your turn to tell me something. That's how this works. I give you information, and you share something. It's the way our relationship works."

The expression on his face went really weird for a moment. I guess he wasn't used to sharing information with a sorority chapter advisor. But he came around, like I knew he would.

"You were right. Shannon Bender wasn't a Delta Beta."

I smiled. "That's a relief."

"She was a member of Mu Mu Mu."

My smile melted like the extra cheese on the still-warm pizza in my lap. *Tri Mu.* Suddenly, I was really uncomfortable with where Ty's information was heading.

And then he said the thing I had been dreading for the past two days. "Based on the information we uncovered on the card in the Witness glasses, it seems likely that Shannon Bender was some sort of . . . Panhellenic spy." He sounded skeptical, like this was something crazy he'd heard about on late-night TV, along with alien abductions and an essential-oil-infused towel that could melt twenty-five pounds off anyone.

I had to say something, anything that would clear the Delta Betas of suspicion. Because I could see where this was going, clear as day.

"Really." I kept my voice as neutral as possible. "That's . . . crazy."

Ty's sigh told me I wasn't totally successful. I picked up the slice of pizza and took a larger-than-normal bite.

"MMM . . ."

"You should tell me what you know about this, Margot."

I pointed to my full mouth. It would be impolite to talk while chewing.

"This is now an official murder investigation. Shannon Bender didn't die of natural causes while wearing a disguise and spy-glasses in your backyard."

Well. There went my spontaneous-head-explosion theory. As I finished chewing, it seemed that I could only tell Ty the truth and nothing but the truth.

"I don't know anything about it," I said.

The look on Ty's face said he didn't believe me. Like I would lie. On purpose.

I put my hand up and made a crossing motion over my Delta Beta pin. "I swear on Mary Gerald Callahan's grave. I don't know Shannon Bender. I've never met her. I've never seen her before I saw her in the yard—" I held up a finger. "And she was already dead, then."

I could see that he was disappointed. It would be nice, I supposed, if I had all the answers to solve their case for them, as I had practically done before. But as much as I would love to solve all the mysteries in the city of Sutton for my good friends at the police station, I had bigger priorities right now.

I stood up. "If we're done, my chapter needs me inside." I handed the pizza box back to him. "Thank you so much for the update."

He accepted the box with a look of resignation. I felt bad for him, I really did. I reached out and patted him on the shoulder and headed toward the tent flap.

"See you tomorrow," he said. He sounded so glum that his words didn't even register until the next morning.

Chapter Fourteen

DAY TWO OF rush started off exactly as the first day. Alarms buzzed at 0700 hours. Boots on ground, the troops stretched and began formations, marching downstairs. At 0800, the doorbell rang. I reached the front door first, as my bedroom was closest. It could have been any number of delivery services, another missive from Panhellenic, or maybe the members who went out for the coffee-shop run.

No. It was Lieutenant Ty Hatfield with Officer Malouf. I nodded at Malouf cordially. Hatfield got my official sorority chapter advisor's what-do-you-think-you're-doing-mister glare. "What is this about?"

"Can we come in?"

It was a trick question. He knew perfectly well I wasn't going to leave two police officers out on the front porch, where everyone could see them.

I pushed the door wider, and when they entered, Ty handed me a paper bag from a certain fast-food restaurant.

Inside was an Egg McMuffin. Hash browns. My stomach growled, and so did I. "I thought we cleared this up last night."

Ty lifted a shoulder. "Nope. We're going to need to question all the members of the chapter."

"No." My flat denial caused Malouf's brows to rise in alarm. But Ty Hatfield was made of sterner stuff.

"Shannon Bender was a Tri Mu, your sorority's archenemy—"

"Don't be dramatic," I said. Tri Mu was more like our arch-nemesis.

"She's found on Delta Beta grounds, caught for spying. There was an argument, a fight, and her death is the result."

"That's not what happened," I said stubbornly.

Ty took out his little notebook. "We'll see."

I realized I was still holding his breakfast, and I offered it back to him. He didn't take it. "I already had mine. That's for you."

My stomach said, oh goodie, but I pushed the greasy bag back at him. "I know what you're doing, and I will not be bribed."

Ty made a regretful sound and accepted the bag. "I guess you don't want this then." He held out a coffee cup, the rich scent tantalizing me. It really would be rude to reject two peace offerings, back-to-back.

My hand closed around the white paper cup, as if my body had no scruples or self-control around caffeine. Strange.

"How long is this going to take?" I muttered, my nose savoring the aroma of the best part of waking up.

He glanced at Malouf. "Fifty women? Plus yourself, Miss..." He checked his notebook. "Martinelli... and the new house brother?" He acted like he was doing the math in his head. "Five hours?"

I had just taken a sip of coffee, and it was all I could do not to spit it back out. "What do you think you're doing? Did you think you could just march in here and pull this?" I hissed. Did he think I could be fooled that easily?

"This is decaf!" I held up the cup dramatically. "And there is no way you're interviewing the chapter today."

Malouf tried not to smile. I wasn't sure what part of the last ten seconds he found amusing because it was all equally horrifying.

Ty lowered his chin as well as his voice. "Do I have to pull rank here? I'm not messing around."

I took a step toward him and made eye contact so he could see exactly how serious I was. "Neither am I!"

"This is a murder investigation."

"This is rush!" I insisted. "You cannot have five hours to question the chapter. We're going to have hundreds of rushees lined up outside that door in two hours! It's impossible!"

"How much time can I have?"

I sighed and consulted my watch, going over the schedule in my head. "Fifteen minutes."

Ty's face showed he was not amused. *Join the club, buddy.*

"I didn't want to do this." He held out his hand, and Malouf handed a paper over. Then he handed it to me. Reluctantly, I read it.

"This isn't over," I promised him.

"It's just beginning," he said solemnly.

"You are going to be so sorry you pulled this."

"You calling a lawyer?"

Oh, how I wished I could be so kind.

I HAD JUST made the call when Ginnifer came into the office, so I motioned for her to close the door. She might as well hear about it now, and this way, I wouldn't have to tell the story twice.

"Casey Kenner," came the voice on the other line.

"It's me, Case."

"Margot!" My heart broke at the love and affection in his voice. I prayed he'd still feel the same about me after I told him the reason for the call.

I went ahead and gave him a brief outline. Shannon Bender's body, the spy-glasses, the investigation, and now a subpoena ordering the chapter to submit to questioning.

"She was wearing a pink-and-blue Delta Beta shirt? That should have been a dead giveaway," Casey said after making the requisite horrified gasps. He always grasped the fashion fundamentals.

"I know!" I agreed. "And now this is going to essentially shut the house down for the second day of rush." I glanced over at Ginnifer. Her face was white, her lips a tight, thin line on her face.

"Well, we're not going to let that happen. I think we both know what we have to do." I should have known that any best friend of mine could immediately assess the situation and make a game plan. It was like we were two halves of a very shiny, glamorous coin.

"I'll take care of things here in town," I agreed, feeling tense about the next steps but also relieved to have a firm direction and Casey's backup.

"I'll make some calls on my end. We can get ahead of this." Casey was all business, which was a relief. I couldn't have handled it if he'd freaked out. Especially since, from the look on Ginnifer's face, I was about to deal with a freaker-outer.

"I love you, Margot. Everything's going to be okay," Casey said before we said good-bye. I knew that last part was a lie, but since it was a lie from his heart, I cherished it.

I took a moment before I addressed Ginnifer, frozen in shock and repressed anger. I totally understood. I would be in the same condition if it wasn't imperative that I take immediate action.

"Ginnifer, you need to get it together." Her eyes were like laser beams, hot and intense. "I need you here, in charge. We're moving forward. We are not letting the police derail our rush."

"But what about the subpoena?" she said through clenched teeth. "We can't just ignore that! It's the law!"

"We're not," I assured her. "But we need to buy some time." I laid out my plan to her. "Can you handle this? I need to know that we're a team, Ginnifer."

She took a deep, vibrating breath before nodding in the affirmative. "You can count on me."

I nodded back. "Good. I'll be leaving soon."

Her eyes widened apprehensively. "Where are you going?"

"The only place that has the power to stop the irreversible damage that we're about to face."

THE WIND WHIPPED through my fleece as I stood outside the student center on campus. I hadn't stopped to put on a heavier coat when I ran out of the house, and the temperatures had dropped overnight. Checking my watch, I saw that I had ten minutes before showtime. Just then, I saw three figures moving quickly across the parking lot toward me. My Plan B A Team had arrived.

Zoe, Callie, and Aubrey looked solemn. They had heard the news and knew what was at stake.

"Thanks for coming," I said after I gave them each a warm hug. "How are things at the house?"

"As good as can be expected," Aubrey said.

"And the police?"

Callie smirked. "They've been interviewing Fiona and Page for the past half hour."

I couldn't help the small smirk that twisted my own lips. Not only were Fiona and Page both theater majors, but Fiona's father was Irish, and her storytelling abilities were legendary. Combined with Page's slight speech impediment, which manifested when she was under extreme stress, Hatfield and Malouf were going to be tied up for a while. And when Fiona and Page were dismissed, Ginnifer was to provide them another two women who either cried at the drop of a hat or had daddies with lawyers on retainer. Meanwhile, the chapter was preparing for the second day of rush prep as planned. At least, until I got the answers I was looking for.

"What about you guys? Are you okay?"

Three sweet faces nodded back at me, full of empathy and resolve. Everything I was doing was for them and the rest of our sisters. And I knew they felt the same way about me.

I looked at Zoe. "Is everything operational?"

"Yes. All systems go."

"And what about you, Callie?"

Callie stared back and lifted her chin. She was a warrior-WASP princess, in her cashmere beanie and pearl-stud earrings. "I'll do whatever it takes."

"Good. Aubrey?"

"You can count on me."

I felt relieved, knowing I could go into battle with my trusted lieutenants on my six, ready to take up my weapon should I be harmed. Or arrested.

Squaring my shoulders, I steeled myself as I entered the student center and said a silent prayer to the patron saint of sorority women to assist me in my hour of need.

Chapter Fifteen

"WHAT DO YOU mean, no?" I demanded, standing in front of the five women in charge of my chapter's destiny.

Under rule 5.2, section D of the Sutton College Panhellenic Recruitment Code, I had exercised the chapter's right for an emergency Rush Council meeting. The Mafia were required to be here, but they apparently weren't required to agree with me.

"Did we not speak clearly?" the Tri Mu representative, Alexandria Von Douton, asked me, with that smug Tri Mu lilt in her voice.

"Now, now, let's be fair. We need to at least get Ms. Blythe on the record with the reasons for her request." God bless Sue Harlow and her Lambda, legality-loving ways.

Von Douton sniffed. "It won't change anything."

I sought out Louella Jackson's attention. As the Delta Beta member of the council, surely she'd be able to somehow help me.

"Do you have something prepared?" Louella asked me, shifting under my pointed stare. "Perhaps it would help if we could consult a memo."

"Or a PowerPoint," Patty Huntington suggested.

"I called an emergency meeting because this was an emergency. I didn't have time to prepare a position statement," I said through clenched teeth.

Patty looked unimpressed. "You are asking this board to postpone an entire day of rush, and you didn't feel it was important enough to *prepare* for this meeting?" She made it sound like I was some frivolous independent who didn't fathom the extreme consequences of rush week.

I had to get into the weeds, as diplomatically as possible. "The police only showed up this morning. If I'd had prior notice, of course I would have drafted a brief and brought in expert witnesses. But this *is* an emergency. Please . . ."

There was the sound of a phone buzzing somewhere in the room. Von Douton reached into her Fendi bag and withdrew a Swarovski-encrusted iPhone. She glanced at the text, smiled, then looked back at me. "Please do go on."

Blinking away my annoyance, I outlined the situation, trying to be as neutral as I could. Yes, unfortunately, a deceased individual had been discovered in our backyard on Friday. Yes, it looked like she was possibly, potentially, the victim of foul play. And yes, now the police wanted to question every member of our chapter today, which would make it impossible for us to conduct our rush parties.

"In the spirit of Panhellenic, which says that we are one for all and all for one, I am humbly requesting that you halt all rush parties today, so that the Delta Beta chapter can deal with this legal irregularity, then focus on what really matters—selecting the next generation of women to join our sisterhood."

The five women exchanged meaning-filled glances. It was weird, like they could all communicate telepathically. Maybe this was something they'd developed after years of serving on the same council together, the next level of female evolution, after the syncing of monthly cycles.

After a minute of silent reflection, I saw Patty, Sue, and Clara-Jane sink back into their chairs, resigned to whatever outcome had been decided. Von Douton arched her eyebrows at Louella, who sighed heavily. When the Delta Beta member, my only ally, sighed like that, the decision wasn't going to be good for us.

Then Louella spoke, and I could tell she wasn't happy about it. "The answer has to be no. With the increased scrutiny we will be receiving from the administration and the press because of this . . . event, any disruption to the schedule could send the wrong signal, that Panhellenic is not equipped to govern itself. A delay would also interfere with the start of the winter semester, affecting everyone's academics, and the administration would not be happy with that. Further, the council has decided that this is a situation that the Delta Betas have brought upon themselves, and therefore, punishing the other chapters would be blatantly unfair. "

This was what I had been afraid of even if it wasn't surprising news. "I really, really, really, would like for you to reconsider."

"Once again, it seems like the word 'no' is not in your vocabulary." Von Douton looked pleased with herself for that little dig. Little did she know that Margot Blythe took that as a compliment.

IN THE COFFEE shop on the first floor of the student center, I sent a simple text to my team. "Go." Then I ordered a triple-shot nonfat, three-Equal latte and waited.

THIRTY MINUTES LATER, my phone exploded.

As outlined in our plan, my girls had successfully unveiled an anonymous Twitter account, broadcasting all the dirt about other chapters. Now it was Casey's turn to start making calls that would ensure that Sutton rush proceeded as planned. He responded immediately to my text: On it.

The barista asked me if I'd like a refill. I smiled, and said, "Yes, of course."

AN HOUR LATER, I received a call from Louella Jackson. I let it go to voice mail, because that's what women do when they're holding all the cards. I was glad that I hadn't left the student center, since I was being summoned back to the Panhellenic Council room for an emergency Rush Council meeting.

I threw away my cup, and when my phone rang again, this time I was pleasantly surprised by the caller. "Margot Blythe," I answered cheerfully. "How can I help you, Lieutenant? I hope my sisters are fully cooperating with your investigation."

There was silence.

"Is this one of those heavy-breathing calls, Lieutenant? Because I've been there, done that, and I didn't get paid nearly enough for it."

There was another brief second before he answered. "I'm just trying to compose myself. I wouldn't want to be rude to a lady."

It was a backwards kind of compliment, but I'd take it. "Thank you, I think."

Finally, he came out with it. "I've been ordered to call off the interviews for today."

"Really?" I tried for innocent and shocked. I'm not sure I fully succeeded at keeping the glee out of my voice.

"The call came from high up. Governor's office."

Wow. Casey had some kind of connections. But then, when 95 percent of elected officials were Greek, it wasn't hard to find like-minded and sympathetic ears in high places. So I've heard.

"This is a mistake, Margot. If there's a murderer on the loose, it's in your best interest to find him or her before there's another victim. Or before you're hurt."

"Me? Why would you even say that?"

"Someone murdered Shannon Bender. Either because they thought she was a Delta Beta or because they knew she wasn't."

A sick feeling in my stomach made me regret that extra latte. Ty was right, of course. But what choices did I have? The Mafia would not listen to reason and postpone rush to let us participate in the investigation.

"Look, I'm about to go into a Panhellenic meeting. When I get out, I'll try to come up with something."

"Something that catches a killer and protects all the women living on Greek Row?" It was almost like he didn't believe I could do it.

"We're on lockdown," I promised him. "There's a curfew for all the houses. I'm watching all the girls carefully. I won't let anything happen to them."

"Even you can't control everything," Ty said grimly. He meant it, but all I heard was a challenge. I was a Delta Beta woman, after all.

THE ENERGY WAS decidedly different in the room when I walked in. This morning, I was the supplicant, and the Mafia was the council on high. This time I was a challenger in an honest-to-goodness gladiator ring.

As if one puppet master controlled them all, the members of the Mafia peered over their bifocals at me, pulled back, and crossed their arms in unison. Being on the receiving end of sorority women doing the exact same thing, at the exact same time was a little disconcerting. I filed that realization away to do some hard thinking on it in the future.

But now was not the time for thinking. Now was the time for action.

"Has the council decided whether rush will be postponed?" I pressed, hoping for a clear decision before the rest of the advisors got here.

"We'll announce that decision when the rest of the advisors get here," Louella said, as if she could read my mind. "So you have one last chance to decide if this is the course you really want to pursue."

It seemed like a warning of some kind, and I couldn't help but wonder whether Louella, the Delta Beta member of the council, really had my back or not. But the time to back out was long gone—if there had ever been such an opportunity.

"No," I declared, wondering why my voice was sounding a little shaky. "The Delta Beta request still stands."

Louella lifted her hands as if she were washing them clean of me, and I steeled myself for the knife that was surely going to come from somewhere—even from my allies.

Chapter Sixteen

As THE OTHER bleary-eyed, sweatshirt-clad chapter advisors filed into the room, led by Panhellenic advisor Maya Rodman, you could have cut the tension with an eyelash curler.

The peacemaker of the Rush Council, sweet Sue Harlow, started off by repeating my request: to postpone rush for all chapters.

Von Douton scowled at the room. "The Delta Beta chapter is under subpoena to cooperate with a criminal investigation." She said "criminal investigation" like it was a bad thing.

The announcement was met with stony silence. I had been prepared for many things. Dramatics, name-calling, flouncing. I had not been prepared for five formidable women to say *nothing*. It was terrifying.

I wasn't the only woman in the room discomfited by the lack of outrage.

"Really? No opinions?" Patty Huntington sounded incredulous. "No objections?"

Sarah McLane's nostrils flared as she slid her eyes toward me. "We understand that the Little Debbies have been given a temporary reprieve."

That was when I knew.

The other advisors weren't just lying back and agreeing to let rush continue because they wanted to be "fair" or "nice." They had an entirely different agenda in mind.

Patty Huntington looked at me. "Is this true? You no longer need to cooperate with the police?"

"Well, I wouldn't put it that way," I said, thinking of my last conversation with Lieutenant Ty Hatfield, who had a point about killers still on the loose. "But yes, a stay has been issued." Because that's what governors do.

Patty and Louella and Sue and Clara-Jane exchanged a look. Only Von Douton was still simmering, seething at me. I wanted to point out that her frown lines were showing, but that would just be uncharitable.

"I don't see that there's an issue here, then," Sue said with a little shrug. "Recruitment will continue as planned, or until there's another emergency at the Delta Beta house."

"You don't work for city government, do you?" I asked her.

Sue's eyes widened.

"She works for the library," Clara-Jane answered. "And what should that matter?"

"Nothing," I shrugged easily. Sue's face had "I put twenty bucks on the Delta Beta 9-1-1 pool" all over it.

"All right then," Louella's voice was clipped as she stood. "That's it then. Everyone needs to get back to work, I should imagine."

The other members of the Mafia stood and followed Louella out the door in short order, leaving me alone with a bunch of well-manicured wolves in Chico's clothing.

I pulled my bag over my shoulder and decided now would be the perfect time to pretend to check for texts, but I was halted with a hand placed on my shoulder. "Not so fast." The tone was menacing, the grip ice-cold through my coat.

I spun, and the other four chapter advisors were standing in a line, their arms akimbo. Only Maya was sort of standing in the middle, like an awkward referee right before the tug-of-war event at the annual Alpha Kapp Olympics.

"Ladies?" I asked innocently, wondering whether I could make it to the staircase and out the front door before any of them. I was a bit younger, but I hadn't been able to work out regularly in months.

"We were being nice to you," the Epsilon Chi advisor hissed. "Since it was your first year and all."

"We felt sorry for you," the Lambda advisor added. "Since the murders destroyed your house's reputation."

"But that ends today." Sarah McLane looked like she enjoyed saying that. "You just remember. You started this."

I held up my hands. "What? I didn't do anything except come here and beg for the Mafi—I mean, the Rush Council, to help even out the playing field."

Sarah smirked. "We know you are behind the Twitter account."

It was only due to years of practice that I was able to lie perfectly with a straight face. "What Twitter account?"

Now Maya chimed in. Maybe she didn't like taking the side of bullies. "The Sutton Rush Anonymous account? The one that's been posting secrets of all the houses all morning?"

"The one that every rushee is now twittering?" the Lambda advisor almost squealed.

"It's not called that," Sarah muttered.

"It's not?"

"If it's anonymous, then it's clearly not me," I asserted, wondering why that had sounded different in my head.

"It hasn't posted anything bad about Delta Beta," Maya said.

Oh, fudge. Surely, the A team hadn't been so obvious. I couldn't check here to prove otherwise, so I had to say something. As in all things, sometimes a woman just needed to fake it to make it. I tossed my ponytail. "Well, maybe that's because Delta Beta has nothing to hide. Unlike some people."

The other four advisors gasped, as if they'd been rehearsing all week. Seriously, the timed reactions were getting weird. But I needed to skedaddle. I had a lot to do in a small amount of time, and with the rest of the chapters out for blood, today might be our best chance to make a great impression.

"You know, it was great talking with everyone, and I so appreciate this show of Panhellenic support—"

"Suck it."

That came from Sarah, and I decided to just be quiet a moment and let that hang out there, like a booger she had forgotten to wipe off the end of her nose. I was the classier person; and even the other women were giving her the judgy side-eye. There were some things a sorority woman just didn't say out loud, even if she was a Moo.

Now was the time to pretend my phone was ringing. "Ah. Yes." I checked the screen. "I know we all have so much to do. Best of luck today, ladies." I gave them my biggest kill-them-with-kindness smile and hustled out of the room.

Chapter Seventeen

THE AFTERNOON WHIPPED by, fast and furious. By necessity, I had to put all thoughts of murder, mayhem, and retaliation out of my mind. It was imperative that we have a successful second day of rush. Tomorrow was not guaranteed: It could be taken away any minute by a cranky police officer or bitter old biddies.

I was so focused on getting everything ready for the day that I even missed a call from Casey. I'd call him after the parties to give him the good news that Delta Beta had successfully recruited the heck out of day two.

Today, the ladies were dressed in matching black loose tops with glittery gold stripes over black skinny jeans with cognac wedge boots. The effect was a preppy chorus line. Ten minutes before showtime, the chapter was lined up in their prescribed order, with ruler-straight posture, flawless makeup, and blinding white smiles.

If I was being honest, I did see a few cracks in our spackle. How could there not be? There had been two police officers stationed in the Rush Dungeon this morning, questioning the sisters about a mysterious dead body that had been found just yards from where they would now be performing the age-old sacred bounce-snap routine. It would fluster even the most professional rusher.

And speaking of professional rushers, where was Sheila De-Grasse? She hadn't attended the emergency Panhellenic meeting earlier, but that didn't mean she didn't know exactly what was going down from her perch in the Tri Mu house.

The social-media attack of this afternoon would have put the rest of the chapters on notice. Maybe they would even be implementing their own Plan B, as I stood here inspecting our daily banner, in the adorable style of an old-time theater marquee: "NOW PLAYING: DELTA BETA." That anonymous Twitter account had taken the gloves off by posting possibly defaming information about the houses—including Delta Beta, as I had confirmed as soon as I was able to check. Though I wasn't sure anyone would believe that our sorority's dirty secret was being "too good" at flat-ironing naturally curly hair.

I couldn't predict what the other chapters would come up with, and, in the case of Sheila DeGrasse especially, what was already planned. Another reason why we had to be perfect. Again.

I ascended the staircase and blew my whistle to get the chapter's attention. It was time to motivate: a heady responsibility, but I was sure I could come up with something to say.

"SISTERS!" I clapped my hands. Everyone went silent and stood at attention. The Gineral must have had them practicing while I was on campus. "We are on the cusp of a day that will live in infamy. Yesterday, we blew apart every single rush record that has ever been set at Sutton. Tonight, we have the best of the best women returning to our house. Don't stop believing! Hold on to that feeling! We are on the edge of glory. The players? They're going to play. All those haters? They're going to hate. And the rest of sorority row? They're going to hear us roar. Because you only get one shot, do not miss your chance to blow. This opportunity only comes once in a lifetime." By the end of my little speech, my positive words had the chapter glowing with pride and confidence. It was just the extra push they needed, right before we opened the doors and started screaming our little hearts out.

Ginnifer tapped me on the shoulder. "Can I say something?" Her eyes were wide and serious; how could I say no? She was working so hard for our chapter, and I had to give her credit for her Latin-American-dictator style.

I ceremonially handed over the whistle, and she took a moment to compose herself. It was gratifying that she was also overcome with emotion at my motivational words, but the clock was ticking, Martinelli. I gave her three more seconds; and then she spoke. Actually, she yelled. "Listen up, DEBS! I have not come all this way to this flipping hillbilly town to see you throw it all away!"

The chapter was stunned. I was shocked. Ginnifer was from Alabama, and she was calling North Carolina 'hillbilly'?" Seemed unnecessary.

"That stunt you pulled today on Twitter was UNACCEPT-ABLE!" Veins popped from her neck. "DID YOU NOT UNDER-STAND THE RULES? NUMBER THREE RING A BELL? NO SOCIAL MEDIA! AND WHAT DID I SAY?" She pointed at poor Kennedi Worth, her hair-sprayed curls were dropping from the fear. "WHAT DID I SAY, WORTH?"

Kennedi shook in her boots. "There would be consequences?"

"SEVERE CONSEQUENCES!" Ginnifer screamed, now with a little vein dangerously bulging on her forehead. I had to calm her down, or someone at the fire station was going to win thirty bucks in the Margot Blythe emergency pool.

I placed a hand on Ginnifer's shoulder blade. "I think they got it," I whispered. "We have a minute before the door opens."

Ginnifer made a visible effort to recover her composure. "I think we got the message across," she muttered.

The chapter's shine of confidence seemed a little dimmer. But I had no time to try to counteract Miss Negativity. "Places!" I yelled, holding my hand up so everyone could see me count down the seconds. "Heads up! Shoulders back! SMILE!"

At the designated time, I threw my hand down like I was the flag girl at a NASCAR race. The front doors flew open, and the best singers in our chapter stood in the doorway.

"We the girls of Delta Beta," rang out in angelic three-part harmony.

Silently, we all counted.

One. Two. Three.

STOMP

STOMP

STOMP.

I lifted an eyebrow at Ginnifer. Their stomps were as fierce as ever.

"WE ARE THE GIRLS! THE GIRLS OF DELTA BEE!"

"WHO ARE THE GIRLS?" asked one half of the chapter, on one side of the entry.

"WE ARE THE GIRLS—THE GIRLS OF DELTA BEE," the other half screamed.

Snap. Snap. Snap.

"DONCHA WONCHA BE A DELTA BEE, TOO?"

Bounce snap.

"YOU KNOW YOU WANNA BE DONCHA WANNA BE . . ."

Bounce snap.

They hadn't missed a snap. I blew out a sigh of relief as pickups started. Maybe Ginnifer's scream-a-thon hadn't negatively affected their confidence.

The first party went as well as could be expected. Maybe the energy level could have been higher, maybe the bumping lagged a bit, but as the week went on, and the ladies' sleep deficits grew, it would be harder and harder to operate at a hundred percent.

As soon as the next party started, the energy level was still down, and I could tell something was off. To identify the problem, I had to join the throng.

Normally, the chapter advisor wasn't visible during rush. She could be in a corner with a clipboard, or on the staircase with a secret remote control for the lights, but she wasn't circulating and greeting potential sisters. But seeing as I was only twenty-six and remarkably well preserved for my age, I figured it wouldn't hurt the Delta Beta image for me to be seen.

Walking around the groups of women, I didn't see or hear anything that explained the shift in energy I felt. As far as I could tell, the chapter sisters were doing everything they were supposed to be doing, if maybe 2.3 seconds slower than they should be.

By the third party, there was a definite change in the rushees. They were hyped up about something, and when I started walking through the floor, I overheard enough proof to know exactly what was going on.

I ran back to the Rush Dungeon and pulled up Twitter. After a quick search, I could see that Nick Holden's account was the culprit. His accusatory tweets about sororities mirrored some of the questions that the rushees were asking the actives during the party. "Do you really circle the fat parts of pledges' bodies?" "Do you force pledges to make out with each other?" "Do you give out free beer?"

Everyone knew the answers to these questions: "Of course not," "Totally their choice," and "That is illegal and high in carbs."

To post these blatantly defaming and insulting tweets about sorority rush was a clear declaration of his intent. He wanted to destroy our way of life, and I had to wonder if he knew what he was getting into.

And although we were fully prepared to field questions about any tacky allegations the rushees were reading on their phones between parties, we were not prepared for what was about to happen.

When a rushee asked Aubrey about the port-a-potty in our front yard, she laughed it off, thinking maybe the girl had just called our atrium by the wrong name. Then someone else asked about the sign on the front of the port-a-potty. Then I was alerted, and because technically chapter advisors could leave the house during a rush event, I made a beeline for the front yard. There, I discovered that the rushees hadn't been confused, or misinformed.

There was, indeed a bright blue port-a-potty in our front yard. The turquoise did not match our theme for the day at all, and neither did the signs painted on the front. "DELTA BETAS ARE FULL OF . . ."

I whipped out my phone to call . . . who? Who would I call? Emergency services? They'd laugh at me, and some guy named Joe in Sanitation would be sent out because he won fifty big ones.

Panhellenic? That was an option, of course, but I would need more evidence before I brought this to the Mafia. I had to be strategic about these things, especially as I had used up all of my goodwill today.

The most I could do at the moment was tear down the signs, lift my chin, and show the rushees outside the house how a Delta Beta chapter advisor reacts when her enemies try to take her down.

Chapter Eighteen

THE CHEERS WEREN'T quite as jubilant after the doors closed today, but I still had to hand it to my girls. Overall, they'd faced severe adversity and survived, with their class and makeup intact. They were true testaments to the ideals of Delta Beta womanhood.

As proud as they were of their accomplishments, I could see the rumblings starting. Some had their phones out and were seeing Nick Holden's tweets about Sutton rush for the first time. If I didn't do something soon, I could have a revolt on my hands, maybe one I couldn't control.

I blew my whistle. "Into the chapter room, ladies!"

As the women were filing in, I grabbed Ginnifer by the elbow.

"You have to let me handle this," I said in a low voice.

She looked confused and a little alarmed. "Handle what?"

"The stuff that happened today. You know as well as I do what sorority women are capable of. We have to allow the girls to let off some steam, or else real trouble is going to hit us."

Ginnifer looked like she was about to say something but bit her lip and reluctantly nodded. I knew that restraint was probably going to be hard for someone like her, but I knew these women a bit better than she did. She had to trust me.

After the ladies settled down, I once again told them what a terrific job they had done. Then I addressed the elephant in the room.

"As some of you are aware, there have been some critics tweeting trying to mess with our heads. This is a psychological tactic, everyone; Nick Holden is trying to get into our heads. And I know that Delta Betas will not be brought down by mental issues. We have our own mental issues, and we're going to stick by them."

I got a couple of strange looks, but I was tired, and I'm sure they knew what I meant.

"Please. Do not stoop to his level. Remember the five rules of recruitment. Do NOT go on social media, tonight, whatever you do. The Mafia will be watching for any misstep, and we are not going to give them that ammunition."

Some ladies still looked different shades of ticked off and confused, but with my message delivered, I dismissed the chapter for dinner. I felt better for one moment, until the doorbell rang, instantly spiking my anxiety. It could be anything on the other side of that door. Thirty third-grader hired assassins with Nerf guns. A flaming bag of dog poop. An Ed McMahon impersonator with a fake lottery check. Who knew what kind of evil plots the other chapters had up their sleeves?

So it was with a sigh of relief when I opened the door and found Lieutenant Hatfield, holding a bucket of fried chicken. Law enforcement and trans fats were not my favorite combination of weapons, but on a day like today, it was the least of my worries.

"Chicken?" He held the bucket toward me.

I shook my head regretfully; the grease would go straight to my hips. He selected a juicy leg, and I decided to start off on a good note.

"I'm sorry about today," I said. "Again." I really was. Ordinarily, a Delta Beta would always cooperate with law enforcement to the best of her ability. But I had been placed in an impossible position.

"Someone in your house knows something about Shannon Bender's murder," Ty said.

"You shouldn't assume things." Ty's eyes shifted from his chicken to me, and I felt encouraged to continue. "Maybe someone from another house followed her here and purposely murdered her to make us look bad." It sounded insane, I knew. But when I told Ty about Nick Holden's tweets, he tossed his half-eaten piece of chicken in the trash can and took out his notepad.

"He's purposely trying to make us look bad, to further his own agenda. Who would do something like that?" I asked after I told Ty what Nick had tweeted about the "Dead Delta Beta" house, pointing out that sorority women were one hundred percent more likely to die at our house. "It was just sick. Twisted." I wrapped my arms around myself and realized that while I had pushed the chapter to overcome the murders of three months ago, I wasn't sure I ever would. The deaths of my sisters would forever haunt me. And that was when it hit me: Shannon Bender was someone's sister, too.

I had known that, logically, as soon as Ty had told me of her Tri Mu affiliation. But right then, I felt it, in my gut. Someone else would be haunted as I was.

"Have you told them?"

Ty looked up from his notes. "Told who what?"

"The Tri Mus. About Shannon Bender."

He shook his head. "She wasn't a member here. She was a member from some school in the Northwest."

That jiggled something in my brain. But I was too overcaffeinated, underrested, and anxious to fully explore it right now. "What was on the card? In the glasses?"

Ty made that face that he did when he didn't want to tell me something. I understood. I often did not want to tell him things. Still. "I want to help. I do. Maybe if you let me see it, I'll be able to see something, recognize something."

His sigh told me he was still reluctant even if his next words didn't. "You could be a suspect."

I threw up my hands. "Really? What was the time of death?"

He looked taken aback, then decided to tell me that the ME had approximated Shannon Bender's time of death to be around 9:00 A.M. on Friday.

"HA! I cannot be a suspect, and neither can the rest of our chapter. Because at the time of Shannon Bender's death, we were having mandatory pedicures downtown at the Sutton Spa Royale."

He looked skeptical, so I threw in the one piece of evidence that always worked on *Law & Order*. "We have credit-card receipts."

"For the whole chapter?"

"All you had to do was ask."

"Pedicures for a mass alibi," he muttered as he scribbled in his notebook.

"Spa pedicures," I added. "Which take nearly an hour and a half."

Ty took a deep breath and closed his notebook. "Would you like to go down to the station with me?"

"In the front seat or backseat?" I had been to the Sutton police station both ways. I definitely had a preference.

"Front seat," Ty said almost gallantly, and I was feeling pleasantly warm with the invitation until he shoved the bucket at me. "You can hold the chicken."

TY PULLED UP the files on his computer, and I watched in silence. There were only five minutes of shaky footage, and I wasn't sure I was going to be any help at all. But I asked to see it again and this time was moved to take notes.

But at the end of the second viewing, I didn't have anything that would help the Sutton Police Department find Shannon Bender's killer. "Nothing?" Ty asked incredulously. "You have nothing?"

I looked down at my notes. "She had a great shoe collection."

Ty looked like that observation caused him pain, but of course I'd noticed the dust bags lying on her hotel-room floor and the distinctive red soles of the heels on top of them. What kind of Delta Beta wouldn't make note of that?

There was only one other thing, and when I mentioned it, I could tell Ty was having a very hard time stopping his eyeballs from rolling into the back of his head.

"So?" he said, reluctantly.

"It just stood out, is all."

"A vase of purple lilies stood out?"

There had been a blip, at the beginning of the recording. Maybe not even two seconds long, like there had been something else that was recorded over. There was a shot of a fabulous chandelier, then the person wearing the Witness glasses had moved her head, down to the center of what looked like a beautiful entry hall, where a crystal vase of deep violet lilies sat atop a shiny cherry antique table. Then the footage ended and restarted with Shannon doing a check in her hotel room of the glasses. Then that was it.

"It's January," I tried to explain. "Lilies aren't big this time of year."

"Okay . . ."

I sighed. That really wasn't why the lilies stood out. But like the shoes, they had, whether because I'm a girl who just likes a nice floral arrangement or because it really was a clue that my brain couldn't interpret at the moment.

"I don't know," I said wearily. "If I think of something else, I'll let you know."

Ty regarded me for a moment. "How much sleep have you gotten this week?"

I blinked. That was a conversation switcheroo. "I plead the fifth," I answered cautiously. You never knew what was considered "illegal" to Ty Hatfield.

"I appreciate the help." His voice sounded formal and sad, almost, and I thought I knew why. Because Ty Hatfield took pride in his work, like me, and he didn't like to let people down, either.

"I need to get back to the house," I said, trying to bite back a yawn. Day two's completion only meant that the chapter needed to prepare for the next day of rush, and there were about three hundred votive candles that needed to be wrapped with gold ribbon and sealed off with hot glue.

Ty nodded. "I'll drive you back." We had just buckled into the squad car when he checked a message on his phone and looked at me. "You wouldn't know anything about a hundred packages of stinky cheese being placed in the heating vents of a sorority house tonight . . ."

I couldn't help but laugh. That was a good one. I shook my head. "You know me better than that. I would never send my girls into HVAC systems." The dust would wreak havoc on their clothes. And just think of their manicures.

Ty chuckled and threw the car into gear.

"Besides, we abide by all applicable Panhellenic curfews," I said solemnly.

We drove for a few minutes, lost in our own thoughts, and when he finally pulled into the Deb parking lot, he nonchalantly asked, "So you've been meeting with Concannon?"

Ty and Brice had some history, but then so did Ty and me. We'd interacted a little in college, a time when he was fifty pounds heavier and not as hot and as assertive as he was now. He was scarily good at recalling details from years ago, and whatever Brice had done to tick Ty off, I knew it was probably serious.

"He's doing a report for the college. And he set up my interview with Nick Holden."

"The reporter? You met with him, too? And you say you don't have time for the police investigation?"

That stung. "Hey, I'm cooperating now. As long as it doesn't interfere with rush." I was just ribbing him a little, but he didn't smile back.

"Margot, this isn't a joke. I'm not asking you for information just because I like hanging around you. It concerns me that someone murdered Shannon Bender while she was wearing a Delta Beta shirt." Ty's hand had reached across the car and brushed my jacket sleeve. "It could have been . . . someone else."

I got what he was saying, I did. "No one's going to be breaking curfew, Ty. Not on my watch. We're playing it safe, from now on."

Chapter Nineteen

I AWOKE EARLY the next morning with my special Panhellenic ringtone blaring "Welcome to the Jungle." "What," I answered groggily. I usually sound a bit more professional when speaking to the Panhellenic advisor, but glue-gunning hundreds of pieces of sparkly gold ribbon had taken until nearly 3:00 A.M.

Poor Maya Rodman stuttered nervously, "Emergency meeting. Th-th-thirty minutes," right before hanging up. Really.

I rolled out of bed and knew I should make an effort, seeing as the Debs had been on thin ice at the last emergency meeting. But on the other hand, I had thirty minutes, and I had not had coffee yet. A girl had to make priorities.

And compromises, I thought, as I jogged down the stairs to the Panhellenic offices on campus. This morning's compromise had been wearing the dirty yoga pants (which were black, after all) with a clean Sutton College sweatshirt. I had also compromised with a drip coffee at the drive-thru.

But I waved my personal Delta Beta coffee mug at the room

when I walked in and smiled like I had no idea what was going on or why this meeting was called.

Because, to be honest? I didn't. And that was kind of annoying.

I'm the type of girl who likes to be in the know about everything, even if I act befuddled. I learned long ago that sometimes it pays to be considered the stupidest person in the room as long as you're secretly the smartest person. Today, it was galling to know that maybe I was the least knowledgeable person.

The advisors took their places at the table, and so did the Mafia.

The door opened again, we all turned, and who should it be but Her Evilness herself, Ms. Sheila DeGrasse.

I hated Sheila for many reasons. I hated what she stood for. I hated that she did rush for the money and not for the love of sisterhood. I hated that at eight thirty on a Wednesday during rush, she had the nerve to walk in here with a DVF wrap dress, a TDF statement necklace, and OTT platform heels. That bitch.

And now, somehow, she had ingratiated herself with the college president and the news reporter who had already produced one television special that tried to take Delta Beta down.

My mean-girl detector was going off, big-time. Sheila was up to something evil. As usual.

Unfortunately, she took a seat at the far end of the table, next to the Tri Mu advisor, as if she knew that I was only drinking drip coffee and wouldn't care if it spilled all over that lovely silk jersey dress she wore.

A bang came from the front of the room: Lo and behold, Patty Huntington actually held a gavel. That's when I knew things had gotten serious.

But none of the Mafia spoke. They sat there with their folded arms, their glares hot and judgmental behind their bifocals. I hadn't felt like this since my mother dropped me off for Catholic education, and the nuns found out I wasn't Catholic—my mother had just needed some free child care.

The seconds ticked away, and I couldn't stand it anymore. Maybe the other houses had all their work done, but the Delta Betas had two hundred stuffed bumblebees to arrange artfully. I raised my hand. "I'm sorry—Maya didn't tell me what this meeting was about."

The room exploded, as every chapter advisor began unleashing her fury.

"Do you have any idea what blue cheese does to lace doilies?"

"It is unacceptable in this day and age! We need our Internet to be porn-free!"

"With God as my witness, someone is going to pay for those lilies!"

Slowly, I began to realize that all of the houses had been the recipients of various pranks the night before, and that the Delta Betas had gotten off easy, with a port-a-potty in the front yard.

While the rest of the advisors were ranting about the injustices done to their house, I watched Sheila. Still sitting, her arms crossed, a stone-cold look on her face. I remembered the rush at ICU and the bedbugs and the ice-cold water and the food poisoning. The Internet hacking and the stinky cheese and a port-a-potty were exactly the kinds of tactics the Moos were paying for, in the form of one Ms. DeGrasse.

Patty Huntington banged her gavel again. "Ladies! This behavior is unacceptable!"

"Since when," the Lambda advisor muttered.

"Since we have been under intense scrutiny from the college, parents, the press . . ."

Von Douton interrupted her. "Nick Holden, to be exact. It has come to our attention that he is here, in Sutton, demanding interviews with those who are connected with sororities."

"Therefore, as of today, we are instituting a new transparency policy," Louella Jackson said.

That wasn't good. Sororities didn't do transparency.

I raised my hand. "What do you mean by, 'transparency'?" Yes, I used finger quotes.

Clara-Jane Booth smiled, just like the kindly grandmother she undoubtedly wanted people to believe she was. "We want to foster a community of open, honest communication. We need to open our doors, share safety concerns, best practices, feel free to tell our stories."

"Sunshine is the best disinfectant, after all," Sue Harlow chirped.

That I could not agree with. Everyone I knew carried little bottles of apricot-mango-scented antibacterial gel to combat the winter colds that ran rampant during rush.

Von Douton spoke up. "That is why we are opening the floor to all of you, to discuss what you've heard about Nick Holden and his plans for his so-called investigative report." Then she glared at the panel of chapter advisors, as if it was our fault for not obstructing the freedom of the press.

This seemed . . . oddly specific. The Epsilon Chi advisor spoke first. "The interfraternity advisor e-mailed me about speaking with Holden." Several other ladies nodded.

"He invited rushees to a round table last week. I know a few of our members were contacted," the Lambda advisor said. "And according to his Twitter feed, he seems to have very strong feelings about sorority life."

"He thinks sororities are outdated and sexist," the Epsilon Chi advisor added.

"He doesn't like us very much." Sarah McLane pointed out the obvious, as usual.

"No, he doesn't," Louella said sharply. She pointed a pen toward the Lambda advisor. "What did your girls say to him?"

"I . . . I . . . don't know. It's rush week."

The answer made perfect sense to me, but Louella seemed shocked. "We have a *threat* on this campus, and you don't *know* what your members are telling him?"

As one, the Mafia shook their heads in dismay.

"I think it's obvious what needs to be done." Alexandria sniffed. "From this point on, anyone who is found to be assisting Nick Holden in his attempts to destroy Sutton College Panhellenic will face severe consequences."

"I second," Louella said.

"All those in favor?" Alexandria didn't finish her question before four hands rose around her.

It was one thing when I had objections to assisting Nick Holden, but coming on the heels for a plea for "transparency," something was fishy here. And I wasn't the only one who thought so.

Sheila DeGrasse stood gracefully. "I'd like to enter an objection to the recent motion."

She was suddenly in the glare of the Mafia's ultracritical spotlight, and I had to admire how she stayed cool as a cucumber. "I fail to see how not cooperating with the press assists this Panhellenic. It won't protect us, it will only empower Nick Holden to come up with his own opinions on the recent events at Sutton. Don't we want him to hear our side?"

I shifted in my seat, acutely aware that Sheila's thoughts were eerily similar to my own.

"Everyone here needs to start cooperating, with each other, with the press, with the police."

The way she said that got my attention. It was funny. In all the hubbub about transparency and dialogue, Sheila was the first one to mention giving information to the police. Was it her guilty conscience?

"You're not from here," Louella pointed out, and many of the women in the room nodded in agreement. "You don't have a vested interest in the long-term viability of this Panhellenic."

Sheila's lips pursed. She clearly did not like being told that. "I've already spoken with Nick Holden and agreed to answer questions on camera."

Suddenly, I realized I was in a very precarious position, as someone who had also already cooperated with Holden and for the same reasons as Sheila. The Mafia was wrong on this call, and Leticia and Mary Gerald would want me to speak up for the rights of anyone who believed in the First Amendment and the right to lie to the press.

"I find myself in the unfortunate position of agreeing with Ms. DeGrasse."

Wait.

Did I really say that?

The rest of the advisors and Mafia seemed to be checking their hearing as well. A Delta Beta agreeing with Tri Mu? It was unheard of.

And very, very suspicious.

Alexandria Von Douton lifted a shocked brow as high as it could go, as frozen as her forehead was. "What, exactly, are you saying, Ms. Blythe."

"I'm saying that the Delta Betas will be thrilled to cooperate with the police, as always." That didn't sound right. "And I also will be participating in Mr. Holden's interviews. Because we can't let the terrorists win."

Some of the women seemed disconcerted by that idea, and some looked ready to attack. I wondered who would win the Sutton town services pool if I called in after being beaten by a bunch of Coach handbags.

Patty Huntington opened a sheet of folded paper that Alexandria had just handed her. "It seems that charges have been filed against Ms. DeGrasse and Ms. Blythe."

"What are you talking about?" Sheila demanded.

"I was cleared of those!" I screeched. "I'm innocent!"

Patty showed no emotion as she read, "The council will therefore apply rule 7.8, subsection D."

That was one of the Mafia's new rules, so it took me a little longer to realize what was about to happen. But when I did, I thought I'd prefer being beaten senseless by a bunch of swinging leather handbags.

Chapter Twenty

THE DOOR TO room 308 of the Fountain Place Inn slammed behind me, every bit as ominous a sound as the clang of the holding-cell door at the Sutton police station.

The last time I had been confined against my will was due to a small criminal misunderstanding. This time, it was over a Panhellenic rule. And I had company. Under rule 7.8, subsection D of the Sutton Panhellenic Recruitment Code, the Mafia had the power to eject misbehaving participants from the recruitment process. Now, I know many sisters around the country would rejoice at this rule, but really, me? Misbehaving? I was a chapter advisor. It was my job to set a shining example for my chapter. My behavior was really beyond reproach.

The Mafia, however, disagreed. Because Sheila and I had just been written up, we had to spend twenty-four hours in solitary confinement, away from our chapters.

I was about to decline this punishment for these clearly trumped-up charges, and shout a few quotes about "give me liberty or give me death" and "no taxation without representation," until Patty Huntington informed us of the fine that the chapter would pay if I did. Let's just say, the Sutton chapter needed heat this winter, so I chose to bravely face imprisonment for my beliefs. Like Mandela.

My last contact with the outside world were quick calls to Callie and Ginnifer, urging them to be strong, stay the course, and recruit the heck out of our legacies. Then I had to take a deep breath, face my situation, and try to make the best of it. One day in a hotel room with Sheila DeGrasse. It could be worse. I could be at the Happy Times Motel down by the interstate.

The Fountain Place Inn was the nicest historic motel in Sutton, and Sheila DeGrasse (of course) had taken residence in the penthouse suite. The room was formally decorated in rose and powder-blue floral chintz, the draperies a royal-blue thick brocade. The suite boasted a small kitchenette and a seating area with a compact pullout couch and Queen-Anne-style chair. It smelled like Thierry Mugler's Angel, but I was almost positive that was Sheila's doing. Irony, thy name is heavy-handed perfume names.

Sheila kicked off her platform heels and took them to the closet, where she froze, as if she wasn't sure what to do next. In that, we were the same. I had no idea what to do, either. The last three months of my life, I had been constantly on the go, my mind racing from one priority to the next, all of it building up to the legacy that I would leave after this week was over.

And now . . . I could do nothing. Maya had collected our phones and laptops until she came to retrieve us the next day. I didn't even have my rush binder with me, leaving it behind when I left the house that morning, frantic and late for an emergency meeting. How could I know that I wouldn't be returning to the bosom of my chapter to hang garlands of plastic flowers and fake palm trees for our Hawaiian-themed day of rush?

Suddenly, my eyes filled with tears. It was the stress. Being out of control and frustrated would make anyone tear up.

At the sound of my sniffle, Sheila spun on her stockinged foot. "Don't you dare play the victim."

Well, that shocked the cry right out of me.

"If you hadn't been such a fuckup, none of this would be happening."

I would have been surprised at the profanity, but it was Sheila DeGrasse who was using it.

"Me?" I stuttered, almost at a loss for words. The woman had lost her grip on reality. "You told them you had talked to Nick Holden first."

Sheila's lip curled. "And then you had to copy me like always!"

"What are you even talking about?" I asked, confused at her nonsense. "Copy you? I wasn't copying you. I was trying to make sure Nick Holden wasn't poisoned by the lies you told."

"My lies? I'm an outsider here, I'm the only one that will tell him the truth!"

She grunted her frustration when she threw her shoes into the closet. I gasped. Those were Louboutons.

"We have to spend the next twenty-four hours together. We should at least try to be civil."

Sheila scoffed. "I tried to be civil when I came to the Little Debbie house before rush started. You called me a skanky sellout."

I opened my mouth to confirm that opinion, then closed it. Sheila might have been a little right about that. Those words were less than civil.

"I'm sorry," I said. Sheila shrugged off my apology, but I wondered if I had really hurt her feelings that night. What had she said? That she was trying to be friends? That we were alike? Here I thought she had possibly been high on her hair spray when she'd said that. And now look where we were. Locked up, like two very-stylishly-coordinated zoo animals.

"I'm sorry," I repeated. "As I'm sure you know, rush can be extremely stressful."

Sheila nodded in agreement. "So stressful." There was a pause before she spoke again. "I have hardly gotten any sleep the past few days."

"I can count up my total weekly sleeping hours on two hands."

Sheila winced. "That explains those circles under your eyes."

I gasped. "I thought we were being civil."

She reached out to push down my hand, pressed against my cheekbone. "We are. I didn't mean it like that." She seemed really contrite. "I almost didn't notice the dark circles because you're looking so thin."

My hand dropped to my belly button. My pants had seemed looser this week, but I'd attributed it to stress and not eating solid food.

Thinking about my stress levels brought everything back. Sheila must have been thinking about it, too, because we both looked at our watches at the exact moment.

"T minus sixty minutes," she said.

I put a hand to my chest as my heart sped up at the thought. "I need to be there," I said, mostly to myself.

Sheila wiped her brow with the back of her hand. "I don't know if Sarah can handle the schedule by herself."

Oh no. I closed my eyes. I had the remote control for the house lights in my purse. How would the chapter know when to start the skit without me there to dim the lights? It felt like my chest was in a vise.

"I can't breathe," Sheila said, putting her hand down and lowering herself to the bed.

"Air," I said, moving to the A/C unit under the window and flipping it to high. The roar of the unit filled the room, and a blast of hot air was shot into my face instead of the cool air I was expecting; given that this was January, when the unit was used for heating. The heat made me feel faint, and I quickly sat down on the other side of the king-sized bed.

After a few minutes, I still felt the adrenaline coursing through my veins. This is not healthy, Margot, I told myself, and bad for my under-eye circles besides. There had to be something else for me to think about aside from whether the Delta Beta chapter was hurtling toward disaster if they couldn't pull off a synchronized hula tonight.

"How bad was the cheese?"

"What?" Sheila asked after a beat.

"The cheese in your ducts. How bad was it?"

A tortured sigh was her first response. "Pretty bad. Someone inserted it in the heating vents in the dining room. We didn't discover it until this morning."

"Accessed the heating vents from the crawl space under the house?"

"How did you know?"

"Just a guess."

Sheila looked across the span of the bed at me, the question plain in her eyes. "Nope, it wasn't me. Or any other Debs."

"Too busy tweeting last night?"

"That was Nick Holden," I assured her.

She frowned. "What do you think he's up to?"

I rubbed my hand over my forehead. It was a good question. Why would a reporter like him try to stir up so much trouble?

"I guess he's just trying to get a story," I suggested.

"How did you know about the—"

"Crawl space that's accessible from the western porch?" I finished that for her and decided to answer truthfully. The statute of limitations was up, anyway. "There was a night, much like this one, seven years ago, when four brave Debs placed smoke bombs underneath the Moo house. The Moos had to evacuate until the firemen said they could go back in."

Thankfully, Sheila didn't run to the courtesy phone to report me to 9-1-1. Who even knew if the dispatch operators took bets on things that happened seven years ago.

I picked up the remote control and turned the TV on and got a sign that God still loved me, Margot Blythe, sorority criminal, after all. *Law & Order* was on.

Chapter Twenty-one

TURNS OUT, *LAW & ORDER* is the universal language that brings us all closer. Sheila and I were soon sucked into the episode with the snotty society mother and her sociopathic, prep-school son, like there had never been any conflict between us. I wondered if the United Nations knew about this secret for world peace.

As engrossing as it was, the show didn't completely make us forget everything that was going on in the world. As the afternoon and evening ticked by, I soon noticed that Sheila would check her watch just when I did—both still on rush schedules, even as we watched the young blond DA verbally tear apart the molesting priest on the witness stand.

Maya had dinner delivered for us, and the Mexican takeout from El Loco Pollo made me think of Ty, with his donuts, pizza, chicken. I wondered if he'd made any progress with the Shannon Bender case. Watching *L&O* was taking my mind off rush but reminding me of the inevitable progress of the legal system. First there was a death. Then there were several visits from world-weary and rumpled detectives. Then the lab came back with a piece of incontrovertible evidence that the detectives couldn't ignore anymore, and they would make an arrest.

Apparently, when rush wasn't consuming my brain, there was room for other, sadder things.

Sheila waved her hand in front of my face. "Hey. They just arrested the stockbroker, and you didn't say, 'so obvious.'"

I cast a quick look at the screen. "Well it is."

"So obvious," Sheila said for me. "I think I've seen this episode about ten times though."

"You're a *Law & Order* fan?"

She nodded. "I travel so much, it's pretty much the only thing that's on no matter where I go in the country."

I knew what she meant. "When I traveled as a sisterhood mentor, I watched it everywhere."

A shadow crossed her eyes. "It's probably why the chapter was in such good hands last year, after the . . . unfortunate incidents."

The murders. I did appreciate her trying to be polite about it.

"And now you have another one . . ." Her voice ran out, like the slowing down of a treadmill that had been unplugged.

I glanced up sharply at her, looking for any sign that she was about to mock me, my chapter, or use this against us in anyway. Just because we'd bonded over *L&O* and tacos didn't mean that I was letting my guard down where the Tri Mu rush consultant was concerned. It was still her job to take us down.

But there was no gloating on Sheila's face. No sign of a malicious intent or sneaky snarkiness. Instead, she looked . . . lost. Maybe a little bereft. Maybe a touch of fright was there.

"Yes," I said carefully, wanting to watch what I said, especially with the expression on Sheila's face. Evil Incarnate Sheila I could

deal with. Emotionally vulnerable Sheila might be more dangerous. "But the police are taking care of that."

"Do they know . . ." And the way she left that open-ended further confirmed my gut feeling that I did not want to get into this
with Sheila. Not here. Not now. Not without my cell phone to text
a warning of impending bedbug invasion.

And I guess that she didn't want to talk about it anymore,
either, because then she turned the volume up, and since it was a
good episode, with Angie Harmon as the tough-talking brunette
DA (as a natural brunette myself, I empathized with her struggles
to break the blond Assistant DA glass ceiling), I closed my mouth
and let the soothing rhythms of *Law & Order* relax me.

Nearly nine hours later, I woke to a knocking at the door of
the suite.

Sheila stumbled to the door while I tried to make sense of the
mystery of what had just happened. Sleep? During rush week?
And in Sheila DeGrasse's hotel room?

If you had told me this set of events several weeks ago, I would
have calmly and firmly escorted you down to the Student Health
clinic and requested a head exam.

Even now, I wasn't sure I believed it, except I felt this strange
peace that could only come from a full night's sleep.

That peace lasted about thirty seconds.

"I got permission from the council," Maya was saying. 'You
guys need to head back to your houses."

She wouldn't tell us more, and when she handed back our cell
phones, they were both dead. I grabbed my tote, Sheila locked the
door to her room, and we walked downstairs to the lobby together.

"Margot . . ." she began.

"It's okay." I put a hand on her coat sleeve, interrupting her. "I accept your apology."

She should have looked overjoyed at my benevolence, but that same sad, stressed expression was on her face again.

"I was hoping we could call a truce."

A truce? "But we haven't done anything to the Tri Mus."

Sheila gave me a look like she didn't want to argue. Well, we hadn't done anything to the Moos that we hadn't done to everyone else, I thought, thinking of the anonymous Twitter account that pushed more than a few Panhellenic buttons.

We were at our cars. "Don't you get tired of all this?" She waved a hand around in the air.

"Sutton's a nice place,' I said defensively. "Maybe it's a little small, but really, it has everything—"

"No, the constant competition. Sorority life. Always being so ruthless and mean."

My car keys stilled in midair as I thought about that. My automatic answer was, of course, no. I loved everything about sorority life, everything about Delta Beta. I even loved the bouncing and the snapping, and the flurry of activities and the constant chatter of college women and the lack of sleep . . .

Okay, there were some things I was probably over.

But I wasn't nearly over most of it. It was clear, though, that something was bothering Sheila. Maybe the great Sheila DeGrasse was nearing retirement, planning to leave at the height of her success, like Posh Spice's first retirement.

I kind of felt sorry for her. She was a wanderer, like I had been, going from chapter to chapter, with no permanent home, no true friends. A hired gun who just wanted to hang up her spurs and relax on a nice piece of property out West. Maybe I needed to stop watching the Western movies that always came on after an *L&O* marathon. Maybe I needed to try harder with Sheila.

"Okay," I said, even while a little Deb voice a lot like how I imagined Mary Gerald Callahan sounded was shouting in my head. "I think we can handle a little truce."

Little TRUCE?

I wasn't really sure what that might entail, but Sheila seemed reassured by it and stuck her hand out to shake on it.

I drove away, wondering whether I had just made a deal with the devil.

Chapter Twenty-two

As soon as I turned the corner onto Greek Row, I knew why Maya had been so insistent that Sheila and I return to our houses. Emergency vehicles blocked one end of the street, and crowds of young women stood in front of each of the sorority houses. I pulled my car over and parked illegally in front of a fire hydrant since every cop in Sutton was at the house with yellow crime-scene tape around it.

Thankfully, it wasn't mine.

Pushing through the crowds, I moved as fast as I could, feeling sick to my stomach.

Then I saw another familiar sight, the gurney and the ambulance and the tall, straight back of Lieutenant Hatfield, his sandy head bent and windblown as he talked to Sarah McLane at the Tri Mu house. My hand covered my mouth. *Oh no.*

"Margot!" I turned and saw Callie and Aubrey running to me, still in their pajama pants and slippers. It wasn't proper attire for leaving the house, especially during first-impression-is-everything rush week, but given that every sorority sister at

Sutton was out here in similar outfits, I wouldn't give it another thought. I clutched them tight to me with the horrible realization that we weren't promised today, or tomorrow. Or the next day. With Callie and Aubrey in my arms, I leaned in and whispered urgently, "Did we do something?"

I let them go and saw that although their eyes were wide, their heads were shaking vehemently. Good. The last thing I needed was this being a smoke-bomb prank gone wrong.

Our attention was again absorbed in the scene playing out in front of us at the Tri Mu house—it felt wrong to call them Moos at a time like this.

"I saw on Twitter that it's a disgruntled rushee who came after the Tri Mus with a steak knife after they cut her," Callie whispered to me.

"I heard it was Sheila DeGrasse finally snapping and throwing a flat iron into a bathtub."

That didn't even make sense. "Sheila was with me all night," I whispered back.

"I think you mean a toaster," Callie corrected Aubrey.

"Why would someone have a bathtub in the kitchen?" Aubrey asked.

There was a reason why Aubrey was our chapter president.

"How was your night in prison?" Aubrey asked, full of concern.

"Well, it wasn't prison exactly," I said, feeling vaguely guilty about my blissful nine hours of uninterrupted, *Law-&-Order*-induced sleep. "But more importantly, how did it go last night? Did the skit go well? What about the cues? Did anyone miss her cues?" I asked in a hushed voice, so that no one could overhear.

Aubrey and Callie hurriedly gave me the CliffsNotes version of the third day of rush. Although there were a few minor errors (how hard is it to play a ukulele, really?), it seemed as if the chapter's vast and concerted effort to be the most prepared chapter that Sutton rush had ever seen was paying off. Our top choices for sisters were coming back every night, and we had been extremely popular with all the rushees. So popular, we were having to cut a substantial percentage every day—heartbreaking. If I could open Delta Beta sisterhood to every woman in the world, I would. As long as they met our high criteria.

Through the crowd, I saw the police setting up a barricade in front of a few reporters and cameramen. There was Nick Holden, at the front of the group, with his head low and talking to the man next to him.

Memories of his unnecessarily venomous tweets about sorority life and the Debs in particular came back to me as I pushed through the crowd and got his attention. He followed me down to the Epsilon Chi house before I turned to speak.

"What was all that about the other night?"

Nick's eyelids dropped, and he licked his lips. "What other night?"

I threw up my hands. "Your tweets during the rush parties! They were uncalled for, hateful, spiteful. Why do you want to cause so much trouble?"

"I'm a public figure, Margot, and people are entitled to my opinion."

"Oh please," I scoffed. "You're a reporter who's trying to drum up controversy."

"I'm trying to open people's eyes and show them what sorority life is all about." He pointed at the Tri Mu house and the emergency vehicles parked there. "And I think I've been proved correct."

"You are disgusting. These are horrible events—"

"That seem to only happen to sorority women. The community, parents, the college, all are starting to see a pattern. Why can't you?"

I felt sick to my stomach when he mentioned a "pattern." Reality was yanking me out of my happy little fantasy world, and I hated when that happened. "What's your end game, Holden," I said quietly.

He smiled ruefully. "I told you in the coffee shop. You must not have been listening."

"The end of sororities?" I had to laugh. It was never going to happen. "Our sisterhoods will survive this."

"No, Margot. Your sisterhoods are self-destructing, and you can't even see it."

Maybe I couldn't see this pattern of self-destruction, but I knew I couldn't even look at him anymore. I spun on my heel and made it back to Aubrey and Callie. I put my arms around their shoulders again, reminding myself that sisterhood could withstand all threats, both foreign and domestic.

"Seriously, guys," I muttered. "Did anyone break curfew last night? Anything I should know about?"

"No," Aubrey answered. "Why?"

"Because Lieutenant Hatfield's headed this way, and from the looks of him, he has some questions for me."

And he did. "Margot." He tipped his baseball cap with the Sutton College eagle on it.

"Was it . . ."

"No," Ty answered, knowing what I needed to know. I breathed a sigh of relief that it wasn't one of my sisters in the back of that ambulance—though I immediately felt like a horrible person. It was still someone else's sister.

"She was rushing. A freshman."

A stab of pain shot through my stomach. I thought that hearing that a Delta Beta had been murdered would be the worst news I could hear, but this was shocking.

"Can you do me a favor?"

Of course, I said yes, and I didn't even regret my answer when I heard what the favor was.

He led me to the back door of the Tri Mu house. I hadn't been there since college, but it still looked the same. On the small, screened-in porch, Sarah McLane sat, completely devastated. As vast as the differences were between Delta Beta and Mu Mu Mu, today I recognized the pain in Sarah's face. One devoted chapter advisor to another, I knelt by her chair and took her hand. A Mu sister stood nearby, tear-stained and vulnerable.

"You—" I pointed at the sister. "Get me two cups of coffee and something sugary. A donut or something." She ran off so fast, I had confidence that she would know exactly where to find pastries here at the Tri Mu house.

I sat there silently, holding Sarah's hand until the coffees and a cherry Danish were produced. From experience, I knew that no amount of platitudes and vague prayers were going to make this any better. Women like us needed black coffee and time to adjust to a new reality. Then we'd be back.

In a little bit, the caffeine and sugar had helped walk Sarah back from the cliff of shock. I knew when she yanked her hand from mine that she was feeling one hundred percent back to normal.

Her mouth settled into a determined line as she stared with vacant eyes at the crime-scene investigation now taking over her chapter's backyard.

"You good?" I asked her.

"Not really," she bit out.

I put my coffee cup down. "Let me know if you need anything."

"Thank you." The words came out through gritted teeth like she was being waxed down there.

My favor done, I started heading back toward the street, when Ty stopped me.

"Thanks," he said.

Of course, I didn't mind helping out, even if Sarah was a Moo. Panhellenic spirit and all. Age-old rivalries took a backseat to tragedy. And I knew what was going to happen—what had to happen. Ty read my mind.

"Even the governor's office won't like this," he said with an edge in his voice.

"No, of course not," I agreed quickly. I wouldn't be requesting any pulled-string shenanigans this time from my PR-specialist best friend Casey.

"I've already put in a call to Panhellenic."

"You're shutting rush down," I said.

"There's a murderer out there." Ty's jaw was hard, and his tone was like he expected me to argue. And why wouldn't he? I'd been completely unhelpful with the first murder investigation, putting up every roadblock I could fabricate. If I hadn't been so obstinate, maybe this wouldn't have happened.

"Come on," he said roughly. "You can't fall apart. This whole street's going to be looking to you to set an example."

My laugh sounded hollow. Me? I'd always striven to be a role model, a paragon of Delta Beta ideals; showing the entire Panhellenic system how to survive a murder investigation was never part of the job description.

But we are all called to different destinies, and apparently, this was mine. I lifted my chin and blinked back my tears. On my long, long list of vital items to do, now I had one more—help solve a murder.

"I have something to show you," I said.

Ty's face stayed composed, with his slightly lifted eyebrow the only sign that he had heard me. "When you have time . . ." I licked my lips nervously. "Come by the house. We might have something that will help."

A curt nod and a tight jaw was all the response I got, and as I walked away, I wasn't sure whether I had just done my civic duty or signed my own arrest warrant.

Chapter Twenty-three

AFTER THE DRAMA at the Tri Mu house, I had never been so happy to return to the drama of the Delta Beta house.

I was in our front yard when I heard voices coming from the tent, set up to shelter the rushees who wouldn't be coming today.

"This isn't sufficient."

The voice was snooty and grating, like gel nails on a chalkboard. Von Douton?

Then I heard my name. "Margot is doing everything by the book."

Ginnifer? Why was she talking to Von Douton about me?

"If you want me to help you, you know what you have to do."

Von Douton was helping us? In what alternative universe? I had to set Ginnifer straight. I whirled around the corner and flipped open the tent door, practically running into Ginnifer, startling the snot out of her. "Margot!"

"What's going on?" I demanded, glancing between Ginnifer and Von Douton.

She looked confused, and I was pretty sure I hadn't given her a brain injury or something. "Oh. Right," she finally said. "No, I ran into Mrs. Von Douton. I thought she might know where I could . . . get a form."

"What form?"

"An extra budget form."

I glanced at Von Douton's Chanel bag and wondered if Ginnifer seriously thought the Mafia carried around extra copies of Panhellenic forms everywhere they went.

"I have those in the office," I explained to Ginnifer.

"She's so conscientious and detail-oriented, isn't she?" We both turned toward Von Douton and the strange note in her voice. "Dotting every i and crossing every T. You're so very lucky to have her."

At the compliment, Ginnifer's face paled, and I guess I would have done the same. Somehow, a compliment coming from a remarkably wrinkle-free Old Moo didn't seem as complimentary as it could have.

Not feeling particularly pleasant, I decided to keep my mouth zipped and just nod and smile as Von Douton excused herself. She was still a member of the Mafia. That deserved some level of respect.

Von Douton's mauve-licious lips turned into a small smile as she walked by. "Good evening, ladies."

As she opened the door to the tent, I noticed something concerning.

"Your shoes!"

Von Douton whirled around, her face panicked as if I'd told her there were big clumps of bubble gum covering the stiletto soles. "I mean, you've got mud all over them. Do you want a towel or something?"

Von Douton frowned as she looked down at her heels. They were caked in mud, nearly up to the red-leather sole. I wasn't being nice because this was Von Douton. I was being nice because they were really hot shoes.

I looked down at the ground; the January grass was dry, our dirt was hard from the winter. Where would someone as chic as Von Douton get her feet so dirty? Unless she was wearing her designer shoes into her spa mud bath.

"No thank you." Von Douton lifted her nose. "I'll have my maid clean them."

I rolled my eyes at her back, and when it was safe, I grabbed Ginnifer's arm. "What did she want?" I hissed.

"She was just walking by . . . I needed a form . . ." Something wasn't right. Ginnifer was smarter than this.

I looked closely in her eyes, wishing I could do that human-lie-detector thing I'd seen on *Law & Order* once. "What did Von Douton really want?"

Ginnifer swallowed hard. "She said something about your not being organized."

Of course she would. That Moo would jump on any chance to point out a Deb's deficiencies. "I don't know how they did this in Alabama, but here? We don't rely on the Tri Mus to bring our forms to us. And for the record, I have a dozen copies of everything in the office. All you have to do is ask me." I smoothed out her shirt and gave her a little squeeze, to make her feel better after contact with Von Douton, but the show of affection didn't seem to relax Ginnifer any, nor did the news that I, as a chapter advisor, was also very prepared in the form-collection area. When we entered the front door of the Deb house, I wondered if such a high-strung, high-maintenance woman as Ginnifer would be able to survive the rigors of Sutton College rush—I mean recruitment—week.

And she wasn't the only one. The house was in a midrecruitment-week state of disaster. Half of the chapter wasn't talking to the other because of some rush-crush drama. Sitting with Sarah McLane had reminded me that it was a good day if no one had died, so I yelled, "PLEASE try not to kill each other for half an hour!" which stunned a few girls; but, for the most part, the message was received. The verbal threats died down to murderous glances, and I locked myself in the chapter advisor's apartment for a long, hot shower and a fresh change of clothes.

I had just pulled on a black sweatshirt printed with the Delta Beta crest and my last remaining pair of clean skinny jeans (what? It was rush week. If there was no time to eat, there was no time for laundry) when I heard the doorbell ring. Steeling myself for some lengthy explanations to Sutton PD's Finest, I answered the door to find not a stern Lieutenant Hatfield, or a slightly more agreeable Officer Malouf, but Louella Jackson, bundled up in a very chic red-wool trench coat and balanced on fierce, patent-leather pumps that I could have sworn Alexandria Von Douton had also worn earlier this week. Seriously. Did they share a personal shopper? And how could I get her number?

She walked straight into the house, as was her right as a Delta Beta alumna, but I was still slightly taken aback by the lack of courtesy chitchat. As she looked around the messy house, I could feel her critical eye as acutely as I had back in college when she informed me that my hand-painted Delta Beta banners were an embarrassment to banners everywhere.

"Hello, Louella." Her eyes slowly lifted to the painted banner hanging from the curved staircase rail.

"I didn't paint that one," I said quickly.

"I can tell."

I won't lie. That still hurt. But I had to thank Louella. Once she described my art skills as "something her Chihuahua could do," I resolved to find other ways to serve Delta Beta, like exercising my people skills and giving free fashion consultations.

Louella started sliding her black gloves off her hand, finger by finger. "I'm here as the Delta Beta representative of the Panhellenic Rush Council."

"You mean Recruitment Council." I couldn't help correcting her, which got me a chilled glance in return.

"As I'm sure you're aware, there's been another incident." I would have corrected her word choice again, but I respected the older generation's need to use euphemisms. They were so delicate, after all. "And unfortunately, the police have made the ill-considered request to temporarily halt the recruitment process."

Based on the determination on Ty's face earlier, I knew it hadn't been a "request" but more of a "shut this place down before I shut your face down" kind of conversation, but again, I deferred to Louella's sensitive nature.

"And the council's decided to grant the request?" I prodded.

"Majority rules," Louella sighed, which not only let me know which side of the debate Louella had been on but also her feelings toward the democratic process, which I sympathized with. Sometimes things were much more palatable when there was a benevolent dictator running things, like a wise yet fun chapter advisor.

"I think it's the best decision," I said, hoping to make Louella feel better about losing her argument. "After all, there are safety considerations."

"It's *rush*."

Given that her opinion had been mine approximately twenty-four hours ago, I was sympathetic. But still. "This was a rushee," I said gently. "We can't let something like this happen again."

Louella's face didn't soften one bit at my reminder. "It's one girl out of hundreds. What are we supposed to say to the ones who didn't die?"

Wow.

Maybe empathy was something senior citizens lost, along with their hearing and their ability to walk in high heels. I had to hand it to Louella, she was still rocking it in that department. But she was a Deb. We kept our [redacted to protect sorority privilege] vows very seriously.

"I'm sure the administration is keeping everyone's interests in mind." I always tried to see the glass as half-full, but Louella was having none of it.

"You mean the administration is listening to Nick Holden and his yellow journalism," she said.

She slapped her gloves in her hand and crinkled her nose at them. "Effective immediately, and until further notice, Sutton sorority recruitment is postponed. We will let the chapters know further developments via e-mail."

That lifted my spirits. "You mean you won't be coming back?"

Maybe that was too chipper-sounding because Louella froze me with her eyes before reaching for the door handle and leaving without another word. I couldn't say I was sorry to have her go, wishing we had a different relationship with the most prominent Delta Beta alumna in Sutton County. Maybe she had to be neutral, on the council for the entire Panhellenic system.

Rush might have been delayed, but the Delta Betas wouldn't

use this unexpected free time preparing for the spring semester or catching up on self-care. We still had work to do.

Luckily, Ginnifer was already on it.

When the chapter convened, Ginnifer had already gotten everything together, which once again made me give her two snaps up for her competence.

Preference night, or "pref" was the most solemn and holy of nights during rush. It was the last night, the last opportunity for the sisters to show what their sisterhood meant, and the last chance for the rushees to make the right decision and put Delta Beta as their number one choice. All across the country, each chapter developed its own unique, timeless, and emotional preference ceremony, usually involving as many candles as possible.

In my job as a Delta Beta sisterhood mentor, I had traveled throughout North America and Canada too, and I had seen many, many preference ceremonies. I had also witnessed many, many accidental fires as a result of all the highly poetic yet highly dangerous open flames. Rehearsal was imperative, to avoid any more 9-1-1 calls.

The first time we had practiced this, Asha Patel lost a lovely spiral of her dark curls and a liberal dose of Febreeze had been applied to the surrounding carpets and draperies to dissipate the smell of burnt hair. The second time, Eliza-Jane Jergenson had somehow lit a chunk of hair on the back of her head on fire. I quietly blamed the helicopter-parent culture for not allowing kids these days to learn how to play with matches safely, opened all the windows and doors of the house, and gave thanks that Zoe had been watching Eliza-Jane's back—literally.

Before we got started, I quickly glanced up and confirmed that the smoke detectors were disconnected. Then I clapped my hands. "All right, ladies, I know it's hard to concentrate today, but let's take advantage of this unexpected free time to really perfect all the details in the preference ceremony."

Our musicians readied their violin, guitar, and piano, respectively. The music chair put her pitch pipe to her lips. I hit the button on the remote, and the lights in the chapter room dimmed.

The chords started, the beautiful swell of the music took me back. This song had graced these halls for a generation, reminding us what was truest and best about being a Delta Beta.

The melody was simple, the words profound. "I'll be there for you, when the rain starts to pour," the ladies sang. "I'll be there for you like I've been there before . . ." Although everyone was relatively composed today, on the actual night of the preference ceremony, there wouldn't be a dry eye in the house. "I'll be there for you, 'cause you're there for me, too . . ."

After the song, there were poems, traditionally read by seniors. This year, Aubrey and Callie were the designated orators, and they stepped forward and recited the verses confidently and emotionally.

Then we entered the danger zone. A large white pillar candle stood on an elaborate pedestal at the front of the room. Each sister was supposed to go, light her gold taper from the Symbolic Eternal Flame of Friendship (c), circle the room three times, then offer her candle to her designated rushee. At this point, there would be a violin solo of "God Bless the Winding Road" as everyone looked in each other's eyes and thought about what sisterhood meant to them. Yes, it sounds awkward. But it's lovely and moving.

Then everyone would file out of the room, (sobbing, hopefully) and whisper all sorts of unsanctioned things like "I can't wait for you to be my sister" and "You're so getting a bid tomorrow," and the doors would close, and we'd do it all over again and mean it just as much to the next group.

Here, in practice, Zoe lit the Symbolic Eternal Flame of Friendship, and the chapter readied their gold tapers.

"Wait!" I cried out. Ginnifer sent me a what-the-hay look from across the room, where she was diligently timing the ceremony to ensure that we stayed within Panhellenic parameters.

"Let's just practice it without the flames," I suggested. Ginnifer very obviously clicked off her stopwatch.

"But we need to practice so we don't burn the house down."

She was right. I was just a jumble of nerves from this morning. Seeing body bags tended to does that to me. Right. We had to do this. For the safety of everyone's highlights.

I nodded. "Let's do it." At my signal, the ceremony restarted, and women began to file down to the Eternal Flame, while the piano tinkled softly in the background.

I almost passed out from holding my breath as each of the tapers were lit without incident, held a safe distance from flammable draperies, clothing or hair-spray-coated tresses, then blown out again at the completion of the ceremony.

"We did it!" I squealed to Ginnifer after it was done, and she looked up from her phone distractedly.

"About time," she muttered.

It was a fair statement, but it ticked me off. The chapter had been through so much, had worked so hard the past few months, and here they had finally gotten through thirty minutes without lighting someone's hair on fire. Was it too much to ask for a little enthusiasm? A little "yay Delta Betas!" "Way to go avoiding fire!"

It was one thing to have impossibly high standards. It was

another never to give credit where credit was due, and I'd had enough of Miss High-and-Mighty.

"You know, I don't think your attitude is very productive," I said.

"What do you mean?"

"I mean, there's a reason why everyone calls you the Gineral."

Several gasps rose around me, from sisters who had filtered back into the chapter room and overheard. The biggest gasp came from Ginnifer herself, who looked shocked and stunned. She clasped a hand to her mouth and ran out of the room.

The look of pain on her face was the second worst expression I'd seen that day. And it was only noon. It made me want to go check back into a room at the Fountain Place Inn and pretend like I'd never woken up.

Chapter Twenty-four

AT THIS POINT, I was 98 percent sure that giving Ty Hatfield my full participation in his murder investigations was the right thing to do. Rush was super important, of course, but the death of a freshman rushee hit me hard, and I couldn't get her out of my mind all day. Her identity was broadcast almost immediately on social media: Daria Cantrell, a freshman business major, from Cleveland. Her last Instagram was being reposted everywhere, a photo of her hand, holding a Starbucks cup, with the hashtag #letsdothis.

As I let Ty into the Deb house, that tiny 2 percent of doubt hung around my head. Voluntarily getting involved in another set of murders I was one hundred percent sure my chapter was not involved in had not been in my rush-week plan.

But Daria Cantrell's Starbucks cup haunted me. How could I not offer up my help to the Sutton Police Department? It could be my Instagram picture next. Or Aubrey's. Or Callie's. Or anyone on Greek Row. Daria Cantrell would never again post a selfie with the hashtag #Iwokeuplikethis. If another woman died or was hurt, I would not be able to forgive myself.

Ty followed me into the chapter advisor's apartment on the first floor of the house, where Zoe was waiting. He took one look at my desk and groaned, closing his eyes like he was in pain. "Please tell me this is not what I think it is."

Well . . . "What do you think it is?" I asked, just to be sure before I implicated myself in anything.

"I think it's a very expensive, very thorough surveillance system." He peered at one of the monitors that held nine different camera angles. "Are those . . ." His mouth kind of hinged open, then he turned his head to look at me. "You bugged the other houses?"

"NO!" I gasped.

"Define 'bugged,' " Zoe said.

"Why didn't you come forward with this before?" He was having a very hard time controlling himself. I took a step back, just to be safe.

"It was—"

"—don't say it—"

"—confidential," I finished.

"I told you not to say that." Ty spoke through a clenched jaw, and I was sort of worried about what his dentist must see in his mouth. He leaned over again, examining the third monitor. Out of six, stacked high.

"You have the Tri Mu backyard . . ." He paused, steadied himself. "You have almost the whole damn Greek Row on camera." He kept staring at the camera feeds, and Zoe and I exchanged nervous glances. I wasn't quite sure that a silent police officer was a safe police officer.

"Ty—"

"Shhh." He cut me off with a hand slicing through the air. "I'm trying to figure out a few things."

"Like?"

"Like how to explain to the district attorney that I got evidence from a private surveillance system."

I knew the answer to that. "Voluntarily," I affirmed with a quick nod. "You got this completely voluntarily."

He frowned. Maybe that was the wrong answer? "What else were you trying to figure out?" I asked.

"Why the hell you didn't tell me about this when Shannon Bender was found dead in your freaking backyard."

I held up both hands. "Because . . ."

Zoe jumped in. "Because I didn't have it up yet."

That was sweet of her to try to protect me. "Because I hadn't given them permission to use it yet. I wasn't sure this was the direction we wanted to take."

"It's a hell of a direction," he said with a wry lift of his eyebrow. "And what, exactly, did you think you would do with all this?"

I knew that Ty had been in a fraternity in college. He was in my class, but I didn't really remember him—he had lost fifty pounds since then and mysteriously gotten way hotter in a uniform and badge—though he remembered me (slightly awkward). But sometimes he acted like he had no clue how sororities worked, like he hadn't paid any attention to the better half of the Greek system.

"We used it for background information, to track deliveries, coming and going of influential persons, what the other houses are using for decorations and outfits."

Zoe moved to the computer and pulled up a database. "Which we then input into the Sutton rush database—it's proprietary," she informed him, as if he were about to market it and take the company public for a billion dollars. I made a mental note to discuss that option with Zoe at a future date.

Ty leaned forward to examine a Web site pulled up on the screen. "Who's Casey Fenner?" He looked at me in confusion. "Isn't that your friend? From headquarters?"

So Ty did pay attention to some things. "No," I answered. "That's Casey Kenner. We just used his name for inspiration."

"For what?" He did that thing he did with his jaw when he was getting impatient. Before I could finesse something that wouldn't make him grind his teeth again, Zoe blurted out the answer.

"Our fake social-media accounts."

"Do I want to know?" he asked me.

"Probably not."

But Zoe was proud of this. I'd come up with the idea for the database and social-media effort as drastic measures, for our chapter to have any hope of surviving being known as the murder house; and Zoe had done the computer-whiz work.

"Casey Fenner is an eighteen-year-old freshman at Sutton College." With a tap on the mouse, she pulled up a Facebook page featuring a normally pretty girl, nondescript in dress and background. "Two months ago, she began requesting to be friends with every girl who was registered for rush." Zoe clicked again, and there was Casey Fenner's Instagram account, her Twitter, and her Vine.

"Oh God . . ." Ty managed to say.

"It was Margot's idea," Zoe said with a note of pride in her voice that I couldn't help but appreciate. I had no guilt about using underhanded methods to get a look at rushees' locked accounts. I was only doing what a potential big sister would do, spotting red behavioral flags.

"You've been tracking rushees from a fake account."

"I wouldn't say tracking," I replied. It sounded like we were hunting rushees for their fur on the Oregon Trail.

"Yes," Zoe said. "Mainly to judge their character."

"Of course."

Zoe didn't pick up on Ty's dry sarcasm. He'd made it clear to me in the past that he thought sororities' emphasis on morality was old-fashioned and dumb. Zoe continued. "To find out if they'd gone to fraternity parties, if they're drinking, or if they run a secret phone-sex hotline. I developed a bot that would flag suspicious posts and turn the rest into data points."

"How have you not flunked out of school?" Ty asked Zoe.

"She's a tech genius," I told him, and this time it was my voice that was filled with pride.

"That's how you knew about the Witness glasses."

Zoe nodded carefully.

Ty straightened up and crossed his arms. "So what can you tell me about Daria Cantrell?"

Zoe looked at me with a clear question in her eyes, and I nodded. "I can give you a full report on all her accounts in the next hour."

"And the footage of the Tri Mu house?"

Again Zoe gave me a questioning glance, and this time Ty noticed. "What's this about?"

"We don't have a clear view of the murder site," I explained.

"How do you know where the murder site was?"

Aha. I was glad Zoe and I had taken the time to prepare before this meeting. I knew Ty would have some tricky questions. "Because we have shots of Daria Cantrell walking down the street toward the Tri Mu house."

"And then she walks on their north side," Zoe took over, pulling the footage up on a separate monitor. In grainy black and white, the three of us watched what was probably Daria Cantrell's last moments on the planet. "And then we lose her."

Ty watched the screen intently. "Where does she go?"

"To the back, I guess," Zoe said.

"We don't have anything back there," I added.

Ty slammed his palm on the desk. The monitors shook, wobbly in their uneven towers. "What good is this, then?"

"Well, we know who put the cheese into the Tri Mu vents," Zoe hurriedly offered. "And we can pretty much tell who put the blue dye on the Lambdas' lily delivery."

"I don't care about cheese. Or flowers," Ty said. "That's not evidence of a murder."

The three of us stood in silence for a long moment, the frame of Daria Cantrell frozen on the screen. Then I remembered something.

"Actually . . ."

Ty's head swiveled toward me.

"We might have something."

"What do we have?"

"We have blue lilies."

"Margot . . ." I liked when Ty said my name like that. Like he was tired of fighting me and had decided to just give in to whatever I wanted.

"I need to see the card from Shannon Bender's spy-glasses again."

Chapter Twenty-five

WE AGREED THAT when I went to the police station to deliver the report on Daria Cantrell's locked social-media accounts and the surveillance footage of Greek Row, I could get another look at the footage on the Witness glasses. I refused to say anything else to Ty about what I was looking for; truth be told, I wasn't altogether sure. The evidence we had linking Shannon Bender and Daria Cantrell's murders was very slim, but something had to be there. Two murders one after another didn't happen that often on Greek Row. Well, except for that time three months ago.

I left Zoe at the computer to download the database and keep sweeping Casey Fenner's accounts. After spending the night in my time-out with Sheila, I took a few minutes to review the most recent recruitment reports from Panhellenic. But that was just busywork to avoid what I really needed to do: update Delta Beta headquarters. Just three months ago, I would have had Mabel Donahue, the Delta Beta international president, on the phone pronto to report the significant irregularities of this rush. But now, as chapter advisor, I found that my loyalties were much different. My first priority was this chapter, not the bigger international sister-hood. Which was surprising when I thought about it, and as I did, a sick feeling crept over me.

The Gineral was in the position I was in three months ago. She was the sisterhood mentor, traveling from chapter to chapter, promoting the interests and betterment of the entire Delta Beta sorority. I knew her job better than anyone: three months ago, I was the longest-serving sisterhood mentor ever, at six years and counting. The mentor's manual was clear: Regular, fully informed updates to headquarters were a necessity.

So why hadn't I gotten a call from Mabel Donahue or anyone at headquarters about Shannon Bender, the high jinks between the chapters, the Mafia's new rules, or the postponement of rush? No one was more plugged into HQ than Casey, who had sincerely responded like he hadn't heard a thing about Shannon Bender's murder. And I would know if he were faking with me; Casey is a wonderful person and a fabulous friend, but he cannot keep a secret from me to save his life.

The only conclusion I could come to was that Ginnifer *had not* reported to HQ. Which was . . . welcome but very suspicious. And possibly meant she was bad at her job. Which in turn meant I would have to report her for not fulfilling her duties as sister-hood mentor; so, report her not reporting me. This was getting complicated.

There was only one thing to do. I had to find Ginnifer and lay it all on table. Before I called headquarters about anything, I had to know who had told whom what.

I headed out of the Rush Dungeon for Ginnifer's quarters on the second floor, in the tiny single room for houseguests, but I was delayed by the crowd of women heading into the chapter room.

"What's going on?" I asked a sophomore near me. I didn't remember there being a meeting or practice. In fact, I had specifically given the chapter some free time and urged them to relax and recharge. I wasn't a complete rush Nazi.

"We all got texts to come downstairs," was the answer. Immediately, I pulled my phone out of my back pocket. No text.

This was bad news. There were only two reasons why someone would anonymously summon the whole chapter to gather without me. The first would be, obviously, a surprise birthday party for me. But I was pretty sure that by now, the chapter would know that (a) my birthday was in July and (b) I had stopped celebrating birthdays at twenty-five. The other possibility was that someone was trying to sabotage us.

My mind shot through the possibilities. More stinky cheese? Smoke bombs? Water balloons filled with gelatin? Check, check, and check. They'd all been done. Whoever was trying to play a dirty prank on my chapter didn't want me there because they knew that I'd foil their evil plan. Well, I'd show them. I pushed my way into the chapter room and made sure I had a good seat at the front of the room, where I could easily jump up and take leadership should the worst occur.

Distantly, I heard a knock at the front door and Ginnifer's voice. Well, at least I knew where she was now. As soon as this was over—whatever it was—we'd have that little chat about her irresponsible (but charitable) lack of reporting to HQ.

Ginnifer rushed into the chapter room, panic-stricken. "Has anyone seen—" She broke off at the sight of me. "Margot!" She was relieved when she ran to me, clutching at my upper arms.

"What's going on?" I asked, instantly on guard.

"The police," she heaved.

"The what?" I asked.

"The police, ma'am." A burly officer I'd never seen before stood in the door to the chapter room, with two other unknown uniformed officers. Strange. I wondered why Ty had sent the new guys. All three of them still had their mirrored sunglasses on, with caps pulled low over their heads. A nervous yet excited ripple of chatter moved through the room at the sight of the policemen, physically imposing and very stern, standing straight in uniforms that seemed . . . sort of tight.

"We got a complaint that there were women here who liked to make a lot of noise."

What? I raised my hand. "I'm sorry, Officer. It's rush week, and . . ."

The officer who had spoken took a few steps toward me and held a finger up to interrupt me. "Who said anything about rushing?"

The one with curly blond hair said, "The ladies like it slow." Then he held up his nightstick and slowly rubbed his palm down it.

Ew?

The third officer held up what looked like a Bluetooth speaker; and suddenly, music was blaring in the chapter room, demanding, "C'mon, rude boy, boy can you get it up?" A few women screamed in surprise. I was one of them. This was very strange behavior from strange Sutton police officers . . . who were now thrusting and grinding their way around the room.

Oh.

My.

God.

Was this?

Were they?

They tossed off their caps, and one managed to unbutton his shirt as if it had strips of Velcro and not buttons, and the other was using his nightstick to . . .

I closed my eyes. I couldn't possibly . . .

I opened them. Yes, I probably should. Just to supervise.

The song was quite catchy, and I had to hand it to our gentlemen callers: They were extremely talented, very athletic dancers. It was really an accomplishment to be able to do that with your hips and glutes and thighs, not to mention the push-up with one hand.

This had to have been Casey's doing, a special surprise to cheer me and the girls up and keep our spirits high. I took out my phone to snap a few pictures to share the joy with him later.

Almost all the girls were enjoying the show, too, except the few who had their eyes closed, or Ginnifer, who must have some serious hang-ups and gone running from the room. Everyone else was singing along and clapping with the most exact rhythm. It had me wondering if we needed to include the lyrics, "give it to me baby like boom boom boom" somewhere in our rush repertoire.

Then the song changed to something about a pony, clearly not about a pony, which was clear when the cute blond dancer was suddenly in front of me. At some point, he'd lost his shirt. And his pants. And now all he was wearing was a policeman's cap and a thong with a fake badge clipped to his hip.

The badge was hypnotic, bouncing in tune to the Ginuwine song. It got closer, the girls cheered him on, then, somehow, mostly because it was a really good song, I was riding the gentleman's thigh, singing "c'mon, jump on it." But when he grabbed my butt, that was totally crossing the line.

He backed off and danced to someone else, and even though I

knew there were about one hundred things wrong with what was going on in the sacred confines of the Delta Beta chapter room, for one shining period of time, we were all young and (sort of) innocent together.

When the performance finished, I led the chapter in a standing O—ovation, I mean. Then I gave them instructions on how to sneak out of the house by the back way. We didn't need anyone on the block to see that we'd been visited by very hot, very muscular police officers during rush week, courtesy of the Delta Beta public-relations director.

Chapter Twenty-six

AN HOUR LATER, when the doorbell rang, the ladies of the chapter gathered eagerly in the front hall, expecting perhaps some firefighters with big hoses or EMTs delivering mouth-to-mouth. There was an audible sigh of disappointment when the door opened, and it was not a crew of off-duty shirtless Marines, but Alexandria Von Douton with her sleek platinum French twist instead.

"Ms. Blythe," she greeted me coolly but with a feral glint in her eyes. "I have the pleasure of delivering this to you in person."

I accepted the envelope, and asked, "Has the stay been lifted? Is rush restarting?"

Her cold smile faltered. "No. Which I'm sure you're quite pleased about."

"No one wants rush to continue more than I."

"I have a hard time believing that considering all the illegal acts you've been promoting this week."

"Illegal?" I sputtered. Was Callie's mom's lawyer friend wrong about North Carolina surveillance laws? How had Von Douton heard about that?

"Don't play innocent with me. You Debs have gone far too long without consequences." Her lips twisted in satisfaction. "Until now."

She turned and left with quite a dramatic flair. I had to give her credit for pulling it off at her age, in those shoes. My begrudging appreciation for a well-executed flounce aside, I opened the envelope with trepidation.

The paper inside was worse than anything I had expected. I headed straight into my apartment, where Zoe was at the computer, and Callie was posting fake pictures on Casey Fenner's Instagram account.

I showed them the letter from Panhellenic.

"Not rule number five," Callie groaned.

"Probation," I muttered, shaking my head. I couldn't believe it. We were getting probation for having men in the house during rush. We were on a break!

"Not double-secret probation?" Zoe asked.

"No," I sighed. "Not this time."

"How did they find out?" Callie asked.

"Clearly, someone posted something about it," I said. I should have known this was going to happen when all the women's cell phones were being held up, capturing the day's almost-nude entertainment. But maybe they just wanted to relive the moment later, in the privacy of their own rooms. I couldn't say.

"On it," Zoe said, sliding Callie out of the desk chair and pulling up Casey Fenner's accounts. This might be one thing I felt actually guilty about. When we were putting the Casey Fenner scheme together, Callie (the standards and morals director, after all), suggested that Fake Casey request to be friends with everyone in the chapter, as well. It would look odd if Fake Casey was only friends with other freshmen, she argued; and this way, we could see whether the chapter sisters were behaving themselves on social media, as well. I felt a little funny about basically spying on my own sisters, but it was for their own good.

In a few quick clicks, Zoe had reviewed everyone's postings from the past hour. No one had posted anything about our surprise strippers. And they were a surprise, which made the whole probation thing superunfair. We hadn't arranged for mostly naked men to appear on our doorstep—Casey had. Hadn't he?

I double-checked with Callie and Zoe and confirmed that as far as they knew, no one in the house had scheduled this visit. I almost smacked my forehead. Of course. How could I have been so stupid? This hadn't been Casey at all. Even though he would have appreciated the dancers' artistry, he knew Panhellenic rules too well to do something like this.

"We were set up," I said. "This was a setup. One of the other houses called the strippers in, then ratted us out to Alexandria Von Douton."

Zoe frowned. "Von Douton? She's the Tri Mu, right? The one that looks like Cruella De Vil?"

Now that I thought about it, Von Douton's fur coat had looked very puppylike that morning.

Zoe moved the mouse and one of the surveillance camera feeds popped up on the screen. Footage of the Tri Mu house sped backwards for a few seconds, then it stopped. "I noticed this a little while ago," Zoe explained. "But I thought it was just some Panhellenic thing going on."

A large black Mercedes pulled up in front of the Tri Mu house.

Nothing happened for a few seconds, then a familiar figure approached the driver's side window. It was Ginnifer. She handed a cell-phone-shaped object through the window, then the object was passed back. The conversation looked short, and Ginnifer soon walked away, in the opposite direction from the Deb house. A few seconds later, the figure who emerged from the Mercedes was clearly Von Douton, her confident stride leading her toward the Deb house.

"When was this?" I asked, unable to decipher the numbers at the bottom.

Zoe checked her watch. "Just about ten minutes ago."

Von Douton's next stop had been to drop off the probation paperwork in my hand.

"The Gineral sold us out," Callie exclaimed.

"We don't know that," I reasoned uncertainly though it was hard to explain why Ginnifer had given Von Douton something through that car window. I had to use common sense. "Von Douton didn't print the paper in her car. She had it before she ever saw Ginnifer."

"The Gineral has had it in for us from the beginning," Callie insisted. "She's always looking for something wrong with us."

Which was true, but . . . "She's also insisted that we follow every single rule," I said. "Why would she do that if she'd just rat us out for accidentally having strippers over?"

"Because we haven't broken any other rule," Callie said.

"Well . . ." Zoe tilted her head toward the computer monitors.

"We did get written up for disobeying the Rush Council," I added sheepishly.

Callie wasn't having any of it. "The Gineral set us up. I bet she called the strippers, then gave Von Douton pics."

I understood Callie's theory, but there was one thing she was forgetting. "Ginnifer is a Delta Beta," I said sternly. "She is your sister, and mine, and she has said sacred vows to uphold our sorority. Accusing her of violating those without proof is just as serious as if she did rat us out to Von Douton."

Taking a deep breath, I looked at the paper in my hand again. It wasn't dated, and it only held the one sentence. "For violation of rule five of the Sutton College Panhellenic Recruitment Code, the Delta Beta chapter is hereby put on probationary status."

Probation wasn't that serious. It was one of those consequences that sounded worse than it was. Like "house arrest." And since I knew that the Debs were one hundred percent following all the rules that anyone cared about, I was confident that this decision wouldn't ultimately affect our chapter negatively.

"I'll talk to Ginnifer," I told the girls, mostly to calm them down and make them feel better that I had everything under control. "I'm sure she was just giving Von Douton directions or something."

"With her phone? Von Douton's Mercedes doesn't have GPS?"

I ignored Callie's well-reasoned and logical points. Now wasn't the time for logic. Maybe I was biased because of my own recent tenure of being the (sometimes) unpopular visiting sisterhood mentor at various chapters, but my intuition still told me that however sketchy Ginnifer's actions were, she was only looking out for the Delta Beta good. "Zoe?" I turned my attention to my adorable tech genius. "Do you have everything ready for the police?"

She unplugged a thumb drive from the CPU and gave it to me. "I found something I wasn't expecting when I was going over

Daria Cantrell's social-media accounts. When she told me, I must have looked as sick as I felt because she asked me with wide eyes, "This is okay, right? We're not getting in trouble?"

"Of course not," I assured her. What else could I say? When it came to Delta Betas at Sutton College, it seemed like trouble was always a possibility.

Chapter Twenty-seven

THE SUTTON POLICE station had always been a huge disappointment to me. On *Law & Order*, police stations are hubs of constant activity. There's always something going on in the background, like a bunch of cops consulting on a case file or bringing in a sweaty, inebriated, homeless person. The set is grim and dim, and you can almost smell the old coffee and stale body odor.

By contrast, here in Sutton, the station was clean and quiet. The building was probably built in the midseventies, but it was well lit and smelled like toner cartridges and floor wax. Like I said, disappointing. On top of all that, there was hardly ever anyone stationed at the front door. This bugged the bedazzled out of me. It was as if they thought criminals wouldn't just walk in and take advantage of all the fresh new toner cartridges, just stacked on top of that filing cabinet over there.

But since I had an appointment, Ty Hatfield stuck his head out into the waiting area, and I didn't have to ponder the annoying cleanliness any longer. I followed him back to his normal office, with piles of paper and files and no gruesome crime-scene photographs or bloody knives in sight. "What did the murderer use?" I asked abruptly, realizing that it had never come up.

Ty looked taken aback. "Excuse me?"

"What killed Shannon Bender and Daria Cantrell?" I asked.

"Who said that one person did it?"

He put his hand out. I knew what he wanted. But he also knew how this worked.

"This is how we do it, Ty. We share information. I give you all our surveillance footage of the entire block plus the social-media records of Daria Cantrell's locked accounts, and you share one teensy, eensy bit of information with me."

"You could be a suspect."

"That would be true, if I didn't have fifty Delta Betas who would swear that I was getting my toenails painted School Boy Blazer navy at the time of Shannon Bender's death by . . ." I let that hang out there, just in case he'd relent.

"And Delta Betas never lie," he said with that tinge of sarcasm that always rubbed me the wrong way.

"Not fifty of them at the same time," I answered smoothly.

"You could be a suspect in the Cantrell murder."

"You know very well that I was incarcerated at the time."

That threw him. "Incarcerated? Ah, Margot, I thought that was our special thing."

So he found it not so much surprising as funny. Really. Whatever was I going to do with a man who thought my being locked up was hilarious?

I calmly informed him where I was during the time of the Cantrell murder. The side of his mouth hitched up. "Yeah, I heard. Sheila DeGrasse said you were her alibi."

Yeah, I thought the fact that I was Sheila DeGrasse's anything was *just weird, too.*

He extended his hand again. "According to the county medical examiner, both Cantrell and Bender suffered head trauma. The weapon was a four-to-five-inch-long spike of some sort."

I rubbed my head at the idea of a four-inch-long spike piercing my skull. "Really? That seems short. That's like the length of a coffee stirrer." I held my fingers apart, easily imagining the length of a little green stick that I poked into my reusable cup every few hours. "Are you sure?"

Ty raised an eyebrow. "It's not just about length."

I rolled my eyes. I'd heard that one before.

"There's also velocity, force of the thrust, technique . . ."

I held up my hand. "There's a *technique* to stabbing someone in the head?" Were there tutorials on YouTube, too?

"Sure." Ty walked slowly around me, a predatory gleam in his eye that sent a shiver up my spine. "Like this."

I felt a gentle pressure on the back of my neck as Ty's fingers pressed against my skin. "This would be a good place. It's tender, exposed. But you'd have to be hard and accurate."

His hand slid up, messing up my hair, but I didn't care. Being touched felt good, even if it was just Ty demonstrating a murder technique. "Here is where the victims were stabbed." He rubbed a little circle on my scalp, and another shiver went through me. "Death would be quick and fast, but the weapon would have to be very sharp to make it through the skull."

"That's it?" My voice was breathy. "Wham bam, thank you, ma'am?"

Ty's arm slipped around my middle, pulling me back into him.

"Someone could do this," he said low into my ear. "What would you do, Margot? If someone grabbed you like this?"

Oh, Ty. He was always underestimating me.

I jerked my elbow back into his stomach, threw my foot back into his leg, and twirled out of his arms. "Then I'd kick him in the balls," I said with confidence. Every Delta Beta took a self-defense course in college.

Ty was doubled over, and for a moment, I was worried I had really hurt him even though I had mostly been pretending. Maybe I was just naturally an excellent fighter. "Ty?" I asked carefully. "Are you okay?" I stepped closer to him and reached out. His pride was definitely hurt. No man liked to be beaten by a woman and especially a tough police officer like him.

His hand whipped out, grabbed mine, and yanked me to him. His arms pinned mine down, I was pressed against his hard thighs, stomach, and chest, and when I looked up at him, the twinkle in his eyes told me he was enjoying this.

"Faker," I accused him.

"It's called technique, Blythe." Up close like this, his smirk was real pretty. I wanted to do something to wipe it off his face.

"I could take you down, Hatfield."

The smirk disappeared, and Ty let go. "I'm sure you could." He stepped away. "Now tell me, Margot . . . why did you ask me that about what killed Shannon and Daria?"

I went ahead and passed over the thumb drive. "There might be a connection between them."

"Do I need to plug this in, or are you going to just tell me?"

Since the answer was buried among ten thousand hashtags, I decided to make it easy on him. "When Zoe was reviewing Daria

Cantrell's Facebook page, she found that Daria had checked in to a location a week ago on campus."

"And?"

"And Shannon Bender also checked in there. It was a conference room that Nick Holden had reserved for his round table on "Real Life Scream Queens of Sutton College.""

Ty's brow furrowed. "That's it? They were in the same room once?"

"With Nick Holden, a reporter who has been tweeting inflammatory things all week long and had the gall to tell me that sorority life was anachronistic."

"Are you accusing him of something?"

I lifted my shoulders. "He's not being very nice."

"Wait, let me get my handcuffs—"

"I'm serious."

"You're serious?" Ty unsnapped the holster on his hip. "I'll just go shoot him then and get it over with. Save everyone the time and trouble of arrests and trials and all that."

I crossed my arms. "You asked me for help, and when I give it to you, you mock me."

Ty's lips flipped up a bit. "Thank you. I appreciate the tip." He weighed the thumb drive in his hand and shook his head. "I still can't believe—"

"That the Delta Betas had the forethought to install security cameras around Greek Row?"

"Security. Yeah."

That was my story, and I was sticking to it. Really, we should get an award or something. Sutton Panhellenic Crime-Fighting Chapter of the Year. If we ever got off probation, I was sure that was going to happen.

I nodded at the drive in his hand. "If you need any help with that, I'm sure Zoe can help you out."

"How many days have you had these cameras up?"

"Just since Sunday."

"Anything interesting that you've noticed?" He held up a hand. "Besides mean boys giving you a hard time?"

I thought of Ginnifer and Von Douton's meeting. It looked really bad, but it wasn't the kind of thing Ty was looking for. "Just the usual. The stinky cheese and the blue lilies and the Internet hacking. From our feeds, we saw the Lambda sisters sneaking into the Tri Mu house to plant the cheese and the Moos waylaying the florist's truck to dye the Beta Gam lilies blue."

"What about the ingenious plot to reverse-filter the Lambdas' Internet router to only show porn?"

Of course he'd pay close attention to that one. "We're not sure; it was probably done remotely."

"By a highly skilled Internet genius in the Delta Beta house?"

I gasped when I realized he meant Zoe. "No!" And made a mental note to ask her later.

"Anyway," I said to get back on track, "I think I need to look at the Witness glasses' card again."

He flipped on his computer screen, and, a few moments later, I saw what I'd thought I see. "There!" I pointed at the lilies in the background of the footage shot by Shannon Bender. "We thought those were irises, remember?"

"Sure we did," Ty said. Typical male, pretending he knew anything about flowers.

"But that would be odd because clearly, from the clothes of everyone else in the frame, this was shot either in the winter or late fall. Look at the jeans and boots and the girl in the Patagonia jacket, here." I pointed at the corner.

Ty squinted. "How did you—That's just a black jacket."

I didn't have time to explain everything to a man who couldn't distinguish Patagonia from North Face from a hundred feet away, and refrained from asking him how he got to be a police offi- cer. "Irises don't bloom in January, and besides, she's clearly in a Lambda sorority house because of that needlepoint crest there on the wall, but it's not the one at Sutton because the Sutton Lambdas don't have green wallpaper in their music room, they have soft rose walls and—"

"Blythe! Spit it out!"

"I'm trying to!" I took a deep breath. "Those aren't irises." I nodded at the screen. "They're dyed lilies. Like the dyed lilies here."

Comprehension began to dawn on Ty's face. "That's another chapter . . ."

"Where the same prank was pulled," I confirmed.

"According to her parents, Shannon Bender graduated from Oregon at the end of the fall semester. They said she'd been home with them since then and just left to visit friends before she was going to find a temp job before grad school started."

"We need to call the Lambda chapter at Oregon and find out if they were the victims of the lily dye job."

"And then what?"

"We know Shannon Bender didn't orchestrate both because she was murdered before the lilies were dyed here."

"So Shannon might have had a friend here who carried out the plans for the flowers?" Ty sounded like he couldn't believe he was having this conversation. And he wasn't getting the point, at all.

"We already know who dyed the Lambda lilies!" I reached for the thumb drive on the desk, the one I'd just given him. "We know the Moos did it! Shannon Bender was a Moo! She obviously came here to visit her Moo friends and help them with rush, and someone in that house killed her!"

"I just questioned the Moo—I mean Tri Mu—chapter yesterday. No one recognized Shannon Bender's picture."

I pushed the drive back in his palm. "There. That's all the evidence you need to put the entire Tri Mu chapter behind bars."

"Margot . . . I need more than some pictures of flowers to arrest sixty people."

"Sixty?" I scoffed. "There's no way that chapter has more than forty-five women. They haven't made quota in two years."

"I interviewed sixty women yesterday."

I quickly did the math. "Those ho-bags have been illegally rushing! I am so reporting this to the Recruitment Council." To pledge women outside the confines of formal recruitment was one of the biggest sins at a small Panhellenic like the one at Sutton. We had rules, gosh darn it. Lots of rules, all written to ensure everyone was on an even playing field.

"I thought you wanted them behind bars."

"That, too," I muttered.

Ty sighed and looked at the ceiling. "I never knew sorority rush was this dirty."

No longer caring that I was speaking to a police officer, I let my anger get the better of me. "They are so going down."

"You know, it's not an open-and-shut case. We're getting anonymous tips from everywhere about the murders."

Something in his voice made me pause and give him all my attention. "Like what?"

"Like anonymous tips about sorority sisters being outside their house after curfew."

As if on cue, there was a knock at the door. "I tried waiting in the lobby, but no one came."

It was Callie, dressed as I hadn't seen in her in days. Gone was her rush-week work wear of fleeces, tees, and jeans. In their place was her usual Callie Campbell style—slim wool trousers and a perfectly pressed oxford shirt with her mother's string of pearls at her throat and at her ears. Her perfectly curled hair and groomed eyebrows made me feel a little self-conscious that I had run off to the police in my casual state. Delta Betas should always put some effort in, especially while meeting with law enforcement.

"What are you doing here, Callie?"

She looked between me and Ty. "I was called in for an interview?"

My hands went to my hips as I glared at Ty. "Did you think you were really going to get away with interviewing one of my girls without notifying me?"

"Hope springs eternal, Blythe."

Chapter Twenty-eight

I HAD NEVER, ever allowed Lieutenant Ty Hatfield to conduct illegal searches, seizures, or interviews of my Debs without my presence, and he darn well knew it. I took my responsibilities as their mentor/advisor/honorary big sister extremely seriously. If their parents were not around, I was going to be there, in a quasi-legal capacity.

Two questions into Ty's interview of Callie, I knew exactly where this was going. "Really? You called her in because of an anonymous tip? On *Law & Order*, they always ignore those—they're from psychics and other crazy people."

"This one was very specific."

I crossed my arms and waited because there was no way in heck my sweet Callahan Campbell, a direct descendant of Mary Gerald Callahan, for goodness' sake, would have broken rule number four and left the Deb house after curfew.

Ty continued, "This one said that at or about four in the morning, you left your room on the third floor of the Delta Beta house, exited out the northwest back door, and proceeded to run around the block, switching up the chapters' Greek letters outside their houses."

That was really specific. I said, "That is ridiculous."

"Did you—"

"Objection!" I said. Callie opened her mouth, then closed it when I glared at both of them.

"Ms. Blythe . . ." Oooh. "Ms." only scared me when it was from someone younger than me. I was not intimidated by Lieutenant Ty Hatfield.

"Do you know who this is?" I wrapped my arm around Callie.

"Callahan Campbell, I hope."

"Exactly! She's Callahan Campbell, the chapter's standards and morals director. She's an excellent role model who's never broken a sorority rule in her life." Callie bit her lip.

Ty raised his eyebrows. "Wasn't she the one having an illicit affair with the house brother last semester—"

"Okay, really—"

"And was recorded having sex in your office?"

Callie winced. "You've gone too far," I said.

"You brought up her character."

Darn him and his accuracy. "Even if she did leave the house and go for an early-morning run, which is an excellent health habit, by the way, and one which we should be commending her for when obesity strikes far too many beautiful, successful college women—what does that have to do with anything?"

Ty speared me with a sharp stare. "Daria Cantrell was murdered at approximately four in the morning. Which makes Ms. Campbell either a potential witness to the crime or a possible suspect."

I stood up, yanking Callie's arm with me. "We're done. Come on Callie, let's go."

"I'm not done," Ty said, his voice rising a little as he also stood behind his desk.

"Are you accusing her of something? Is she being arrested? Based on an anonymous tip?"

"No, but—"

I held up a finger. "After all the help I've given you today, this is how you repay me?"

"Margot, I have to look at everyone, not just the suspects you give me."

I pushed Callie toward the door. Ty called out behind me, "I don't arrest people just because you tell me to!"

"And I don't sit down and shut up just because you tell me to!" I yelled back over my shoulder.

It might not have been the most ladylike thing I've ever said, but it was probably the truest.

BACK IN THE safety of the Delta Beta house, I marched Callie into my apartment living area. "Spill," I ordered her.

She twisted her hands, and when she turned her big brown eyes at me, I knew.

"Callie!" I exclaimed.

"It was hilarious!"

"You broke rule number four!"

"I didn't see anyone, and no one saw me!"

"Someone did and knew what time you left and what door you went through. Unless . . ." A crazy thought entered my head. "That was all just made up?" Maybe it was a psychic's lucky guess that someone named Callie Campbell left the Delta Beta house at 4 A.M.

"No, that was all correct."

"The northwest back door?"

She nodded glumly. The Delta Beta house sat at the end of the street and backed up to a greenbelt and the Sutton College golf course. It was probably one reason so many people dropped dead bodies in our backyard—it was very private. The northwest back door faced the woods. Unless someone was sitting in the woods watching us in the middle of the night (and that would be super-creepy), that meant . . .

I covered my mouth with my hand. This couldn't be happening again. Callie saw my distress and asked what was wrong. I briefly debated telling her my suspicions, but since her name had been reported to the police, I thought she deserved to know.

"It had to be someone on the inside who saw you leave."

Callie's eyes narrowed. "Ginnifer."

"Don't leap to conclusions," I warned her, but I had to admit, I had the same thought. Little Miss Follow the Rules would have had a fit if she'd seen Callie leave the house during curfew. And that was why it also didn't make sense.

"Why didn't she report you to Panhellenic, then? Why did she make an anonymous tip to the police?"

"Because she hates me. She hates the whole chapter."

I can see why Callie thought that. The Gineral had definitely earned her nickname.

"Has anyone seen her?" I asked, trying to think all this through.

Callie shook her head no. I moved to the computer and paused as a terrible notion hit me.

"You really ran around the block and switched everyone's letters?"

Callie's adorable dimples flashed at me. "It's funny."

Under normal circumstances, she would have been right. But

her midnight prank had, in all likelihood, been captured by our security cameras' footage. Footage that we had just handed over to the Sutton PD.

Sometimes being the Crime-Fighting Chapter of the Year had its definite disadvantages.

Before I did anything crazy, like accusing Ginnifer of narcing to the cops about our beloved S&M director, I went to the corner of the backyard to double-check the vantage points. Walking in an arc confirmed that unless someone was lurking about under the tree cover, there was no accidental way to see Callie sneaking out of the house last night. I would ask Zoe to check our cameras, but they wouldn't be able to see into the woods. Maybe next year, we should talk about upgrading to an infrared system.

I was walking back inside when my phone blew up—and judging from the sounds I simultaneously heard from the house, everyone had been alerted to some kind of drama. I said a silent prayer to the patron saint of long-suffering chapter advisors and prepared myself for the worst. As soon as I heard "GreekGossip," I knew I'd found it.

GreekGossip.net was the nastiest, filthiest, lie-infested Web site on the Internet. The message boards were crawling with trolls and fraternity guys who probably looked like trolls, spewing sexist, elitist, racist, every kind of bad-ist vitriol about sororities. Each college had its own forum for Internet meanies to post polls like "Which chapter is the sluttiest?" and "Who has the ugliest pledge class?" The site was a stewpot of negativity; and everyone who pledged anywhere read it regularly.

I didn't read GreekGossip.net because I liked it. I read it to stay on top of the rumors and the public perceptions about the chapter. For instance, when our previous chapter advisor was murdered three months ago in the midst of rumors of a phone-sex ring, my best friend Casey Kenner, the PR genius, and I had stayed up all night long posting on the boards, shooting down the gossip about Delta Beta—and adding red herrings about other chapters, just for fun.

So when I walked inside the house, and the entire chapter was buzzing about a new thread on GreekGossip.net, I knew that it was probably a bunch of lies. But that messiness could still be a huge pain in the seat of my lululemon yoga pants.

I walked straight to the kitchen and poured what was left in the coffeepot into a cute Delta Beta mug emblazoned with our mascot, Busy Bee. There was no time for a much-needed latte. Our day off from formal recruitment was more dramatic than a day full of preplanned conversation and supercute coordinated outfits.

Aubrey, Asha, and Zoe were clustered around a laptop in the dining room. I pulled out a chair across from them. "How bad is it?"

"For whom?" Asha asked.

I perked up a little at that. It was actually a good sign that no one was in hysterics. Maybe it meant that the GreekGossip. net trolls had decided to pick on another chapter for once. When Asha read the posting aloud, there was almost nothing I found offensive. Another first from GreekGossip.

"The Sutton College Tri Mu chapter is really the lowest of the low," Asha read. I sipped my coffee. So far, so good.

"Their rush tactics show that they are a desperate, skanky bunch of ho-bags who couldn't rush their way out of a Walmart bag," Asha continued.

"Wow," Aubrey said. "That's harsh."

None of us corrected her. Aubrey's twin sister was president of the Tri Mus, so we tried to be tactful in her presence.

"The whole row has today off," I observed. "Some Beta Gam or Epsilon chick got bored and decided to start something." I didn't really see what the fuss was about. It was more of the same for GreekGossip.

Asha shook her head. "It wasn't started by a sorority member."

"A frat guy?" I asked. It wasn't unheard of, the fraternities got a kick out of starting stuff with sororities, as they did with the annual prank wars in the fall.

"If Nick Holden is in a fraternity."

Crap. I swiveled the laptop toward me and saw that a user named Nick Holden had started a topic on GreekGossip: Tell the Truth about Sororities.

"WHY?" I asked no one in particular, but Aubrey answered anyway.

"I heard he's had trouble getting people to cooperate with his interviews."

That made sense, given that it was rush and the Mafia had essentially threatened anyone who participated in his journalistic strategies. "But this is the way he gets his scoop?" I asked no one, again. It seemed desperate and shoddy.

Then Asha kept reading. "'The Tri Mu hired rush consultant is a beyotch who travels around the country starting shit with other chapters. This shows you what kind of people the Moos are. They purposely brought this beyotch in to divide Sutton Panhellenic like she did at the last schools she went to. At the University of Oregon, Colorado State, Tufts, Immaculate Conception, and more, she has done horrible things to people.'" The post ended with "Don't pledge MU MU MU or you will be joining the biggest bitches ever!"

I flinched a few times during the rant. It got pretty specific about some other aspects of Sheila, speculating about her weight (unfair) and her nose job (totally up for debate). I knew if it were our chapter singled out, we would be worried about rushees reading it and the negative PR impact. But in the end, anyone who knew anything about sororities also knew that the stuff on Greek-Gossip was 90 percent bull. Surely, Sheila DeGrasse had heard worse over the course of her storied and evil career.

Chapter Twenty-nine

"THEY SAID WHAT?" I screamed at the laptop screen.

It didn't take long for the Tri Mus to rally on GreekGossip.net. They really had way too much time on their hands if all they were doing was sitting around reading this stupid Web site.

Asha, Aubrey, Zoe, and I were clustered around the computer, our mouths slack from shock at the fingers that were now being pointed at us. Yes, it was a lie. But it was the worst kind of lie EVER, and one that we had no way of combating.

"I can't accept this. It's so blatantly untrue. I'm the social director! I know the truth!" Asha was getting dangerously worked up, and Aubrey put an arm around her shoulders.

"This is going to kill us with the rushees," Zoe muttered.

"They won't believe this. They can't believe it. Right, Margot?" Aubrey lifted her worried eyes to me. Once again, the women were looking to me to show leadership.

I was about to reassure them, to tell them that it was all going to blow over, that anyone who had seen the Delta Beta chapter would know this post was a lie, but I was interrupted by a call on my cell phone. The number was unknown, but I picked it up anyway.

"Hello?"

"How could you?"

"Who is this?" I asked. Really. It could be anyone these days.

"I thought we had an understanding!"

"Sheila?"

"We had a truce!"

Oh. The truce. I made a face. She was serious about that?

"We had a truce," she said it again, like it had been really important to her. "And then you and your Little Debbies go and post about us?"

She sounded really hurt.

"It wasn't us." I was pretty sure it wasn't. "Why would we do such a thing?"

"You and I both know why. You wanted revenge for when I beat you at Immaculate Conception."

Hearing it coming from her made me go shivery all over. "I don't do revenge."

"Well, I do. And if you think this posting about how none of the fraternities will mix with the Debs because of your unfortunate bouts of mouth herpes was bad, you just wait until you see the rest of what I can do, Margot Blythe. Nobody breaks a truce with me and gets away with it."

"What are you saying?"

"I'm saying you should make sure your sisters don't break curfew."

She hung up after that chilling statement, and another round of goose bumps rose on my upper arms. Her words ping-ponged around the inside of my head. Curfew . . . Revenge . . . Immaculate Conception . . . Oregon.

Holy caramel macchiato. The original GreekGossip posting listed Oregon along with Immaculate Conception in the list of schools where Sheila DeGrasse had wreaked havoc. The same school that Shannon Bender had just graduated from.

It was a huge coincidence. But Sheila DeGrasse had just proved herself to be a completely unreasonable, vengeful shrew who had just threatened my entire chapter and spread an anonymous rumor that the Debs were sorority non grata for the Sutton fraternities. If she could do something that horrible, what else would she do?

I leaned over and reread the responses to Nick Holden's inflammatory thread. What if . . . what if . . . my mind raced with dark and unfounded suspicions. There was so much to unpack, but I had to start taking decisive actions if I wanted to end the threats that were hanging over the Delta Beta house.

I grabbed my jacket, purse, and car keys and headed out the door. If Sheila DeGrasse was going to threaten my chapter, her experience from Immaculate Conception should have told her what was coming next.

SIX YEARS OF serving as a sisterhood mentor and helping chapters during rush had taught me many things. I knew how to apply lip gloss so that it didn't end up on my teeth after hours of smiling, singing, and talking. I knew how to look a rushee in the eye and see if she was lying about the extent of her marijuana experience. And I also knew that sometimes anonymous message boards and Twitter accounts weren't going to be enough to fight vicious lies spread by jealous girls.

Sometimes, you had to get your own hands dirty and get down in the Alpha Kappa Jell-O wrestling ring yourself.

So here I was, standing outside Nick Holden's room at the Fountain Place Inn. I knocked loudly and was shocked when the man himself opened the door. Shouldn't he be out reporting on something?

He answered the door and checked his watch. "Margot? Did we have an appointment?"

On the way over, I had debated how to play this, but now, standing in front of a famous news personality, with a reputation people could trust, I decided to just come out with it. "You're posting replies to yourself on Greek Gossip."

Holden's eyes grew round as a camera lens. I held a hand up to stop his sputtering.

"It had to be you. All those details about Sheila DeGrasse's work history. Only someone who has done background research could know all that."

"It's common knowledge."

"No, it's not. Especially her working at Immaculate Conception University. I'm the only person in Sutton who knows what she did there. And I didn't post those things."

"The Internet is a big place, Margot. And they let anyone come in and write whatever they want."

"It's pretty unlikely that someone else who was at ICU four years ago happened to stumble upon your posting and decide to answer it. And, within two minutes of the original topic." Holden's usual suave, confident, anchorman demeanor had faded to something uncertain and shaky.

"Why don't you come in, and we can discuss it."

Instead, I took a step back. "I don't trust you," I told him. "And

I don't like what you're doing here. You're purposely causing trouble. And I have to wonder if the college administrators know what you're doing."

Genuine distress crossed his face now. "I haven't done anything wrong. I'm hustling is all. You don't understand cable news. It's brutal out there. Gossip, innuendo, backstabbing, and that's just your friends."

I shook my head. I was a sorority woman in the middle of rush. I think I had him beat in that arena, but he still wanted to prove a point. "I wouldn't have to do all this if your Panhellenic hadn't told everyone not to talk to me."

"They don't have that much power."

Holden sneered. "Oh yeah? Last week I had thirty women show up for a round table on sorority rush. I asked them all to come back to film an interview, and you know how many showed up? Zero."

"It's rush week," I explained to a clueless male for the four-hundredth time that week. "People are busy!"

"I have a deadline. And if you and your witches won't bring me the story, I'll get it one way or another."

"You're poking the bear, Holden. And if you don't stop, it's going to poke back."

"Is that a threat? Are you threatening me?"

"No." I sighed, but I had to wonder why he had immediately jumped to that conclusion. Did I look like a girl who threatened people? Maybe it was my sassy new blond highlights that made him think that.

I was almost back to my car when my cell phone rang—Ty Hatfield.

"I'm only calling you because I know how you'll be if I didn't tell you." He ground out the words.

"Tell me what?"

"I received a second anonymous call."

Please no.

"About another Delta Beta breaking curfew and leaving the house last night."

Sheila FREAKING DeGrasse!

I tilted my head back to see the third floor of the Fountain Place Inn.

"Thank you very much for letting me know, Lieutenant." I popped the trunk to my car.

"Blythe? What is that sound?"

"Have a good day, Lieutenant."

The last thing I heard before I hung up was Ty saying something about how my being polite was suspicious. Unwarranted—I was always extremely polite to all public officials.

And to motel maids.

Ever since we came up with Plan B, I'd kept a blond wig and glasses in the trunk of my car. Let's just say there were some possibilities for cloak-and-dagger operations, and I was thrilled that I was finally going to use them. I considered being a natural brunette my curse, ever since my mother told me at twelve years old that blondes really did have more fun—and she could tell because my father's girlfriend was a blonde.

I expertly donned my disguise, and fifteen minutes later, I had charmed a member of the housekeeping staff into letting me into Sheila DeGrasse's suite. The smell of her Angel perfume hit me like a baseball bat; I was going to reek of it the rest of the day.

This was a very impromptu, very poorly-thought-out plan, but I just had to see Sheila's room and double-check that there wasn't some huge piece of evidence against Callie. I would run in and out, making a quick sweep before I could get caught.

"I'll just be a second," I told the maid. "I think I left my bronzer here last night. And you know how us girls can't live without our golden glow in January." I wasn't sure she understood me, but I took advantage anyway and started poking around Sheila's room. I pulled out drawers and opened the lid of her suitcase and was in the bathroom rifling through her makeup bag when I heard Sheila's voice greeting the maid.

A quick glance around the bathroom confirmed that I had no place to hide unless I jumped behind the shower curtain, which wasn't an option. If I was getting caught snooping by Sheila, I was going to get caught in style.

I flung open the bathroom door. "Found it!" I cried, lifting a compact into the air. "Thank you so much," I said to the maid graciously. I pretended to notice Sheila. "Oh, you're here."

She crossed her arms against her chest and tapped her long red fingernail against her sleeve. "What do you think you're doing?"

"I accidentally left my bronzer here last night. But I found it, so I won't bother you anymore."

Sheila didn't move aside to let me pass. "That's my bronzer."

"Oh?" I inspected the container more closely. "That's strange. We use the same shade." I held it out to her. "Here you go. I'll just be on my way."

"Leave us," Sheila snapped at the maid, who apparently was being tipped very well because she skedaddled and shut the door behind her before I could make my move.

We faced each other down, and I was about to come up with

something glib about being in her room again when I saw some-thing terrible. I never thought I could be horrified about a pile of designer shoes. That shot of designer shoes that I'd reviewed multiple times on Ty's computer. I had assumed they were Shan-non's, somewhere in her room. But they were here, the pile of dust bags with the logos that I could never afford on a chapter advisor's salary. At least, not without some major birthday money from Great-aunt Dorothy.

Maybe I'd been too sleep deprived the night before to think straight; but today, a glance inside Sheila's closet confirmed it was the exact same view that Shannon Bender's Witness XV–99 glasses had captured before she died.

Now was the time for me to escape the clutches of evil Sheila DeGrasse, to jump in my car, and drive straight to the Sutton police station to present further solid evidence of who killed Shannon Bender.

"What's got you so scared, Blythe? Is it that you finally got caught breaking a law?"

I rolled my eyes, mostly at the irony that a murderer was accus-ing me of being a criminal. "I've done nothing wrong!"

"It's called breaking and entering!"

"It's called just entering when housekeeping lets you in!" I yelled, then remembered, *don't yell at the murderer*. It was a good rule. One I needed to remember.

I raised my hands innocently. "I thought I left something here. That's all. Can I go, please?"

"This is just like you. You pulled the same stunts at Immacu-late Conception. And somehow you think you can just skate by with your pretty hair—"

"Thank you."

"And your stupid way of talking."

"I'm from Florida!"

"And why do you keep looking in my closet?" Sheila demanded. I hadn't realized that I was. "Did you put something in there? Firecrackers? A jar of ants? A bag of dog poop?" Sheila gasped. "If my Manolos smell like poop because of you—"

"You'll what? Kill me?"

Sheila looked like she'd been slapped. I went on, though antagonizing a rush consultant was never a good idea. "That's right, I've figured out what you did to Shannon Bender."

Right then, Sheila's face crumpled, and she burst into hysterical sobs. "You are evil, Margot Blythe! Just evil! I would have never taken this job at Sutton if I'd known you would be here. How could you accuse me of killing my own sister?"

Wait. What?

"Your sister?"

"She was my great-grand-little sister at the Oregon Tri Mu chapter. She came to Sutton because of me! And then your Debs ripped the life from her, and the police won't do anything to you!"

I threw up my hands. "We have an alibi!"

"How do you do it?" Sheila demanded. "How do you always convince people that it's not your fault?"

"Because it's not!"

"It never is!" she spat.

We were going around in circles. "I'm telling the police about the shoes, Sheila. The footage on Shannon's spy-glasses . . ." My voice trailed off as I put the pieces together.

"Shannon came from Oregon to Sutton to help you."

Sheila nodded mournfully.

"And you were going to use her to spy for you!"

"You pulled the exact same stunt at Immaculate Conception."

I opened my mouth to argue, then shut it. Technically, there might have been a Plan B during that rush, too. But at least it didn't result in someone's getting killed.

Sheila sank onto the side of the bed, her shoulders slumped, her mascara in black streaks down her face. "Go ahead and tell the police. It's the kind of low, conniving move you'd make."

"At least I'm not doing it anonymously!" I pointed my finger at her, and she had the grace to look shamefaced. "Callie may have made a poor decision, but it wasn't criminal."

After a beat, Sheila's brows drew together. "Who's Callie?"

"Callahan Campbell? Callie? Our standards and morals director?"

Sheila lifted her shoulders. "So?"

The nerve of this woman. "You turn in an anonymous tip to the police, and you don't even know her name? You're not very good at this."

Sheila shook her head slowly. "I didn't call about Callie." Then she said a name.

It took me a minute to process what Sheila had just said.

Finally, I could repeat it. "Ginnifer Martinelli?"

Chapter Thirty

Sheila nodded warily.

"This doesn't make sense. Why would Ginnifer leave the house in the middle of the night? How do you even know this?"

Her face shuttered. "That's privileged information."

Sure. "Ginnifer is our visiting sisterhood mentor. She would never break the rules," I insisted, even as Callie's accusations were ringing in my ears. *She hates me. She hates the whole chapter.*

"Like you never broke the rules?" Sheila's sarcasm cut to the bone. She had me there. But while I might have broken teensy eensy little rules here and there, it was always to benefit the greater sisterhood. Ginnifer, on the other hand . . . I wasn't entirely sure what she was up to.

I had urged Callie to take the high road, to consider Ginnifer's side of the story before we jumped to any conclusions. But if the Tri Mus knew that Ginnifer was breaking curfew and rule number four, that was going to not only look bad on the Debs but also potentially bring the police straight back to our front door.

One curfew breaker was suspicious. Two looked like a conspiracy to commit murder.

"I'm . . ." I paused. "I'm sorry about your friend," I decided to say. Something about the flow of tears and the stricken look on Sheila's face made me believe that whatever stunts she had pulled, whatever lies or half-truths she was still telling, she was genuinely devastated by Shannon Bender's death. Fresh tears flowed after I said that, and I sat next to her on the bed and pulled her hand into my lap.

"But I still have to tell the police about your connection to Shannon," I said quietly. "It's not personal, but until they catch her killer, we're never going to be able to finish rush."

Sheila wiped her nose. "Shannon would not have wanted this. Tri Mu meant everything to her. She only wanted to make our sisterhood great."

I bit back a response about dreaming impossible dreams and squeezed Sheila's hand supportively. "I'm also sorry I came here," I finally said. "I don't really know why I did. Except when I thought you were threatening Callie, it got me a little crazy."

Sheila nodded. "You'll do anything to protect your sisters. It's the only thing I respect about you."

I bristled a little but realized that even if Sheila didn't appreciate my many other exceptional qualities, she had pinpointed one of my best. Like a lady, I graciously accepted the backwards compliment.

"We have to find out who killed Shannon," Sheila whispered.

"And Daria," I added.

"She was just a freshman. It breaks my heart that she never got to pledge."

"I know."

"What if it happens to someone else?" she asked, with a raw edge to her voice. "Sutton Panhellenic will never recover. No one will ever pledge here again. And Shannon's death will be for nothing."

"They'll find the killer," I said with as much confidence as I could muster.

Sheila didn't answer, and we sat in silence, both lost in our own worries, when she suddenly said, "There's an ice-cream social going on for the rushees right now."

"I heard that." I didn't want to give anything away.

"It might be a good place to try to get some information about Daria Cantrell."

"True. I bet she had a lot of friends going through rush."

"With the GreekGossip thread, there's going to be a lot of chatter."

I turned to face Sheila. "We didn't post that information about you."

Sheila bit her lip. "I didn't start that rumor about you."

I dropped her hand and shoved my butt off the bed. Yeah, right! "You already admitted it on the phone!"

"I thought we were lying to each other on purpose!"

"Why would we do that?"

"Because that's what Debs and Tri Mus do!"

Oh. She had a point. "But we really didn't start that thread about you."

She lifted a skeptical brow, and I decided to let it go. In the grand scheme of things, the Tri Mus believing we wrote mostly true information on GreekGossip wasn't the worst thing in the world. Besides, time was running out.

"Are we doing this or not?"

Sheila stood decisively. "Just let me get my wig."

THE RECRUITMENT ICE Cream Social at the student union was Panhellenic's attempt to keep the rushees involved and interested even with pref night delayed because of a murderer's being on the loose. The e-mail invitation from that morning explicitly stated that representatives from the chapters were not going to be there, so that the rushees knew this wasn't a formal rush event.

I checked my blond wig, glasses, and face in the rearview mirror. I was twenty- six, but on a good day, in just the right light, with makeup that had the high-tech fine-line-blurring particles, I could probably pull off a mature, sun-damaged twenty-one. That would have to do. Maybe with sunglasses covering my laugh lines, I would be a convincing twenty-year-old.

Maybe.

If I was barely pulling off twenty-one, Sheila looked closer to a PhD student. Her short red bob, fedora, and trench coat were exactly what I would wear if I was a double agent in East Berlin in 1987. But hey, at least everyone was wondering who the German graduate student was and not looking at me.

The ice-cream social had been thrown together hastily, and it showed. Maya had bought about ten boxes of ice-cream sand-wiches and Creamsicles and laid them out on a table with Happy Birthday paper napkins and some half-chilled bottles of water. As Panhellenic events went, this one did not reflect the high enter-taining standards of the majority of chapters at Sutton College.

The turnout was also lower than I expected. Back in my day, women who hoped to pledge a sorority would have taken every opportunity to present themselves favorably to the chapters—or to the fellow rushees. After all, psyching out the competition was a huge advantage. Showing up to a social event such as this, impeccably turned out, head high, and beauty-queen smile plastered on would have earned a girl mega points in Greek society.

So I had to wonder if the low turnout was due to rushees not caring as much about making an impression, or negative attitudes about rush in general, given the ridiculous situation with the Nick Holden campaign. If women were dropping out of rush before pref night, Sheila's worries would be confirmed, and the future of the Sutton Greek system could be at stake.

As we had discussed on the ride over, Sheila and I split up automatically, the better to canvass the room and start as many conversations as possible. We would mix and mingle and artfully direct topics toward Daria, and information that could lead us to why she was outside the Tri Mu house the night before. Between Sheila and me, we had nearly twenty years of rush-conversation expertise. No one could squeeze info out of a rushee like an experienced sorority woman.

Sheila moved to the left side of the room, and I surveyed the right side. Months of preparation for rush meant that I recognized many of the faces in this room. I had personally reviewed hundreds of letters of recommendation for these women, assigned points to their resumes, uploaded their photos in our database and, of course, been following their social-media accounts as Casey Fenner. There was no reason why I shouldn't use this opportunity to try to woo some of our top choices to choose Delta Beta. Along with trying to solve a murder. I was nothing if not efficient with my time.

I slowly rotated throughout the room, keeping my face averted from Maya Rodman's semiwatchful gaze. Soon I found a likely group standing in a corner to join. I recognized several of their faces from the first two days of rush, including a double legacy— someone whose mother and grandmother had both pledged Delta Beta—named Tanya Pyles, an English major from Atlanta.

Not only could I find out what she might have heard about Daria Cantrell, I could get some information on how likely Tanya was to pledge Delta Beta. Although I was probably imagining the strange looks at my wig when I inserted myself into conversation, I rapidly steered the conversation around to Daria Cantrell.

"I never met her," I said sadly, not having to pretend that emotion. "But from what I read on GreekGossip, it sounds like she was awesome."

"You know," Tanya piped up, "you can't believe everything you read on that Web site."

I nodded in agreement. "Like anything to do with mouth herpes is probably a complete lie."

A tall girl with black curls looked at me funny. "Which chapter has mouth herpes?"

"None," I forced myself to say because saying "Tri Mu" would probably give me away. "So no one knows why Daria Cantrell was walking down sorority row that night?"

"I heard she was doing research for that new Nick Holden documentary," the tall girl said.

"No," another woman said. "I have a friend in the Epsilon Chi house. Daria had left her purse in their tent and gone back to find it."

"At four o'clock in the morning?" I asked skeptically.

"There was a big fraternity party that night," Tanya offered. The other women all nodded knowledgeably, and I made a note to confirm the party with Zoe. Even so, it seemed like Daria's presence on sorority row in the middle of the night had been completely accidental, which made her murder all the more tragic. She had been in the wrong place, wrong time.

"I'm sure everyone knows she needs to take a buddy with her wherever she goes, just to be safe," I said. The women's expressions told me I might sound a wee bit too advisorish with that instruction. But safety was really important. "Like now." I grabbed Tanya's hand. "I need a buddy to go to the bathroom with me."

Tanya shrugged and followed me out the door of the meeting room and down the hall to the ladies' room. I was mentally high-fiving myself over a sneaky yet practical way to get Tanya alone to nonchalantly mention how awesome being a triple legacy in Delta Beta would be, when I saw Ginnifer walking toward the bathroom as well.

I still needed to talk to her about turning in the Debs to Von Douton. But if she saw me now, she could blow my cover. I stopped suddenly in front of the water fountain and told Tanya to go ahead. "I'm dying for a drink."

With a roll of her eyes, she headed into the bathroom, holding the door open for Ginnifer, who didn't seem to recognize me, or notice me for that matter. I counted to twenty before going in, but just as I reached nineteen, I caught a familiar whiff of Angel perfume. Turning to greet Sheila, I saw instead Alexandria Von Douton walking into the ladies' room. Did they give the perfume out in Tri Mu bid-day baskets?

Now I wouldn't be able to dirty rush Tanya or confront Ginnifer, not with Von Douton in the bathroom. But since I still had to go, I went in and found an empty stall.

Before I could do anything, I heard Ginnifer's voice. "We're done."

Von Douton's silky reply reverberated around the pink tiles of the ladies' room. "Rush isn't."

There was a flush, and through the crack of the door, I saw Tanya go out, wash her hands, and leave. When the door closed behind her, Ginnifer hissed, "I'm not calling again."

A sour taste rose in my mouth. Callie's accusations were, indeed, true. Ginnifer had sold us out to Von Douton. But WHY? And how?

"They have to go down," Von Douton said. "This is how it works at Sutton."

"There's nothing left! They're on probation, rush is delayed." Ginnifer's voice rose shakily. "What do you want me to do?"

"Exactly what you've been doing. Until it's safe."

I pressed my cheek against the cool stall, trying to stay quiet until Ginnifer and Von Douton's heels clicked away out the door. I still didn't understand why Ginnifer was working with Von Douton? A sisterhood mentor collaborating with the enemy? Just how was I going to explain this to headquarters? How I eavesdropped in a ladies' room wearing a wig? And the scariest thought—if Ginnifer and Von Douton were collaborating—had they collaborated on other, more sinister activities?

Like murder?

When I left the bathroom, Tanya was waiting for me, leaning up against the wall, checking her phone.

"You waited for me," I said dumbly.

She shrugged. "You needed a buddy."

Maybe she'd be a good Delta Beta.

Then she checked her phone again and giggled. "My mom is going to freak out."

"Why?" I asked, trying to seem nonchalant.

"The Delta Betas. Another one got snagged by the police."

"What?" My voice cracked.

"For murder." She rolled her eyes. "You'd think they would learn how not to get caught."

I had never found my phone at the bottom of my purse so quickly. I had about two hundred messages. I swore a word that nice legacies shouldn't use, spun on my heel, and left Tanya in my dust.

My car was squealing out of the parking lot when I realized I'd left Sheila behind at the student union. Once Sheila knew what had happened, I was pretty sure she'd understand why I'd broken our second truce.

Chapter Thirty-one

FOR THE FIRST TIME, I was gratified that the front lobby of the Sutton police station was unmanned and empty. As far as I was concerned, no one needed to know that I was here—or who the most recent occupant of the holding cell was.

I stormed past the reception desk, where no one sat, and into the hall, where no one stopped me from going straight to the depressing gray cell with the disturbing drain in the middle of the room. But before I made it, Officer Malouf stepped out of a nearby office. "Ms. Blythe, you can't go back there."

I stopped short. "Oh. Of course. I forgot, I'm sorry."

Malouf's eyes softened. "It's okay, I know you're probably a little distracted."

I nodded and looked over my shoulder. "Should I go back to the reception area and sign in with the officer up there?"

Malouf frowned. "Officer? What officer?" He moved past me, back toward the front door. Rookie. I turned and picked up the pace down the hall toward the holding cell.

Malouf realized what I'd done right away, but I had a head

start, and the cell wasn't that far away. Ty was there, and so was Callie, backed up against a wall with markings for Ty to take her picture.

"Callie!" I called out, my voice breaking, going to her with my arms outstretched.

"Crap." Ty lowered his camera. "Malouf! What did I tell you?"

"She looked so sincere!" Malouf exclaimed.

"Of course she did, she's Blythe!" Ty looked exasperated. I thought he'd gotten over that with me months ago.

I pulled Callie into a tight embrace. "Let her go, Margot. I'm not done here." Ty sounded less exasperated but still not super-empathetic.

"You are done here. We're all done here."

"I told you, you don't get to decide who gets arrested and who doesn't."

"Well, if some people made better decisions, I wouldn't have to insert my opinion."

"Margot, it's okay." That was Callie, and she sounded a little strangled. I loosened the grip on her throat. "I'll be okay."

Sweet girl. So brave. So noble. "I know you will," I assured her. "When we're back at the house, and your dad's lawyer is on the phone."

"Blythe . . ." The warning in Ty's voice was real.

How many times did I have to explain this to him? "As chapter advisor, I have a quasi-legal duty to represent the interests of the sisters of Delta Beta—"

"Even if they confess?"

He was just being stupid now. I wasn't even going to deign to respond to such a ridiculous hypothetical. "And I would be abdicating that responsibility if I let you book innocent, God-fearing women—"

"Margot!" Callie pulled away from me and put her hands on my shoulders. "I'm so sorry."

Ever since I first met Callie Campbell, she had burrowed into a special place in my heart. Apologizing to me for the possibly libelous acts of the Sutton PD? This earth did not deserve to host such an angel. "Shh . . . We're going to get this taken care of," I assured her.

"I confessed."

I blinked. Then I looked at Malouf and Hatfield to see if they had spoken in the soft Southern feminine voice. Neither looked like they had just finished uttering two unbelievable words. I swore to heaven that I would get more sleep and cut back on the coffee because I was clearly having some sort of caffeine-induced hallucination.

Callie was still standing there, cool as a tall glass of cucumber water, looking into my eyes expectantly. "Okay." I nodded my head. "We'll get you out of here right now."

"Margot . . ." Her voice was distant, now. Coming from a very far-off place . . .

"Okay," I repeated. "We're going."

Far off down the tunnel, I heard Ty shouting. "She's going down!"

Then something came up and smacked me in the face.

I WOKE ON some sort of examining table in a back room. I had been covered with a thin polyblend blanket that smelled like solvent and stale coffee. Curiously, my stomach rumbled.

My hand went to my forehead and patted around my skull, which hurt like the dickens. My cheekbone was especially raw and achy. I closed my eyes and felt myself tumbling back down a smooth black tunnel, and I didn't fight it. Instinctively, I knew it was the safest place for me.

At some point, I was aware of lights again. And voices. And pain. "Ms. Blythe?" I was pretty sure the voice belonged to Officer Malouf, and when I cracked one eye open, I confirmed that. He held his police baseball cap in his hands, rubbing the brim between this thumbs. "Ms. Blythe, you're awake now." He seemed relieved by that.

"Did I fall asleep?" I asked even though I knew the answer was negative. Nice girls like me did not fall asleep in police stations.

"You passed out, I think. Are you thirsty?" He reached behind him and lifted a water bottle. My throat felt scratchy and dry, so I motioned for the bottle and took a big drink.

It was all coming back to me. Rush and murders, then the unthinkable. My poor brain only accepted the world in one incarnation. Accepting the words that had come out of Callie's mouth? It was too much. I wouldn't process it now.

I took a deep breath and asked the only question I could. "Where's Callie?"

"Right. Lieutenant Hatfield said you'd probably want to chew him out first."

"No." Yet again another nearly incoherent statement. In what world would I chew out Ty Hatfield *before* I visited my own sister? My priorities would always be sisterhood first, chewing Ty Hatfield out second. He would never understand me.

"I want to see Callie," I informed Malouf, and put all the authority and weight of my office into that demand. Rather than deny a formidable sorority chapter advisor, he acquiesced and led me down the hall to the place I'd hoped I'd never see again.

Three months ago, I had briefly stayed in this holding cell, a large square with concrete benches and fluorescent lights and lots of gray bars facing the hall. Callie had been here, too, when her then-boyfriend Hunter was arrested for burglary and messing up my nice clean office. But now, Callie was on the inside, and I didn't even have a knife or a shank or a pack of smokes to give her.

She was on the bench, her knees pulled up to her chest, when she saw me. Her face was determined, with no trace of a smile or her cute dimples to indicate that she was going to laugh, and cry out, "gotcha," and tell me this was all a joke.

"Callie!" I put my hands through the bars, and she rose to meet me, clasping my hands. "What's going on?" I whispered fervently.

"Are you okay?" Callie looked concerned about me. I could not love her selflessness more.

"I'm fine," I insisted. I paused before I asked the next question. I'm not good with facts that alter my worldview. "Did you ... really?"

"I did." She said it plainly, so that I didn't misunderstand her this time. "I confessed to the murders of the girl in our yard and the other girl at the Tri Mu house." If I weren't holding on to her hands, I probably would have lost my balance a little bit.

"Why?"

She glanced briefly at Malouf, then back to me. "I . . . I don't know."

"Why did you confess to this?" An awful thought occurred to me. "Does your mother know? Your sisters? Your grandmother?" The idea was horrifying. An entire lineage of Delta Beta womanhood would have its reputation demolished. Sweet Mary Gerald. Would we ever recover from the scandal?

Now tears formed in Callie's eyes. "No. They don't know yet. Unless . . ."

"It's on GreekGossip," I had to tell her. "That's how I found out you were arrested."

"Damn," she muttered, and with that swearword, I could see just how fast incarceration damaged innocent souls. Her big brown eyes pleaded with me. "You have to talk to them, Margot. You'll have to tell them that everything I've done, I've done for all of us."

"You're going to tell them soon," I said. "When you get your phone call."

She shook her head. "I already used it."

Of course, I should have known that a smart, classy woman like Callie would have a criminal lawyer on retainer. Debs are nothing if not prepared for all eventualities.

"We're going to get you out of here," I swore. "I don't understand why you felt the need for self-defense, or whether you're truly, medically insane." I lifted my voice, to make sure that Malouf overheard me. I knew from *Law & Order* that it was important to start laying the groundwork for these defenses as soon as possible. "You have, after all, been talking to imaginary people at the house for a long time."

Callie frowned at me, but I just squeezed her hand. She'd thank me eventually.

"I'm going to support you," I told her. "We're not going to stop until we've found the real killer. We'll have a hunger strike, and I'm going to get *Dateline* out here and maybe we'll film a documentary like the one that freed those Satanists in Arkansas."

"Margot." Callie was staring at me intently. "Don't. Just forget about me. Focus on the chapter, on rush. I'll be fine."

"I'll never forget, Callie," I said bravely, wiping a tear from my cheek.

"Seriously," she said between gritted teeth. "I confessed. I deserve to be here. You need to do what you need to do."

I didn't understand her. I didn't understand why she'd done what she did or why people kept blaming us for murders on sorority row. I certainly didn't understand when she asked Officer Malouf to escort me back to the sorority house as if she didn't want me around her sobbing hysterically.

When I was all curled up in my bed in the chapter advisor's apartment in the Deb house, I felt like my whole world had been turned upside down. Everything I'd worked for, for the past three months, was gone. Rush was in limbo. Our house was under a cloud of suspicion. And I had gone to an ice-cream social with a Tri Mu, for heaven's sake. Nothing in Margot Blythe's world made any sense.

Chapter Thirty-two

I WOKE UP to the sound of an argument. This was not unusual in a sorority house. What was unusual was that one-half of the argument participants seemed to be male.

"She's had a head injury!" the man said in a raised voice.

"She's had a trauma!" That was the female.

"Exactly!"

"She needed rest!"

"I need to see her!" Why would the man need to see me?

"She's busy!"

"You just said she needed rest!"

"Because rush is starting again!"

I sat straight up in bed. How long had I been out? I swung my feet out of the bed and entered the tiny living area of the apartment. There was Lieutenant Ty Hatfield in his waterproof police jacket and jeans, and in his face was the chapter president herself, Aubrey St. John. She saw me, then pointed a finger in his direction. "You woke her up!"

He threw his hands up. "Head injury!"

Aubrey came and took my face in her hands. "You look better. The swelling's gone down."

"Swelling?" I asked.

"At the hands of the police." She gave Ty a nasty look over her shoulder. "We'll probably sue them for a million dollars."

Ty's jaw worked as he threw out his hand toward me. "She did that when she fainted and fell on the floor."

Aubrey rolled her eyes. "Next you'll be telling me that the hose just accidentally turned on. You didn't mean to use the pepper spray. The police dog was just trying to play."

"Would you tell her, please?" Ty asked me with frustration all up in his voice.

I was still about three sentences back, though. Gingerly, I pressed against my cheekbone. "Ouch," I said. It did feel tender and swollen.

"Great," Ty muttered.

"What time is it?" I asked.

"Eight," Aubrey said.

"Oh wow." I peered out the window. "It's not dark yet?"

"Eight in the morning. She let you sleep all night long," he said, with another gesture toward Aubrey.

"You were tired," she assured me. "You cried yourself to sleep."

"Head injury!" Ty reminded the room.

"Police brutality," Aubrey sassed back.

"A million dollars does sound good," I said. Ty looked up to the ceiling like he was praying.

Aubrey patted my shoulder. "I'm glad you're feeling better."

I wasn't. I was just awake and achy and a little foggy with all the craziness that had happened the day before. Even though as a chapter advisor I was now used to busy days, a day that started out with me waking up in a bed with Sheila DeGrasse and ending with my sorority sister confessing to a murder (I hope) she didn't commit was one for the books.

"Did I hear something about rush?" I asked Aubrey's back, as she had turned to shake out some Advil out of a bottle.

"Yes! We got a call from the Recruitment Council. Pref night is tonight." She handed me five Advil. "We have so much to do. Not to mention the chapter is a wreck from hearing about Callie."

The name made me feel sick to my stomach. Which could also be the sign of a concussion. I considered the painkillers and tossed them back without water. A strong woman had to overcome all sorts of things during rush.

Aubrey gave me a little hug. "I'm so glad you're feeling better. I don't know what we'd do if you were taken from us, too." While I appreciated the sentiment, it reminded me of Callie and also brought back all the feelings.

"Aubrey—" And then I broke off.

"It's pref night, Margot." I heard the plea in her voice, and I understood. We only had so many things we could control in this world. We couldn't control cancer, or global warming, or when no amount of hair products could keep the natural curl out of our hair. So we clutched tight to the things we could control. Like lighting candles and singing. And choosing our sisters. In the middle of a crazy, unpredictable world, Aubrey and the rest of the chapter wanted normalcy and predictability. If I couldn't give them anything else, I would give them that.

"Okay." I nodded and looked around the room. Time to break out the rush binder. "We should probably start decorating ASAP."

I was rewarded with a smile that only Aubrey could give me, and I knew I had made the right decision.

Until Ty Hatfield ruined everything.

"No."

"What do you mean, 'no'?" I asked, more than a little exasperated. He was the one of the reasons I couldn't control things for my chapter.

"You and I need to talk."

I hated him. I really, really did. Now was so not the time to deal with the police, but I could tell from the expression on his face that I could do this the easy way or the hard way, and the hard way might end up with me in a cell next to Callie. Which, while dramatic, wasn't going to help the Debs make quota. "Fine," I said. "I'm going to shower and change first." I was still wearing the same clothes from yesterday, and I'm pretty sure there's a rule about wearing the same outfit to a police station twice.

ALMOST AN HOUR LATER, I realized that Ty Hatfield wasn't driving me to the police station. In fact, we were going the opposite way, to the old downtown part of Sutton. When we pulled up in front of Joey's Diner, I almost didn't want to get out of the car. What did Ty have up his sleeve? He walked around and opened the door for me, and I had no choice but to step out onto the curb. We entered, the bells over the front door jangling, and in a low voice, I asked, "What are we doing here?"

He gave me an inscrutable look and put his hand on my elbow, leading me to a booth by the front window, where anyone could see me with the finest member of Sutton's Finest. This whole thing was suspicious.

I hadn't been to Joey's Diner since I'd relocated to Sutton, but when I was a student, late-night meetings of study groups were fortified with constantly refilled pots of Joey's coffee. The diner still looked the same; somewhere around the millennium mark, Joey's kids decided to stop updating the place and apply for historical-landmark designation, which the town had granted. Now, the original 1950s checkerboard linoleum and chrome fixtures were complemented by the seventies macramé potted ivy hangings and the eighties Robert Plant and Genesis music on the jukebox.

Ty slid one of the laminated menus across the teal table at me. "What are you going to have?" he asked.

"Coffee." It was mostly an automatic answer, but also one of self-preservation. I didn't know why Ty had brought me here, and I had to stay on my toes, preferably with a pot of coffee in my bloodstream.

Ty shrugged out of his jacket, and from this close-up, I tried not to notice how nice his shoulders were, or the way his plaid shirt folded up around his lean but muscular forearms. They were efficient arms, meant for getting a job done quickly and well. Like handcuffing one of my sisters.

The thought made me push my menu away, and Ty noticed. "Seriously, you should eat something."

"I'm not hungry."

"When was the last time you ate?"

"Last night," I snapped. "I had Mexican takeout with . . ." Oh right. I amended my statement. "The night before last," I informed him.

Ty stared at me for a moment, a strange expression in his blue eyes. I thought he was about to argue with me, but then he slid out of the booth and went to the counter to order. A few minutes later, he was carrying a tray full of food back to our table. He set a basket of fries, a plate of pancakes with bacon, a glass of orange juice, and a milk shake down on the table.

In college, Ty weighed about fifty pounds more, and his nickname was "Fatfield," so I was really proud of him for being confident enough to pack it away now.

He pushed the milk shake toward me. "You have to eat."

"I just wanted coffee," I replied stubbornly.

He flicked the straw at me. "Drink."

Since I was a woman with a healthy respect for authority, no matter what Ty Hatfield would have people believe, I reluctantly took the straw between my fingers and sipped.

My eyes popped open. "Coffee! It's a coffee milk shake!"

Ty's smile surprised me almost as much as the flavor bursting in my mouth. He was smiling because I was smiling, and it was a nice feeling. "I had them put a shot of espresso in a vanilla milk shake. I didn't think there was any other way to get the calories in you."

Wow. "Thank you," I said. "It's really good."

We sat quietly and drank for a minute or so, me from my espresso shake and him from his orange juice. It was companionable and pleasant, and I almost forgot why he'd asked me out.

Wait. "Why did you want to talk to me?"

Ty took a moment before he answered, pouring a big dollop of ketchup on the side of the French fries before he did. "I haven't investigated that many murder cases here in Sutton."

Hmm . . . I reached over, took a fry, dunked it in ketchup, and ate it while I waited for him to get to the point. "It's a small town, but it's also a college town, so we get pretty lively on the weekends, more than our fair share for a town this size."

The fry was crispy and hot. I took another one. "Before you came to town, there had only been two unnatural deaths since I've had my badge. One was a drunk-driving incident. The other was a woman who shot her abusive husband in the crotch and let him bleed to death in their bathroom."

I chose not to dunk my next French fry into the ketchup.

'Of course, we have a fair amount of other crimes in Sutton. Some pretty significant, theft, hit-and-run, drunk driving, assault."

I got a funny feeling from the way he was looking at me. "I haven't assaulted anyone." I sniffed before draining my milk shake.

"No," he agreed. "You haven't. Not that I know of." His eyebrow went up, and I realized he was making a joke. Ha.

I pushed my glass away and toyed with the edge of the bacon hanging off the plate with the pancakes. It was a deep red-brown, just the slightest bit of burned on the end. I broke off a piece and realized that I was actually interested in Ty's stories about Sutton. If I were a different woman with different priorities, I would have enjoyed a brunch with Ty. Hearing crazy stories about crime in Sutton, funny things and sad things. I would have enjoyed just spending time with him: He was kind (when he wasn't arresting me or my friends), steady, and quite nice to look at. Like now, with his sandy hair combed away from his chiseled, clean-shaven face and his shirtsleeves rolled up, his fingers moving up and down the orange-juice glass.

I had a sudden sharp memory of the "police" who had visited the house and wondered if Ty knew about the "rookies" that were going around impersonating Sutton's Finest. If Ty ever listened to Rihanna . . .

I shoved the strip of bacon in my mouth.

"I'm surprised, Blythe."

"Hmm?"

"You haven't asked me the question I know you're dying to ask."

Oh crap. How did he know?

"What's the point of all this?" He directed the rhetorical question toward the table and lifted his eyes to mine. "All of these crimes in Sutton and the first time anyone walks straight into the police station and volunteers to confess? Your girl. Callahan Campbell."

I dropped the second piece of bacon I had selected back onto the plate. Now we were getting to it. Maybe he thought I was supposed to be proud of her civic-mindedness? Even the Delta Betas standards and morals code didn't require our members to voluntarily confess to felonies they didn't commit. And I know Callie didn't murder two people. Especially ones she didn't know.

"I'm suspicious, Margot."

I jerked out of my thoughts. What had I done now? "About what?"

"Why this young woman, by all accounts a smart, accomplished, leader, waltzes into the police station and confesses to murder. Especially one she has an alibi for."

The pedicures! A wave of fresh hope hit me. "Did you check her toes?" I asked.

Ty frowned. "No. But you said she had a receipt."

"Oh. Yeah."

"The only thing I could come up with is that someone like Callie might confess if she was trying to protect someone."

The way Ty was looking at me right now was throwing all my brain cells off. I couldn't think right while under the scrutiny of such a hot, straight guy who had bought me breakfast. I now understood how prisoners at Guantanamo felt. I had no choice under this pressure.

But I also had no answers for him. "I don't know. I don't know why she's done this or whom she could be protecting. I just know . . ."

I realized I did know some things that Ty didn't know, and before he broke his jaw clenching it like that, I attempted to reassure him. "Okay. I just figured this out yesterday. I haven't been holding out on you." I spilled on Sheila. Also, I made it clear that the inn's housekeeper had kindly and enthusiastically volunteered to unlock the door of Sheila's suite for me.

I explained about her shoes and her friendship with one of the murder victims.

"So she knew Shannon Bender," Ty said, almost to himself. "That explains her hysterics when I questioned the Tri Mu chapter."

"I really think they were friends," I said weakly, thinking of the fragile truce part two I had with the rush consultant.

Ty leaned back in the vinyl bench, and it made a creaky, sticky sound behind him. "That explains why Shannon was here. But who would have a motive to kill someone that no one knew? Especially when all the Debs were at the salon?"

"She was wearing a Delta Beta shirt . . ." I broke off. This was one of the things that had been running through my head for the past four days that I had just kept ignoring because, really, it was unthinkable. "Maybe someone hates us enough to kill one of us."

Ty rubbed his chin. "But Sutton College isn't that big a place. Someone who had that big a vendetta would surely know all of you. Unless it was someone who was new to Sutton."

She hates the whole chapter.

I leaned away from the table and smell of the fries and bacon. It couldn't be.

"Could this Sheila person be lying about being close to Shannon

Bender?" Ty half asked me, half asked himself. "I think we'd know by now if there were more new people hanging around the row."

She's had it in for us from the beginning.

I had to tell him. I didn't want to tell him. Now was the time to tell him. Even though I had no proof, of anything. Not really.

I swallowed, hard. My throat was scratchy. I was probably coming down with something. It was pretty common after rush for an entire chapter to be laid low with a virus. It was only natural after spending so many hours together, inside, during winter.

"There's Ginnifer," I said slowly.

"Ginnifer?" Ty asked, his face blank.

"Ginnifer Martinelli. You met her at the house after Shannon Bender . . . She's the visiting sisterhood mentor."

Realization showed on his face now. "Ah. The Mini Margot."

"Mini me?"

"Exactly."

Ginnifer was shorter, more compact, but with her darker hair, okay, maybe I could see it.

"What about her?" he asked.

"She's new."

"She's a Deb."

"I know!" This was so hard. So, so hard. It was antithetical to everything I was, everything I stood for to voluntarily give a Deb sister to the police. Even though I'd set up the arrest of a Delta Beta last semester, it didn't mean that I hadn't prayed right to the very last moment that I had been wrong, that it was some sort of *Law & Order* murder-mystery game that I hadn't been invited to.

I focused on keeping my hands folded, the fingers gripping each other and forced the words out of my mouth. "She's made a lot of girls unhappy at the house, and Sheila somehow knows that Ginnifer left the Deb house and broke curfew and . . ."

Ty reached over and put a warm, steady hand over mine. "Where is she now?"

I shook my head. "I don't know. She's been hard on the girls. I called her a name. She turned us in for breaking a rule. Then, yesterday, I was wearing a wig, and I saw her in the bathroom . . ."

Ty's fingers twitched. "It's okay," I told him. "You can write things down."

Immediately, his hands went straight for his pocket to retrieve his pad and pen. "Spell her name."

I did, and curiously, somehow just the fact that he was taking notes alleviated some of my guilt. Maybe I wasn't tattling on a sister for no reason. Maybe I was actually looking out for truth and justice and the Delta Beta way.

"What rule did you ladies break?"

Oh. Um. Man. How was I going to explain this one? "Rule number five." Ty wrote that down, and I hoped he would find that sufficient. But of course, a detail-oriented man like him had to ask a follow-up.

"What's rule number five?"

"It's the . . . um . . ." I thought quickly. "No outside help rule."

Ty looked skeptical. Probably because I sucked at lying. "All right, fine!" I spat it out even though I knew exactly what he'd say. "Rule number five is no men in the sorority house."

Just as I expected, his lips twisted in a half-amused, half-sardonic way. "You don't say."

Don't ask don't ask don't ask.

"And what exactly were these men doing in the Deb house?"

"They were serenading us," I snapped. Technically, stripping was almost the same as serenading.

"And who did Ginnifer report this egregious rush infraction to?"

"The Mafia."

Ty's eyebrows jumped up. "No, it's just their nickname. For the Panhellenic Recruitment Council," I assured him hastily, in case he started worrying about organized crime infiltrating Sutton.

"I think I remember that from my Alpha Kapp days." Then he paused, frowning at his pad. "In fact, that's the second time I've heard that name recently."

The Mafia? Dang. I really hoped I had been wrong about that organized crime wave.

Ty tapped his pen against the Formica tabletop. "Callie was talking about that. With her grandma."

"Her grandma? She called Elizabeth?"

"Please tell me you don't memorize all of the sisters' grandmothers' names."

I waved my hand. "I spent part of Christmas break with Callie's family in Richmond."

Ty looked relieved at that answer. Maybe he thought memorizing fifty women's family trees was excessive?

"No, she didn't call. She had a visit from her last night."

That didn't make sense. "Elizabeth Campbell?" I clarified.

Ty shrugged. "I didn't catch the name."

It didn't matter. "Callie only has one grandmother still living. Elizabeth Campbell is eighty-five years old and extremely inspirational."

"Okay . . ." Ty still didn't see where I was going with this.

"Do you know why she's so inspirational to me?"

"There are so many possible reasons, Margot."

I ignored that tone in his voice and went on. "Because two weeks ago, eighty-five-year-old Elizabeth Campbell left the country with her wine club to study rare vintages around the world. The first stop of their two-month trip was Argentina."

Ty's brows snapped together. "Oh."

"So that means that Callie was talking about the Mafia with another woman who was pretending to be her grandmother." I whipped out my phone and pulled up the Panhellenic Web site. "Was it this woman?" I pointed at Alexandria Von Douton's face in the picture of the Mafia.

"No." Ty was definite. "It was her."

He was pointing at Louella Jackson. The Delta Beta Mafioso.

I slid out of the booth and said something that I never thought I'd say, "You're taking me to jail. Now."

Chapter Thirty-three

In the end, Ty didn't agree to my plan of putting Callie in an interrogation room with a single lightbulb hanging over her head. He said they didn't "do that" anymore though my friends Olivia Benson and Elliot Stabler would beg to differ. But he did think that playing "good cop/bad cop" was a worthwhile idea. At least, he didn't use air quotes and say that was "frowned upon."

I marched straight down to the holding cell to see Callie. "Look, missy, you've got a lot of talking to do. Don't make me call your mother."

"I thought you were going to be good cop," Ty muttered.

Please. And miss my chance to be bad cop?

Callie's eyes opened wide in fear. Then she remembered that she was a hard-boiled tough criminal now. "So?"

I pointed up at all the cameras in the ceiling. There were two high up above the cell and at least three down the hallway. "Did you really think they weren't going to notice, Callie?

"What?"

"We have proof of your grandma visiting last night," Ty inserted.

"And it wasn't Elizabeth Campbell," I added. "Unless she can fly back from Buenos Aires at a moment's notice."

Callie's shoulders slumped.

"You tell me who it was right now, little lady. Don't make me look at those tapes," I threatened, pointing up at the ceiling again.

"Fine," she said grudgingly. "It was Louella Jackson, from the Mafia."

Ty and I exchanged a glance, and I gave him a little nod. His ID had been correct. "What did you two talk about?" Ty asked.

Callie pressed her lips together, but as soon as she saw my finger snap back toward the cameras, she relented. "Louella called me yesterday and convinced me to confess to the murders."

"Why?" I asked.

"She said it was for the good of Delta Beta. That rush could go forward if they had a suspect and that Nick Holden would back off his push to close down the sororities if there was no more danger to the girls. She came in last night to make sure I was still on board."

My heart melted a little bit hearing that. Callie truly lived up to her ancestor's legacy. I was proud to call her my sister. Except for the fact that she was in a jail cell. "Okay, Lieutenant. Let her out."

Ty jerked his head back. "Excuse me?"

"Let. Her. Out."

"I can't."

"What do you mean you can't?"

"I still have a confession," Ty said, his arm gesturing toward Callie. "And to release someone who confessed would be idiocy on my part."

"She just said she didn't do it!"

"No she didn't!"

I started to argue again, then realized he was right. Callie hadn't taken back her confession. "Go ahead, Callie. Do it."

Her wide eyes went damp. "I'm sorry Margot. She said she couldn't vote for rush to restart unless the police had a suspect. I have to do this for Delta Beta's sake."

I was speechless. This was a *Sophie's Choice* situation. Do I sacrifice one sister for the good of them all?

Or do I trap the enemy in an underground bunker and toss grenades in the air shafts?

If history had taught us anything, it was that Margot Blythe was always ready to go to war for her sisters.

No one was happy to be there. Of course not. It was two hours until preference night, and every chapter, nervous as all get-out, had a to-do list as long as a Project Runway marathon.

But rules were rules, and once again, I nimbly used the Panhellenic regulations to my advantage for an emergency meeting. Every single woman in the room gave me the evil eye, even Maya, who was usually pretty sweet. "Where's Sheila?" I asked the Tri Mu advisor.

Sarah just smirked. "She's getting shit done." Uncalled for.

Patty Huntington banged her gavel and called the meeting to order. "This one was called by the Delta Beta chapter advisor," she huffed. "After we just calmed everything down, too."

I stood and calmly greeted everyone. It wasn't the first time I had been the most unpopular person in a roomful of Panhellenic women. As a Delta Beta sisterhood mentor, I had had many opportunities to address Panhellenic councils around the country and suggest corrections to their approach to Greek life. In college, they actually honored me at the Panhellenic banquet my junior year with an engraved silver plate that read, "MOST LIKELY TO SUGGEST SOLUTIONS TO EVERYTHING." I got the sarcasm.

So this was not my toughest room. It would rank up there, but I had faced worse scenarios.

"As many of you know, rush—I mean recruitment—was restarted because the Sutton Police Department arrested a suspect. Therefore, our esteemed Panhellenic Council deemed it safe for rushees to once again walk the streets. However, I have proof that we—all of us—are still in danger for our lives."

I said that really dramatically, and thankfully, there were many gasps and shocked faces in the room. "Because the real murderer is still out there!"

Genuine fear was in the chapter advisors' faces, and I could see they were just like me. They didn't want another innocent woman to die without knowing the pleasures of sisterly love.

The council, on the other hand, was another story. To a woman, they were stony and unfazed by my dramatic declarations.

"Do you have any evidence to bring to this council of this allegation?" Von Douton challenged. Seriously, this woman was obsessed with "evidence."

"I know that the woman who was arrested is not a murderer. Ergo, the real murderer is still at large. Waiting." The logical theory was thanks to my major—I was a philosophy major if you couldn't tell. The extra flair at the end was all those nights rehearsing skits for the Epsilon Chi Sing-A-Thon my sophomore year.

"You mean that you called us all here to tell us that the Delta Beta who confessed to a double homicide is innocent? *Quelle* surprise!" Von Douton sneered at me.

"Technically, a double homicide means that two people were killed at the same time, which is not the case here," I informed her, drawing upon my vast criminal-law expertise.

"You would know." Von Douton's snide remark made some of the women actually giggle. Like that was appropriate.

"And yes. The Delta Beta who confessed is innocent."

"If she's so innocent, then why did she confess?" Patty Huntington's thick Southern accent only made that question seem more reasonable, and many women around the room nodded.

I placed a hand on my heart. This is where things were going to get really emotional. "Because she loved her sorority"—I waved my hand to encompass the rest of the room—"and Greek life so much, she sacrificed herself so that rush would go on." Everyone was hanging on my every word. It was an unbelievable story, one full of loyalty and true crime. And now, betrayal. I thrust my finger at Louella Jackson. "And because that woman ordered a young, impressionable postadolescent to confess to a crime she didn't commit!"

That did it. The room went into a tizzy. The advisors were whispering and nattering, their eyes round and concerned. And the Mafia was . . . well the Mafia was rather stoic.

I hadn't expected that reaction. Maybe they were a little uncomfortable, but there was no shock, no outrage there. I suddenly got the distinct impression that I was in way over my head.

Patty Huntington banged her gavel. "Enough! Ms. Blythe, you are out of order."

"And her chapter's on probation," Von Douton singsonged. Oh how I loathed that old Moo.

"Ladies, please." Louella addressed the room in a stern voice that was the opposite of the genteel words she had used. "I would like to address the charges. Yes, I urged Callahan Campbell to confess to these crimes. But I did so because of the overwhelming evidence provided to this council that proved that she was guilty. Evidence that I will be providing to the Sutton Police Department after this meeting is over."

She tapped a manila folder in front of her. What could be in that folder?

As if she could read my mind, she went ahead and described the contents, which included proof that Callie Callahan had set up surveillance cameras around Greek Row in order to track her victims before she murdered them in cold blood.

"Oh for Pete's sake!" I cried out. "Callie didn't do that! I did that!"

The room went silent as the grave.

Patty Huntington and Clara-Jane Booth and Sue Harlow all looked very regretful. Alexandria Von Douton looked triumphant. Louella looked . . . satisfied?

I was trying to process that when the members of the Mafia shared a glance and a nod, as if they were listening to their hive mind. "Louella, as the Delta Beta representative of this council, it's your responsibility . . ." Patty's voice trailed off as Louella sat straight and faced me.

"Ms. Blythe, under rule 24.4 subsection d of the recruitment regulations, I regret to inform you that the Delta Beta chapter has been removed from the formal recruitment process."

In the distance, there were more shocked gasps and maybe a curse word. I could do nothing as I felt the icy-cold shock in my nervous system.

This was the death knell for the Sutton Delta Beta chapter.

Chapter Thirty-four

TOSSED OUT OF formal recruitment . . . I could barely process such a tragedy. The hours of blood, sweat, and tears. All the paint, tulle, and twinkly lights. The fights over the perfect stuffed-animal placement, the heated debates over flat iron versus curling iron. The bouncing practice!

I wandered through campus, not ready to go back to the house and tell everyone what had happened—what I'd done. But who was I kidding? Someone had probably posted all the gory details on GreekGossip.net already. Or Maya had delivered the proclamation, torn up all the invitations to pref night at our house, and hung crime-scene tape all around the beautifully landscaped grounds.

The last time I'd felt this devastated, I'd just learned that one of my sisters had betrayed my chapter. Now, the sister that had betrayed Delta Beta was me.

The shame of it knocked me back into a nearby bench. I put my head in my hands and let the tears come, as the memory of another bench, next to the Jackson Memorial Engineering Building, floated to the surface. We had been so proud of raising the money to dedicate that bench to my pledge class. Our kissing booth at the student center had raised nearly five hundred dollars before we were shut down by the administration for possible sexual-harassment violations. The location was perfect, too, since the Jackson building had been named for Louella's husband, a Sutton College alum, and a pioneer in advanced nail-gun technology. As a pledge, I had been so excited to learn that, until I realized his invention had nothing to do with fingernails and everything to do with drywall. That was back when I idolized all Delta Beta alumnae, when I believed that they were nice old ladies who only had our best interests at heart.

Kind of like how my chapter thought of me. A nice old lady no longer. The sobs started again and were interrupted by two Hunter boots stopping in my field of vision.

I looked up. "You!"

Ginnifer was in the same clothes she'd worn when she was recorded by our cameras giving something to Alexandria Von Douton.

I scrambled to my feet, pretty sure I could outrun her in those rubber boots. But if she decided to take me down, those boots would help her. We were pretty evenly matched.

"Margot, I just heard the news."

"GreekGossip?"

The grim expression on her face was all the confirmation I needed. I let a curse word fly, and Ginnifer's eyes widened in shock. But if there was ever a time for me to use the "d" word, it was now.

"Have you called headquarters?" I couldn't believe this question, of all questions that I needed immediate answers to, was the one that popped out. I think we could both tell I was not operating on all cylinders, anyway.

When Ginnifer shook her head slowly, alarm bells went off. There was something seriously, seriously wrong here.

A sisterhood mentor who wasn't calling headquarters regularly? And who hadn't updated them on a chapter's being kicked out of rush?

Her confirmation of this major breach of protocol was the last piece of the puzzle.

"You've betrayed your sisterhood."

Ginnifer's hands twisted, and there was a strange plea in her voice. "You have to understand . . ."

I'd tried giving her the benefit of the doubt, but now I had to address the damning evidence. "You've been meeting with Von Douton, you ratted us out, about the strippers, about Callie, about the surveillance system."

It was a guess, but it fit. No one else inside the chapter had been caught multiple times with the enemy.

"Why would you set us up like this?" My shriek was probably heard all the way across campus at the Frito Lay Agricultural Hall.

Ginnifer's hands twisted frantically. "I didn't know what they would do, Margot. I thought some information here and there would be safe. I mean, how was I to know that Sutton rush was so bloodthirsty?"

"You NARCed on us!" I already knew about part of it, of course, but now so much more made sense. But not all of it. "But you were always trying to make sure we followed the rules!"

Ginnifer stepped toward me, and I took a step back. I didn't know if I trusted her enough to be in my personal space. "Yes, I did. Because . . . I didn't want to tell them anything. And because

I wanted a clean rush for once in my life, and I thought Sutton was my chance."

A single tear spilled out of her eye, and it would have made a beautiful addition to a pref-night ceremony, except for the fact that she was admitting her betrayal of Delta Beta.

"I wanted to follow in your footsteps. The legendary Margot Blythe, the greatest sisterhood mentor who ever lived, and here I got the chance to learn from the master, to sit at your feet and soak up all your wisdom."

This made no sense. "But you kept yelling at me with your megaphone."

Ginnifer ducked her head. "I was insecure."

Oh, okay, I guess I would be insecure if I were a young sisterhood mentor and had been assigned to work with me. I had been pretty awesome at my previous job.

Key words: HAD BEEN. I was sucking at my current job. Exhibit A: Getting chapter kicked out of rush. For years, future generations of sisterhood mentors would learn how NOT to advise a chapter by studying my actions of this week. I rubbed my forehead, as if that could forestall the horrible migraine that was coming. "Yelling is not the most effective way of communicating."

"It seemed to work okay . . ."

I had been talking to myself, but I didn't point that out. "I have to call headquarters to tell them everything." I shuddered at the conversation with Mabel Donahue that was to come. Explaining how the chapter had gotten kicked out of rush AND there were two unsolved murders being blamed on our S&M director AND how I had failed to provide proper leadership for the sisterhood mentor? I wondered how far I'd get with my wig and glasses. Maybe I could talk to Ty about witness protection.

And the worst part of it was, I didn't have any answers to give Mabel, when she asked me why I didn't keep a closer eye on Callie, or Ginnifer, or . . .

"Wait." Ginnifer looked up with pathetic, puppy-dog eyes. As if I was going to feel sorry for her. "Why, Ginnifer? Why give all of it to Von Douton? I don't understand that part. You said you wanted to be more like me, and I would never, ever betray us to a Moo sister."

Ginnifer looked miserable. "It's going to come out anyway. Since you'll probably ask for an investigation . . ." She let it hang out there like there was some chance that I would give her a hug and tell her it was going to be all okay. Maybe when Moos flew.

She saw the "no chance" written on my face, and continued, "Ms. Von Douton has a granddaughter at Alabama."

That was Ginnifer's alma mater, I remembered, and I gestured for her to get on with it. "And her granddaughter had information about certain activities that I encouraged during rush there."

"You didn't," I said.

"She was going to tell headquarters about all the tequila shots we gave to the rushees," she said. "Then there were the bribes."

"For Leticia's sake!" I clapped my hands over my ears.

"It wasn't a big deal, we just . . . called the Department of Homeland Security on the other chapters. Just the two times. Their study-abroad activities were really suspicious."

It was all the proof I needed that she was morally deficient. Betraying our chapter hadn't even been the first of her crimes: She'd had years of experience performing possibly illegal activities. I reached into my pocket to feel the comforting shape of my cell phone. Three little numbers, and I'd get Sutton emergency services. I didn't even care who won their bet this time. I'd shout

Ginnifer's name right before I was attacked with a spike to the back of my head.

"Did you hurt people, Ginnifer?" I asked quietly, even as my hand shook withdrawing my phone. "Did you kill Shannon Bender and Daria Cantrell?"

A half sob erupted from her. "No!"

She sounded sincere. She looked stricken. But I'd been fooled by her before. "I don't know if I can believe you," I said, even as my grip eased up on the phone. I don't know what it was, but I didn't feel unsafe. Just betrayed.

"I did it for Delta Beta!" she cried.

She didn't know how many times I'd heard that before. "I have to tell headquarters everything."

At that, she turned and ran away.

After I went through the Starbucks drive-thru, I realized I couldn't avoid my responsibilities any longer, even if they were the worst duties ever.

I still had taken vows to these women here at Sutton and Delta Betas throughout the world. Those vows must be honored even if I did it wrong.

At the Delta Beta house, I called everyone into the chapter room. They had all heard the news, and there was a mix of confusion and emotional pain in every question that I couldn't answer.

When I apologized to the chapter, I meant every word. I was sorry we wouldn't make quota. I was sorry we wouldn't pledge new sisters. I was so sorry our headquarters would likely pull our charter, and everyone would be homeless.

That was the extent of my positive thinking. I was out of rainbows and sunshine and baby ducks. The time had come to face facts.

My Michael Kors watch said pref night was starting in five hours. I headed to my apartment, determined to find solace in the flask I had hidden in my lingerie drawer and a pint of cookies and cream that I'd been steadfastly ignoring during rush-work week.

After pulling on a pair of flannel pajama pants and my coziest, most comforting fleece from sophomore year, which had seen many postbreakup pints of ice cream, I poured a dose of Fireball into my Delta Beta shot glass, toasting Mary Gerald Callahan and Leticia Baumgardner. I had barely made a dent in the cookies and cream when there was a knock at my door. I ignored it. As I was about to be fired, I figured the members better get used to not having me around. The knocking grew insistent, then downright pushy.

"All right!" I yelled. "Come in!"

In a whoosh, the door flew open, and there was Sheila De-Grasse, looking all pulled together and chic and evil in a black sweater dress, tights, and thigh-high boots that totally should have been mine.

She arched an eyebrow at my flannel and fleece. "Oh, honey," she said, her tone pregnant with pity.

"What are you doing here," I mumble-glared at Sheila, who had the gall to burst in on my pity party in a seriously fierce pair of four-inch red boots. To her credit, she didn't back down from the girl on the couch clutching a pint of ice cream and wearing pajamas. She tutted and looked pointedly at my cookie dough. "And you call us the Moos."

Sheila needed to go. She was disturbing the coma I was trying to put myself into. I was about to suggest that she shouldn't let the door hit her on the way out, when she said something that stunned me.

"Callahan Campbell is innocent."

Well, the substance of her statement didn't shock me. But the bald assertion of a truth that I didn't find the need to argue with from a Tri Mu was pretty incredible. And suspicious.

"I know," I haughtily said. "I've been telling everyone that. Thanks for the update."

Sheila's lips tightened at my sarcasm, and I felt sorry for a nanosecond for letting my depression get the better of me.

"Don't you want to know why I came over?"

Depressed Margot wanted to throw a blanket over her head and tell Sheila to go back to the farm. But, naturally, Curious Margot won out, as she always did. "Yes," I said.

"I have proof of Callahan's innocence. And I thought you'd like to be there when I gave it to the cops."

"Down at the police station?"

Sheila nodded.

This could be a trick. No matter the status of our truce, I still was wary of Moos bearing gifts.

"No," I said definitively. "When Lieutenant Hatfield has something to tell me about the case, he'll give me an update."

Sheila's brows rose in interest. "Oh. You two are that close?"

Not really. "It's professional courtesy," I informed her. Not that she would know anything about that. She didn't look convinced, so I went on. "I have a very firm policy of not intruding on police work. I don't even know where the police station is."

Sheila let out a bark of laughter. "You don't trust me."

There it was. "No." I admitted it because—why not. Let's lay it all out. "After what happened today? I was stabbed in the back by the Mafia. Like Caesar, they each took a turn, the Deb, the Moo, the Lambda. And the rest of the advisors didn't do anything. I would have stood up for them, insisted that any chapter leaving rush weakened all of us. We're stronger together, but no, they saw I was weak, and they all did nothing. And now you waltz in here, with your shiny hair and your Angel perfume and hot boots, and I'm supposed to believe that you don't have an ulterior motive?" My voice had risen, it was shaking and on the verge of hysteria. "I may have been born on a Tuesday, but it wasn't last Tuesday."

As tough as Sheila was, I shouldn't have been surprised at how she stayed ice cool during my shrieking. I had to give her credit for that. It was probably a character trait that helped her become the preeminent rush consultant in North America: staying chill while frantic, hormonal sorority women screamed at her. Finally, she spoke, calmly and scarily. "You're absolutely right."

"You really need to stop agreeing with me!" I half yelled.

"I do have an ulterior motive." Sheila's eyes shimmered. "Normally, I'd let your chapter hang, ensure a fantastic pledge class for my client, and move on. But I want justice for Shannon. You were right at Panhellenic. If Callahan Campbell isn't exonerated, the police are letting the real killer go free."

Truce or no truce, I didn't ever know if I'd trust Sheila De-Grasse. But that ulterior motive I understood. I dug my spoon into a big chunk of cookie dough and took a bite. Then I stood. "I'm taking my own damn car."

"Are you going to change out of . . ." Sheila waved a hand at my uber-casual attire. "That?"

I lifted my chin defiantly. "No." Getting dressed up for events hadn't helped anyone so far. Maybe, after all these years, underdressing was the key to success after all.

Chapter Thirty-five

BEFORE WE LEFT, I called Ty to give him a heads-up, and once he heard the bare details, he asked to speak to Sheila. After a quick conversation, she hung up the phone.

"He said he'd meet us at the house," she said shortly, turning on a pointed red toe toward the other end of Greek Row.

I waved arms at the front of the Delta Beta house. "Hello? We're here."

Sheila lifted an eyebrow. "Not your house. Mine."

Oh, crap. This was getting worse and worse. It was bad enough when I thought Sheila might be tricking me into turning myself in at the station. But if she expected me to enter the Mu Mu Mu house without a weapon (for self-defense, of course), she had better check herself.

Ty said that he'd meet us there, and he wasn't kidding. By the time I'd followed a good ten steps behind Sheila down the block, Ty was standing outside the Moo house.

"Are you living here?" I grumbled at him.

"I had some business in the area." His face was perfectly blank, and I couldn't detect any of the low-key snarkiness that he usually flung my way. Maybe since Sheila was here, he thought he'd be more professional.

He started to follow Sheila inside, then did a double take, his sharp gaze taking all of me in, the fleece, the slippers, the flannel. Then he reached out and smudged something on my chest with his thumb and looked at it more closely. "Ice cream?"

My face burned. "So?"

"Just glad to see you eating something, Blythe."

Sheila sighed heavily. "I hate to interrupt the flirting, but pref night starts in two hours."

Ty's attention snapped to her. "Yes, I know. Let's get this done and see what you have." Since when did Ty pay attention to the rush schedules, much less act like they were a priority? The two walked through the front door of the Moo house with purpose, and I lagged behind, not used to entering the Moo house—invited, anyway.

There was something fishy going on. A Tri Mu wanted to help a Deb, the antisorority police officer was quick-stepping because of a rush deadline, and I had failed to notice the dribbled melted ice cream down my jacket. My whole world had gone topsy-turvy.

I had a vague recollection of the layout of the Tri Mu house from studying the schematics back in my undergrad days, so it wasn't unfamiliar as we followed Sheila up a back stair and into a TV room that had clearly been taken over by their version of a Rush Dungeon. The same piles of paperwork, photos, receipts, random pieces of bedazzled costumes graced their workroom as they did ours. Their computer system was similar to ours, as well. Several monitors and laptops and cords and . . .

"OH. MY. GOD."

I froze at the tone in Ty's voice. "Is that . . ."

Sheila nodded slowly, with the same vein of caution that I had when Ty had discovered our high-tech surveillance—scratch that—security system.

"Does this have something to do with the remote-control plane?" I pointed at the toy on the desk, a black-plastic spider with propellers on top.

"That is a Sonssuto Uber Vision," Ty said, as if I should understand it now.

"Top-of-the-line," Sheila added. Those words I understood better, but I still wasn't sure. When Sheila stepped forward and hit a button on the flat screen, and aerial photography popped up, I got it.

"You used drones?" I screeched. "You spied on sorority row from the sky? What's next? Do you have a satellite intercepting our calls?"

Sheila crossed her arms and rolled her eyes and got all huffy. "Like you have any room to talk, Margot. Don't think that we don't know about the bug you put in Sarah McLane's car."

Ty tilted his head at me, his eyes wide. I threw my hands up. "That wasn't us! Why would we bug her car!?"

"Because it's where she goes to talk so no one listens in at the house."

"Lord help you all," Ty said in a mysteriously exhausted voice. "Do you have anything useful here?" The question was for Sheila and, after a moment to collect herself, she nodded and pulled up footage of the night that Callie broke curfew and ran around sorority row mixing up everyone's Greek letters. Apparently, the Tri Mu drone flew at four hundred feet and had an excellent camera range. According to the time stamps, Callie had just reentered the

RUSHING TO DIE 243

Deb house about half an hour before Daria Cantrell arrived on sorority row.

Sheila had done something extraordinary. By bringing this evidence to the police, Callie Campbell had been exonerated. I couldn't wait to go to the jail and be there when the doors burst open, and she was free as a bird. I was about to suggest that next course of action when Ty leaned over the desk, drumming his fingers on the white-painted wood and peering in to the monitor. "Where does Daria come in?"

There was a moment of silence before Sheila admitted, "We don't have the murder on film."

Ty's head dropped low, a lock of blond hair falling in his face. I wanted to pat that tense spot between his shoulder blades where his shirt stretched tight and taut.

Sheila moved the mouse, and a scene came up. "This is all we have." I recognized the street in front of the Tri Mu house, and it got bigger and bigger, and it looked like the drone was coming down into the bushes.

"I'm sorry," Sheila whispered. She went on to explain that the drone was programmed to come in each night for charging, and it had right before the hour that the ME said Daria Cantrell had been attacked in the Delta Beta backyard.

Ty shook his head slowly. "Two high-tech surveillance systems of this block and not a damn picture of anything that will help me catch a murderer."

Sheila shot me a look, and I tried to look ignorant of the other security system.

Then she refocused on Ty, with renewed purpose. "We actually have something else. It's about Shannon's murder." At Ty's sharp glance, she resumed the explanation in a hurry. "I just went back and looked for it today, after the Panhellenic meeting. You see, Shannon was my dear friend. A sister. At first I thought that it had to be a Deb and I was angry and I assumed that a Deb had to be involved, given the location and, well . . ." She trailed off as she glanced at me, a heavily charged expression on her face. "Their reputation."

That brought out a thick sigh from me. "Really?"

Sheila continued, "For the longest time, I couldn't understand why you weren't arresting someone from there and battling with my own demons about Shannon." Sheila pressed her lips together and gave her head a little shake. "And when I heard about the Delta Beta chapter's mass alibi, I came up here to prove them wrong." She pulled up a file on the laptop. "And this is what I found."

The black-and-white footage was remarkably clear for being filmed four hundred feet in the air. I wondered what those drones could catch people doing. Illicit things. Nose-picking things. Could it see my PIN number when I went to the ATM? How could this technology be in the hands of untrustworthy American citizens like Sheila DeGrasse?

There it was, the Delta Beta house. And then came the entire chapter, spilling out of the house in our matching black sweatshirts that day. I remembered it so well. We had still been organized and motivated and hopeful that all our hard work was going to result in a kick-butt pledge class that should have been coming this time tomorrow. The thought that we'd never have that was like a punch to my gut.

Then everyone loaded up in cars and drove off to the day spa, where we'd all had pedicures done, first the seniors, then juniors and sophomores.

The drone drifted toward the Epsilon Chi house to the south, and Sheila put her finger to the screen. "There's Shannon." She whispered it, but I could still hear the tightness in her throat.

We saw Shannon get out of a car and head toward the Deb house. "Was she going in?" I asked. Sheila nodded. "Did she have the security code?"

A guilty look crossed Sheila's face when she glanced at the drone on the table. Guess that answered my question about the capabilities of the device to record PIN numbers.

On the flat screen, Shannon turned toward the woods behind the house, as if she had heard her name called.

Then, barely visible in the bottom right-hand corner, a pixelated figure approached Shannon from behind, lifted a hand, and struck her in the back of her skull.

I gasped, involuntarily, even knowing what was about to happen. Sheila had turned away, her arms wrapped around her middle.

Even Ty took a deep, steadying breath before saying, "I'm going to need all of this."

Sheila nodded, and Ty got out his phone to call someone to pick up evidence. I sank down in a chair, my brain on overdrive as it processed all that it had just seen. Once again, I had a sickening feeling that my subconscious knew something, had picked up on a key clue, but before I could stitch the strands together, Ty was lifting my elbow.

"We have an appointment," he said in a tone that brooked no argument from me. But then he said, "Pref night starts in an hour and a half," and that made me wonder all over again.

Chapter Thirty-six

THIS TIME I didn't even notice that Ty drove me back to the police station. My brain was replaying the drone footage over and over again. There had to be a link there, but the harder I tried, the more I had nothing. Which was probably the right result. After all, the drone had nothing on Daria Cantrell's murder, just a dive into the bushes.

When we walked through the front door of the police station, we were immediately met with a waiting room full of very angry sorority women with hand-painted signs saying FREE CAMPBELL! and CALLIE FTW! and PLEDGE DELTA BETA! Clearly, the rush supplies had been repurposed for this impromptu sit-in; I had never loved my girls more, for their dedication to social justice and their commitment to recycling.

Ty barely gave me a chance to lift my fist in solidarity and shout "power to the people" when he hurried me through the waiting area and down the hall toward the sound of Callie's voice shouting. I pulled away from his hand to go toward the holding cell and got a scowl in return. "We don't have time, Blythe."

I held up a finger. "One sec, I need to let her know that Sheila has evidence that's going to set her free."

"One minute," he growled, and while I was thankful, I also wondered what his big hurry was.

Callie had her hands around bars, shaking them and yelling at the top of her lungs. Normally, this was not appropriate behavior for a young woman who should be exhibiting the highest qualities of Delta Beta womanhood. But considering she was in the clink, I was giving her a pass. "LET ME OUT!" she practically howled. "I RECANT MY CONFESSION!"

She trailed off when she saw me. "Margot!" she cried out in relief. "Finally! Did you hear?" she demanded of Ty, tight on my heels. "I'm recanting my confession." Callie looked back at me. "That bitch Louella Jackson totally broke her promise to me! Aubrey told me what happened. Louella voted us out of rush, so why should I do anything to help her? Screw her."

Again, given the circumstances, I was very much supportive of Callie's word choice, despite my usual feelings to the contrary. I crossed my arms and gave Ty a "when you gonna let my sister out of jail" look. He held up both hands in surrender.

"Malouf is coming down to process her paperwork after he gets the evidence from the Tri Mu house."

Callie immediately pounced on that. "Evidence? The Moos killed someone? I knew it!"

"No, the Moos have evidence that clears you," Ty said; then he corrected himself with a quick shake of his head. "I mean the Tri Mus."

I allowed myself a small, satisfied smile at his slip. Finally, he was getting the idea.

"Now we have to go." Once again, he grabbed my elbow and pulled, just hard enough for me to know that he meant business.

"Margot? Where are you going?" Callie shouted at my back, as I was whisked away. "Where are you taking her?" I supposed that was directed at Ty, and I looked up to see if he'd respond in some way. It was a little thrilling, to tell you the truth. After being swept away for an impromptu brunch at Joey's Diner, I could get used to Ty Hatfield's being all manly and taking charge and special-ordering me coffee milk shakes.

If that wasn't a sign that I was getting my groove back, then the little zing I was getting from Ty's capable hand on my arm definitely was.

He led me to a back part of the station I'd never been to before and paused ever so slightly before slapping his palm against a door clearly marked "men's locker."

"Everyone decent?" he called out.

I flinched, pretty sure I didn't want to walk in and surprise some half-dressed Sutton cops. Not all of them were as young and hot as Ty Hatfield.

Then a body came out from behind a locker, and I jumped and bit back a scream until I saw who it was.

"CASEY!" I squealed, leaping into my best friend's arms for a ferocious hug. I hadn't realized until I saw his Rock Hudson smile and Cary Grant twinkle how much I had missed him this week, dealing with all the usual rush drama with a couple of murder investigations besides. When he squeezed back, I knew he felt the same.

And in case you're wondering if Casey was going to kiss me, since I am obviously the light of his life and he's super good-looking and dedicated to Delta Beta to boot, the answer is, unfortunately, no. Casey likes to kiss the nonfemale half of the population. Lucky for them.

He let me go, then grimaced as he caught sight of my togs. "Oh, honey..." he moaned in dismay. "What have they done to you?"

Self-consciously, I pulled down my fleece and tried looking out of the bottom of my eye at any more possible streaks of dried cookie dough ice cream that might have appeared. "I had a moment of weakness," I said. "Did you hear? They threw us out of rush!"

The Cary Grant twinkle in his eyes disappeared, replaced by a mean Richard Belzer frown from *Law & Order*. "They're not going to get away with this," he swore.

I loved that spirit, but I didn't see what we could do about it, since pref night was in . . . Out of the corner of my eye I saw Ty check his watch. Then Casey checked his. "Okay, boys." I took a step back so I could better assess their lies. "What's going on? Why is Casey here? In a locker room?"

The two exchanged a mysterious look, and my stomach dropped strangely. There hadn't been anything, nothing really, between me and Ty. So why were my palms getting sweaty at the thought of secret assignations between him and Casey in the Sutton PD shower room? It wasn't my flannel pants, was it?

"Basically, Lieutenant Hatfield thinks I'm the shit," Casey said. That didn't help the sweaty, gurgly feelings.

Ty spoke immediately after that. "I called Casey in to help with an undercover operation."

Casey clapped his hands and bounced, mouthing the words "the shit" and I had a pretty good idea that "undercover operation" wasn't a euphemism for role-playing good cop/bad cop in the Sutton PD shower room.

"Undercover operation . . ." I echoed, looking Casey up and down. He was as nattily dressed as usual, tonight in a black-and-white hound's-tooth coat, a yellow-and-black polka-dot tie with his mama's Delta Beta pin serving as a tie tack.

He was dressed in our sorority's official colors, so I could only come to one conclusion. "You're going to pref night?"

Casey reached into his inner breast pocket and pulled out a pair of what I could only presume were the finest Witness spyglasses that Casey's Delta Beta credit card could buy. When he settled them on his face, the effect was astonishing. The man could really pull off any accessory. It wasn't fair.

Ty gestured toward Casey. "Meet Mr. Peter Jones."

Casey hissed at Ty. "I thought we agreed. I'm Pedro San Diego."

"What kind of a name is that?" I crinkled my nose at Casey, who eyes lit with excitement.

"I got hooked on a telenovela in Texas. You're going to love it. Think *Law & Order* with backstabbing mothers-in-law and really hot Latin guys."

I wasn't so sure about the backstabbing part, but Casey was kind of an expert when it came to hot Latin guys.

"Okay," I rubbed my hands together. "I got it. How about . . . Lorenzo San Diego."

"For Christ's sake!" That was Ty.

"Oooh . . ." That was Casey. "I like it."

"Does it matter what fake name he has?"

Casey and I both swung around on Ty, our mouths dropping open in disbelief. I didn't even know what they had taught him in police academy, but a fake name was everything in undercover operations.

"Fine," Ty said through gritted teeth. "Lorenzo."

"What name am I going to use?" I asked, my mind burning with possibilities. Perhaps I could assume the identity of Carmen

San Diego, Lorenzo's mysterious and sexy globe-trotting twin sister.

Ty quirked an eyebrow at me, and Casey pressed a fist against his mouth the way he did when he had something really bad to tell me about a celebrity crush.

"What?"

"Oh, honey . . ."

Ty interrupted Casey. "You're not in on this one."

"That's not fair!" I exclaimed. "I'm just as good as he is!"

"It's hard for anyone to be as good as I am," Casey said reassuringly, and really, I couldn't argue with him on that. But I still didn't want to be left out of whatever it was they were planning.

"I can do this," I promised. "I won't let you down," I added when Ty didn't immediately agree.

He shook his head. "You can't pull this one off. You're too old."

Casey gasped in horror at that one, and I was about to react similarly when I remembered all the suspicious looks I had received at the ice-cream social. It was definitely time to find a decent dermatologist in Sutton.

"And everyone would recognize you," Ty went on quickly.

Wait. People would recognize me? I peered at him and Casey. "What are you two planning, anyway?"

Chapter Thirty-seven

ONE OF THE reasons I loved Casey Kenner like a sister was his creativity. No matter the crisis, he always had a brilliant plan. So I was astonished to find out that this sting operation was the brain baby of one Lieutenant Ty Hatfield.

"Are you sure?" I queried Casey for the tenth time, watching carefully for one of his tells. When he lied, he smiled charmingly, as if those deep, big-screen-ready dimples would distract anyone from sniffing out the truth.

But he stayed absolutely serious when he answered me for the tenth time. "Yes, Margot. Obviously, I wouldn't have chosen to do this."

I palmed the still-warm laminated press badge that Ty had fabricated for one Lorenzo San Diego, reporter for UnoVision. Fundamentally, I objected to any intrusion into the sacred rites of pref night, but I had to agree with Ty that this was the best way to get Casey into the houses. Since the college already had told all the chapters to cooperate with Nick Holden, they were already primed to answer questions from an even handsomer if unknown Lorenzo San Diego.

"You really think this is going to work?"

"Sure it will."

My head jerked up at his nonchalance. Now that was suspicious. I knew Casey Kenner better than I knew anyone. He was rarely this blasé about supersecret, undercover sting operations. When I met his eyes, I saw a shadow that belied his breezy tone. "What? Why are you worried?"

Casey frowned as deeply as his Botox would let him. "It's about the chapter. It's all I can think about. Even if we catch the killer, will it be enough to salvage the Debs' good name?"

The thought sent me back to the Fireball and Chocolate Chip Cookie Dough zone. Casey's fears weren't unwarranted. Rush had been a disaster: The Delta Beta name had been dragged through the mud, then stomped on, then another pile of mud unloaded on top of it. A chapter couldn't bounce back from a week like this easily.

I could see it all play out in my head. The next two semesters, Delta Beta would be operating at a deficit; incoming freshmen would hear all about "the murder house;" and the numbers of young women willing to attach themselves to a chapter of assumed thugs and criminals would dwindle down to nothing. Headquarters would close the house down, no longer willing to associate or fund the few losers that were left. And nearly one hundred years of Delta Beta sisterhood at Sutton would be erased.

I didn't know what I could do to stop the inevitable slide, but I did know that two women had to be avenged. And my best friend Casey had to play a vital role.

"It will be okay," I assured him, pulling up every ounce of bounce from my mostly depleted reserves. "You're the best sorority public-relations guru in the galaxy. If anyone can rescue Delta Beta, it's you."

Casey got a little *verklempt* at that. "I won't let you down."

I gave him a hug, and Ty stepped in. "We're on," he said, his words tight and crisp as the khakis he wore. "Your first party is in thirty."

"Where?" I asked.

"Mu Mu Mu."

I groaned loudly.

"Is there a problem, ladies?" Ty deadpanned.

I ignored that and squeezed Casey's hand. "You can do this."

Casey tossed his hair off his forehead. "Damn right I can."

Ty DIDN'T WANT me undercover, and he didn't want me in the police van, either. Things were said that could never be taken back, like "Damn it Blythe," and "Do you ever listen to anyone with an ounce of sense?" But I pointed out all of the convincing arguments why I should be allowed to watch Casey's live feed, like, "What are you going to do, arrest me?" And eventually, we came to the mutual conclusion that I was staying.

This was my best friend we were discussing, after all. The man who was going into the lion's den to draw out a killer. Well, we hoped that's what Casey would do. It turned out that Ty shared the same suspicions as me; that whoever had murdered Shannon Bender and Daria Cantrell was deeply invested in rush, either from the inside or out. Sorority recruitment was the only thing that linked the two murders besides the similar blows to the back of the head.

Ty's theory was that, if Senor Lorenzo San Diego appeared during the final round of rush parties, the killer was sure to make a move and, hopefully, a mistake. We had the Delta Beta cameras and the Tri Mu drone on high alert, and police officers were hiding in cars all around sorority row, keeping a close eye on the affairs. Per Ty's request, Sheila allowed Zoe to link the Tri Mu drone to the Deb surveillance system; Zoe was now monitoring the whole block with a police officer watching over her shoulder.

I used all my mental energy to focus on Casey's safety and any clues that he could dig up regarding the murders. As long as I spent one hundred percent of my brain waves on solving a crime, I wasn't thinking about the Deb chapter's not getting ready for its preference ceremony lit by the glow of a hundred candles. All that fire-safety training gone to waste.

The Sutton Police Department surveillance van sat at the end of the street closest to the Delta Beta house. It was emptier on that end of the street since no beautiful rushees were following the side-walk to our front porch, gracefully lit by probably ten thousand twinkle lights twirling around the porch columns. The van was quite small on the inside, not as roomy as *Law & Order* episodes would have you believe. Ty and I sat shoulder to shoulder, hip to hip on low stools facing the monitors that showed the view from Casey's Witness glasses, listening for sounds from his small mic.

We had eyes and ears everywhere, but the problem, as I saw it was we didn't know what we were looking for. According to Ty's theory, our killer was probably between the ages of 18 and 108, was either a man or a woman, had visited sorority row a few times, and had something sharp that s/he killed potential rivals with. You know, the typical profile.

Ty and I both looked down at our watches. Showtime.

Silently, we counted down to the start of the first party. Seeing it through Casey's eyes was pretty wild. I hadn't been in line to enter a rush party since I was an eighteen-year-old brunette virgin. It was clear from the visuals that Casey was getting a lot of attention, but he was handling it with the confidence and charm of Ryan Seacrest.

The doors opened to the Tri Mu house, and their welcoming song was soft and gentle, something about friends and stars and blah-blah. Nothing could be as moving as the song that the Debs had planned to greet rushees with, about eternal friends like stars.

Casey followed the line into the Tri Mu house and instinctively, I clutched Ty's arm, as if I were the one headed into the lion's den. The Witness glasses were extraordinarily clear, and we saw everything as Casey purposely turned his head constantly, giving us a 180-degree view around the Tri Mu house. "Too bad he can't turn around," I murmured under my breath, then, because Casey and I have an undeniable psychic connection, Casey spun around slowly.

"He can hear you through my mic," Ty whispered.

Oh.

"Oh?" Casey was saying to the woman talking to him. "I thought you said you liked my outfit. I was just showing you that my back looked even better than my front."

I snickered. Even undercover, Casey was a hoot.

The girl assigned to answer Lorenzo San Diego's questions was at a loss, and I felt sorry for her. Clearly, her chapter advisor had not prepared her well for public-relations duties. Casey took over the conversation like the PR pro he was.

"Tell me all about the pref-night ceremony," he prompted her. "What will the typical rushee be experiencing tonight?" She looked relieved to be able to talk about something other than the giant, well-dressed, masculine elephant in the room.

"We've all worked so hard on it, to show girls the true meaning of sisterhood . . . It's pretty special . . ." The girl blushed as she looked down at Lorenzo's reporter notepad that Casey had insisted on, for "authenticity."

"I like your decorations," Casey said. "Are any of them particularly sharp? Maybe four or five inches long?"

"Um . . . no?"

"Are any of them electrical? Poisonous? Could someone strangle an enemy with these twinkle light strands . . . ?" Sweet Casey was trying to get intel for the police on possible murder weapons even when he could be violently attacked by a frustrated Moo any second. Judging by the expression on the woman's face, Lorenzo San Diego's questions were the type of hard-hitting journalism that would earn him an Emmy if he were a real journalist. I was so proud of Casey and his professional fake-reporting skills that were surely going to quickly ferret out the clue that would help us solve the case. Which was also a problem.

"This isn't good," I whispered to Ty. "I have a bad feeling about this."

Sending Casey into the Tri Mu house was pretty much the same thing as sending up a giant bat signal into the sky. "Here's the guy that's going to catch you. Better attack him first."

"This was stupid." Fear lit up my chest, making me feel all hot and squirmy. "What are you looking for, anyway?"

Maybe Casey heard that because he started to turn his head slowly again, giving us a clear rotation of the view while his rushee was leading him back toward the Moo chapter room for the preference-night ceremony. Nothing looked out of the ordinary, but it didn't quell my nerves, jangling through my system, fast and electric.

Then the Witness glasses jerked and fell. And everything went black.

"SHIT!" Ty punched the side of the van and lifted the small mic to this mouth. "Casey? Your glasses. Pick up your glasses. We're not getting a feed here. Are they broken?"

"My glasses!" Casey's voice was still clear as a bell, thank goodness, but the screen was still pitch-black.

"Oh no! Are they broken?"

My hand shot out and squeezed Ty's arm. I recognized that voice. It couldn't be . . .

"Let's get you some tape or something," the woman's voice suggested, smooth and silky.

"I think they're okay," Casey said. A pause. "There. Can you see me?"

The question was for us, but the person he was talking to might not know that. "Of course I can. But they're still dangling on the side." A pause. "Is that a wire hanging out?"

Abort! Abort! "She knows!" I whispered.

Casey laughed. "I know. They're the newest in sun-deflecting technology."

God, he was good. But he wasn't going to be good enough for Sheila DeGrasse.

Ty flicked a switch on the radio box and pried my clenched fingers off his arm. "Margot? Who is it?"

What if I was wrong? I was going off a voice for heaven's sake. "It's Sheila DeGrasse! The Tri Mu rush consultant!"

"So?"

"So she knows about the Witness glasses since she was the one who put them on Shannon Bender's face!"

Ty's mouth turned down slightly. "Okay, but has she done anything to make Casey?"

No. She was being cordial and helpful, and we both knew it. Even so, when Ty switched the mic back on, I was still nervous as a pledge at her first fraternity social. Threats were everywhere, disguised as helpful people offering cold drinks in red cups.

"You're still black," Ty said to Casey. "But if you're good to go, so are we."

I wasn't! I wanted to shout, but I kept quiet. I should have known better.

"This is very informative," Casey said. I could only assume that meant he wanted to keep going. My head fell into my hands. I had nothing to look at, anyway, just the terrifying pictures running through my imagination.

"You're a reporter . . ." Sheila purred at Casey. I wish I could tell her she was so barking up the wrong gay tree. "How interesting. Do you know Nick Holden?"

Then we heard Nick's morning-show voice say hello.

"Do they let just anyone into the Moo preference ceremony?" I asked rhetorically.

Ty shushed me and nudged up the volume, as sound was all we had to go on now. "Yes, Nico. Remember me? Lorenzo San Diego. We covered the presidential election together."

Wow. Casey even bullshitted big. It was so inspirational.

"Lorenzo, yes, what are you doing here in Sutton?"

"Sorority murders are the biggest story of the year."

"My story, last I checked."

"Oh, Nico, that's what you said about the election. You can't call dibs on these things, you know."

Before we could hear Nick's response, we heard Sheila whispering something about the preference ceremony starting.

The sounds of music grew louder, and I could only assume that they were entering the Moo chapter room, where the preference ceremony would begin. A chorus swelled . . . what was that? Electric guitar? An opera singer? What the hell kind of music did the Moos think inspired a lifetime of friendship?

I felt a sudden movement next to me. Ty's hand had jerked up to the volume on the radio system. "Repeat that?" he asked Casey.

Sure enough, there was a scratchy sound just underneath the swelling rock aria that was assaulting my eardrums. Feedback from their stupid stereo, probably. Cut up in that mess of noise was Casey's voice saying, "Yes, ma'am."

Crackle. Crackle.

"Step out for a moment?"

My head jerked up. That wasn't Sheila's voice. It was someone else.

"Of course," Casey replied.

"No!" I half shouted.

But he couldn't hear me. I stood up the best I could in the cramped van, and Ty's hand clamped around my wrist. "Blythe!"

"I'm going in! We don't have visuals or audio, and you're just going to let him walk off with some murdering Moo?"

Ty's grip didn't let up, but I saw the doubts that flashed through his eyes. We had lost control of the situation if we'd ever had it to begin with, and I couldn't let my best friend be the next sister with his brains poked out.

Suddenly, a light flashed inside the van. The monitor had a picture again, but the Witness glasses clearly weren't transmitting from Casey's face.

"What the fudge!" I exclaimed right before Ty yanked me back onto my stool and shushed me.

"We have visuals," Ty told Casey on the radio. "Where are you?"

Either Casey couldn't hear us, or he couldn't improv an answer fast enough. "I understand, ma'am. But yes, I have permission to be here from the college press office. My badge is right here."

Ma'am?

I stared so hard at the monitor, I'm surprised two laser-beam holes didn't appear in the glass, and I finally realized what I was looking at. The glasses were on a table. It must have been a glass table because I saw shoes below on the carpet. First I recognized Casey's trademark Gucci loafers with the golden bit. Then a set of woman's pumps.

Size seven.

With a red sole.

And a dirty heel.

And it all came together.

I leaned over to Ty's radio, and shouted, "Look out, Casey! Behind you!"

Chapter Thirty-eight

THE LAST THING I heard before I leaped out of the van was a scream. Somewhere along the sidewalk between the van and the front door of the Tri Mu house, Ty Hatfield and five other Sutton cops appeared out of nowhere and beat me to the sorority house, guns drawn and authoritative voices yelling. It would have been the most brilliantly exciting moment of my life if I wasn't torn up with worry about Casey's safety.

The sudden invasion of a platoon of gun-waving, shouting police officers caused a panic in the Tri Mu house, which meant that no one paid much attention to me, following in the wake of the law.

I followed my nose and soon heard Casey's voice. "I said, get down on the ground!" Which was very authoritative of him. Then I heard Ty shouting, "Someone call EMS," which made me panic.

A couple of the cops acted like they didn't want to let me into the scene of the crime, which seemed to be a small study room. After I shouted, "FBI," I shoved and slipped under elbows and saw

Casey, sitting in a chair and clutching the back of his head with a bloody pocket square.

I went straight to him, ignoring the "hey you!" and "Blythe!" that came from the officers around me. It was only after I looked in his eyes and assured myself that he was okay that I faced the culprits.

Ty's eyes met mine, filled with more than his usual natural skepticism, silently asking me, "are you sure?" I nodded slowly, knowing that I had a lot to explain and guiltily glad that Casey would be able to back up my theory: that Louella Jackson and Alexandria Von Douton were coconspirators in the deaths of Shannon Bender and Daria Cantrell.

With a resigned sigh, Ty reached into his jacket pocket and slapped some cuffs on Louella, while Officer Malouf handcuffed Von Douton. "I'll meet you at the station," I called out to him, as they marched the women out the door, past the gaping mouths of a houseful of rushees, Tri Mus, and Nick Holden's camera.

It was over an hour later before I walked through the front doors of the police station. While the other officers had been questioning women at the pref party, I had stayed by Casey's side as the EMT guys checked him out. He had a major scrape down the back of his skull, not deep enough to require stitches.

While I waited for Casey, I got a call from Maya, the Panhellenic Advisor. She was convening a chapter-advisor meeting right there on the Epsilon Chi front steps. I gave her ten minutes, but it didn't take that long for her to declare yet another change in Sutton rush procedures. With the craziness going on at the Tri Mu house, nobody argued. When Casey and I pulled out of the street, three Sutton College buses had pulled up at the end of the block to transport all the rushees back to campus for counseling and, hopefully, a hug or two. They didn't sign up for this insanity in their rush registration.

Outside the Sutton police station's interrogation room, Ty scratched his chin and frowned at me. "How did you know?"

"It was the shoes. I always notice the shoes."

"Really?" Ty asked. "That's not an urban myth?"

I shrugged my shoulders. "Not for me. Louella and Alexandria have been wearing amazing footwear all week. That's what killed the girls, right?"

Ty nodded. "A four-inch-long stiletto from Alexandria Von Douton's closet. Reinforced steel with a sharpened projectile of some sort. Kind of like a nail gun."

Ouch. Sounded like Louella's husband had developed some specialized technology for savage old ladies.

"Reinforced steel would sink down into dirt easier, wouldn't it?"

He looked unsure for just a moment, then he realized where I was going. "The mud on the shoes."

"Have you questioned them yet?"

"No. I was waiting for you to tell me what you knew."

I was beyond flattered.

"And I wanted to make them sweat a little."

The thought of those two old ladies wringing their hands in anticipation of being questioned about committing murder didn't make me feel good, but something in my gut told me that all of the women of Panhellenic would be a lot safer with these two locked up.

I decided to start with the beginning. "Shannon Bender was a stranger in Sutton. No one even knew she was here, and those that did wanted her to complete her spy mission. If someone wanted her dead, it was because of who they thought she was—someone working for Nick Holden, whom she had met with earlier that week."

"And Daria?"

"Also went to Nick Holden's round table. That's the only connection between the two women." But it was enough, unfortunately.

"In nearly all of the footage that we and the Moos have recorded, there's a silver Mercedes parked just off camera. That's Alexandria Von Douton's car. Ginnifer's been feeding her information all week."

Ty slid his ever-ready pad of paper and pen out of his coat pocket. "Ginnifer? She's the Mini Margot, right?"

"Yes." I held up a hand before he could ask his next question. "Von Douton was blackmailing her for rush violations at another school—nothing superillegal."

Ty's eyebrow flick showed he didn't quite believe that, but he let me move on.

"When we watched Sheila's footage of Shannon's murder, there was something that bothered me. It looked like Shannon was responding to someone in the woods, but then she was killed from behind." I explained that we had thought someone was watching us from those woods and suggested Ty get someone down there to check for high-heeled footprints in the dirt. "I didn't realize what it meant until I saw the shoes with dirty heels behind Casey. There had to be two murderers. They weren't strong enough to take one person down, so they had to work together to take them down by surprise."

Ty's hands dropped to his side, his pen and paper momentarily forgotten. "You really figured all this out while we were watching Casey's feed?"

"I didn't figure it all out. Just the important parts." Just enough to keep Casey alive.

"What did you miss?" Ty asked me, watching me carefully.

"Why." My voice broke. "Why us, why rush, why Shannon, why Daria. Why in the hell would a Deb help a Tri Moo with anything, much less murder?"

Ty thought about it for a second, then nodded. "Then let's ask."

After a quick debate, we agreed on starting with Louella. And because Louella and I were technically sisters, Ty allowed me to talk to her.

The room was small and airless, with nothing but two metal chairs, a plain table, and the requisite two-way mirror. Louella looked extremely peeved when I came in. "What is going on out there? I need my medicine. I told the police I need my medicine."

I walked into the room with every intention of playing the role that Ty and I had agreed on. I was going to be the sympathetic sorority sister, ready to engage all the Delta Beta resources to protect and defend one of our own. But this bitch had always rubbed me the wrong way.

"Louella, you were caught digging your heel into the back of a man's skull," I snapped. "I'm not sure what kind of medicine helps with that."

There was no contrition in her eyes. "It was self-defense. He attacked me. I think he was going to rape me."

"With his back to you? I'm pretty sure you remember that it doesn't work like that."

She flinched. "He was going to attack Alexandria. Then me. He was a crazed sex fiend. Why else would he come to the sorority house looking for a story? And his name was Lorenzo," she added, as if that was obviously the name of a violent rapist.

I'd let her defense attorney explain all the evidence we had showing that "Lorenzo" was not only perfectly pleasant but had been invited back to a private room by two senior citizens.

Instead, I sank into the chair across from her and sighed sadly. "Oh, Louella. I don't know how to say this, but . . ." My voice trailed off, and it got her attention. "I think the Tri Moos are out to get the Debs."

"What do you mean?" she asked sharply.

"I mean, they're setting all of this up. Alexandria just told Lieutenant Hatfield that you plotted the murders of Shannon Bender and Daria Cantrell because you hated the Moos so much."

Louella's head jerked like she'd been slapped. "She wouldn't!"

"She's a Moo. They'd do anything to bring us down."

I must have been a really good actress, or Louella needed new glasses. Her face dropped, then her hands started to shake, as reality started smacking her in the face. The doubt, then fear showed in every expression, and I almost felt sorry for her.

Almost.

"Alexandria and I have been best friends for nearly forty years," she said in a shaky voice. "She wouldn't betray me."

"When Lieutenant Hatfield comes in, tell him it was her idea." How I managed to say that with a straight face, I had no idea. After all, Casey was going to testify that it was Louella who spiked him with a Manolo Blahnik.

Her eyes clenched closed. "No. I won't betray her. That's the Delta Beta way."

At that, I couldn't help but roll my eyes. This lady had pledged way too long ago. "What happened, Louella," I said as gently as I could. "If you're protecting her, you must have had a good reason."

Louella sat up straighter and lifted her chin. "Forty years, the council has run Sutton rush. The five of us determined long ago that we would ensure that the Sutton Panhellenic system would survive no matter what."

So far that didn't sound crazy. I loved the idea of Panhellenic alumnae working together to provide a steady guiding hand to the system we all cherished.

Louella looked dismayed. "But then you came to town."

Oh please. "What did I do?"

"You came, and the murders started."

"You know I didn't actually murder people?"

"Yes, but they happened. You weren't strong enough to stop them. Then the press came. Then the critics. Now the college is actually debating ending their support for Greek life." Her lips pressed together, as if she was trying to stop herself from crying. "All these years, we were in control, and now the college wanted us to be transparent." Yes, she used finger quotes. 'Talk to the press,' they said. But the press were the ones trying to close us down! We had to stop them."

"By murdering people?"

"We had to ensure that Nick Holden did not get further information to harm our way of life."

I decided to repeat myself. "BY MURDERING PEOPLE?"

"We didn't mean to," Louella moaned, pulling her wool coat around her. "I had no idea I still had so much upper-body strength."

"What you had was the equivalent of a nail gun in your shoe."

Louella's eyes teared up. "My husband gave those to me and Alexandria before our trip to Paris five years ago. He didn't want us to get raped by Gypsies while we were touring the Eiffel Tower."

This woman had quite an imagination. I could psychically feel Ty's eyes rolling behind the two-way mirror, so I tried to get her back on track.

"So you were just going to knock Shannon Bender down? And then what?"

"She was clearly working for him. A stranger in that ridiculous Delta Beta shirt could only be Nick Holden's spy. We just wanted to get her attention and talk some sense into her, make her realize what she was doing."

"So why Daria?"

"She was the second one?" Louella clarified. It was all I could do not to stand up and play bad cop on her. She didn't even know Daria's name.

I managed to control myself and nodded; Louella managed a look of pained regret. "She overheard Alexandria and me in the Tri Mu yard discussing the first incident. She said she had Holden's card and was going to call him, tell him everything. Can you imagine what would have happened then?"

"Yeah, Nick Holden was going to have information that you committed murder." Louella didn't appreciate my sarcasm.

"It was an unfortunate consequence."

"Why attack Lorenzo?"

"It was our sacred responsibility to protect the rush process." She looked despairingly at me. "And here was yet another reporter—a Mexican one—who had come to our home—on pref night!—with Nick Holden and expected us to just lie down and let them destroy everything that we'd worked for, for forty years. It wasn't right, what they were trying to do."

I pushed back from the table, sick to my stomach, my skull

pounding like someone had been tapping a steel-toed work boot against my forehead. "You're right, Louella. You need some medicine." She was unhinged.

Her face was unreadable as I glanced at her one last time before I left the room. Maybe she really thought herself some sort of warrior-protector of Sutton Panhellenic. But a couple hundred young women who only wanted friends and a good time in college didn't need anyone to take them quite so seriously.

I walked out, saw Ty, and threw up my hands. "I quit," I said. "She's all yours."

Louella Jackson was no sister of mine.

Chapter Thirty-nine

ALL I WANTED to do was take Casey back to my apartment, tuck a blanket around us, and watch *Friends* on Netflix for three or four days. But duty called. And by duty, I mean the Panhellenic advisor.

When I showed up at the Commons ballroom, I had no idea what to expect. Maya Rodman met me at the door and filled me in, with a new, no-nonsense attitude. "I'm exerting my authority under Article G, section two of the Panhellenic manual," she said in a voice that dared me to argue. After the most draining twenty-four hours of my life, I wasn't up to nitpicking.

"Okay," I said simply.

"This is how it's going to be, and if you don't like it, you can quit."

Little did she know that was exactly what I was going to do. I shuffled off into a corner and joined the other chapter advisors in submitting to Maya's usurpation of the entire Sutton Panhellenic system. In a few minutes, she took the stage and addressed the assembled crowd, a mixed group of sorority women and rushees.

She apologized for the way the week had gone. Then she explained how rush was going to finish up tonight.

For the next two hours, rushees and sorority women circulated among the room, tentatively at first, then more enthusiastically as time went on. Natural conversations flowed, people relaxed, and here and there I even spied a Deb and a Moo chatting, or an Epsilon Chi and a Lambda laughing together. The young women acted like young women do: shy and bold, funny and serious. Finally, Maya took over the microphone again and invited anyone who wanted to join a sorority to the adjoining room, where they would rank their preferences on sheets of paper and go home, safe and secure and, hopefully, future sisters.

It was casual and informal, and when Maya handed me an envelope of those who had chosen us, I felt a strange mix of gratitude and regret.

The preference ceremony that the Debs had practiced over these past few weeks was both life-affirming and awe-inspiring. Imagine all the Disney princesses in glittery dresses singing in a forest, lit by three hundred white candles, about what friendship means to them; now take that image and multiply it by ten. We would have knocked the socks off of any rushee who entered our sacred meeting space.

But there was something amazing about Maya's alternative plan. No pressure, no stress, no frantic whistles or megaphone shouting. The peaceful, chill vibe of two hundred young women getting to know each other might be just what we all needed to begin to heal this crazy collection of sisterhoods.

Back at the house, I gave the envelope to the rush team, we carefully drafted our bid list, and e-mailed it back to Maya. I instructed Zoe to dismantle the security system and asked Aubrey to make sure the whole chapter knew they could sleep in the next morning. I wasn't sure what our bid day would entail, but I knew everyone deserved a good night of sleep.

By the time I finished delegating tasks, I found Casey sprawled out asleep on my bed. I wondered if that was advisable with the bloody head wound but couldn't interrupt his sleep. And then, for the first time in months, I found myself with absolutely nothing to do.

I lasted all of two minutes.

The temperatures had dropped severely that evening, and I zipped up my fleece and held my arms tightly to my chest as I left the Delta Beta front yard and turned to the south. I could see my frosty breath in the dim light of the crescent moon overhead and wondered if Sheila's drone would be able to see it, too.

Walking just to walk, I passed the other sorority houses, curious if they were all up preparing for the next day or if their advisors had said "screw it" too. Judging by all the lights blazing in the Moo and Lambda houses, it seemed I was the only one who had used up her allotment of energy on this rush.

Yet another reason I was no longer fit to be a chapter advisor. The next morning, I planned to call Mabel and offer my formal resignation. No matter what happened with the incoming pledge class, the entire chapter deserved someone who could have navigated the past few days with a little more integrity and a lot more circumspection.

I was about to turn the corner and head west when a car's lights flashed at me. A Sutton police cruiser pulled to the curb, and the one and only Lieutenant Ty Hatfield emerged from the driver's side.

"What are you doing out tonight?" I asked him.

"I could ask the same of you."

I took a deep breath and plunged my hands as far as they could go into my jacket pockets. "Just needed some air."

"No curfew?"

I shook my head. Maybe there technically still was one, but Maya had turned all of the rush rules upside down today. I doubted anyone cared.

Ty stepped closer to me, and it made me feel warmer, just having him in arm's reach. "Thought you should know that the rest of the Panhellenic Rush Council has been arrested."

I gasped in surprise. "Why?"

"Conspiracy." Ty made a face. "Who knows if the DA can make it stick, but once Von Douton and Jackson's statements reached her desk, she couldn't wait to get her hands on the whole crew."

"Wow." I couldn't believe it. The whole Panhellenic was really going topsy-turvy.

"Between you and me, sounds like the DA might have gone through rush at Sutton some years back."

And it sounded like she hadn't had quite the same positive experience that I had. Rush karma.

"You doing okay?" Ty's question startled me.

"Me?"

"You've eaten today, right?"

I opened my mouth to say, "of course," but realized the last thing I'd eaten was a few bites of ice cream.

Ty scowled. "You realize I have a job to do, right? I'm a police officer. I can't be your personal fried-chicken-delivery service."

I got huffy at his out-of-nowhere flash of anger but then checked myself.

The pizza, the fried chicken. The breakfast sandwich. In his

weird, offhand way, Ty Hatfield had been making sure I was surviving on more than lattes and hair-spray fumes this week.

I dropped my chin a little to hide a smile that was sure to annoy
him but couldn't resist patting him on the long, strong upper arm
of his. "Thanks. I'll make sure to get a healthy breakfast."

We stared awkwardly at each other for a long moment. What
did we have to say to each other when we weren't a seriously impressive crime-fighting duo?

"So maybe—"

"I was thinking—"

We talked over each other, then we both stopped, with a little
nervous laugh.

"Maybe we can get coffee sometime," Ty suggested, the warm
light in his eyes taking off the edge of his usual gruffness.

"Or donuts," I replied.

That made him bite back a smile. "Don't get fresh, Blythe," he
said as he backed away toward the squad car, keeping his gaze on
me the whole time.

The twinkle in his eyes is what made me say, "You wish, Hatfield." And with that, a true grin cracked on Lieutenant Hatfield's
legendary stern exterior.

I turned and felt a thousand times lighter as I headed back to
the Deb house. Maybe I was failing at being a chapter advisor, but
it looked like I still excelled at a few essential life skills.

Chapter Forty

BID DAY WAS the best day of rush week. All of the hard work and toil and tribulation we went through, it all came down to that life-changing moment—when twenty new pledges were dropped off in front of your sorority house and ran, screaming and crying, into the arms of the virtual strangers who would instantly become their best friends. It's not as weird as it sounds.

I woke up in a strange position on my couch, with drool pooled on the Delta Beta T-shirt quilt that someone—hopefully Casey—had tucked around me. Casey was nowhere to be seen, and after I brushed my teeth and retied my hair back into a more orderly ponytail, I opened the door of the chapter advisor's apartment into a new world.

The sun was shining. Women were laughing and giggling and running with baskets of sorority gifts and mason jars of flowers and Starbucks cup carriers.

God bless them so hard. Aubrey pulled to a stop outside my door and handed me a Venti cup. "Special delivery!"

I would have kissed her if my mouth hadn't instantly planted itself on the coffee lid.

After the first shot had gone down, I was able to ask her. "What's going on?" She lifted her hands to the grand stairwell, where a giant, hand-painted, bid-day banner was hung, bright with jungle animals. "We're just waiting for the pledge list to finish their cards and name tags. Everything's done!"

Wow. "Really?" I asked in a mix of admiration and guilt. They'd all been working so hard while I had slept until almost noon, not caring about anything sorority-related for a good eight hours.

Aubrey seemed to always know what I was thinking. "Well, we had a lot of help from your assistant. The chapter couldn't have gotten this all together without him."

Casey. I smiled and looked for him in the crowd of women. There he was, giving posing tips for the innumerable pictures that were going to be snapped today. How lucky was I to have a best friend who was not only excellent at organizing events but generous enough to share his techniques for photogenic perfection?

The next two hours flew by in the bustle of giddy activity, and I couldn't help but be lifted and encouraged by the women around me, who couldn't wait to welcome new sisters.

The buses came, the pledges flew out into the Delta Beta open arms, and it was like everything was all right again. Like no one had ever died or been arrested. I knew that this was the true strength of our sisterhood, our resiliency; but somehow I found myself standing back from it all, an observer for once instead of jumping into the bouncing, squealing mass.

I felt a person come up beside me—Sheila DeGrasse. The expression on her face told me that I wasn't the only one in a slightly more somber mood today.

"Happy bid day," I greeted her.

Sheila pressed her lips together in a half smile. I knew she had to be thinking of Shannon Bender, so I put my arms out and dragged her into a tight hug.

When I let go, we both took a step back and stared. Did we just . . . Did that . . .

Sheila took a deep breath, then said, "Thank you."

So I had hugged a Moo. It was weird, maybe, but in the moment it had felt like the right thing to do. "Of course," I sniffed. "That's what Debs do."

The smile that appeared on her face now was tentative, but true, and even the most hard-core Delta Beta could appreciate when the first tenuous bonds of friendship had been extended.

"How's your pledge class?" Sheila asked.

"Amazing," I assured her. "We took the best baby bees on the block."

"Panhellenic frowns on calling new members, 'babies,'"

God, she couldn't help herself. "Are we really listening to anything Panhellenic says anymore?"

Sheila snorted. "Good point."

"Where are you off to next?" What did a rush consultant do between rush seasons?

"I'll be in Florida," she said, and while the words were casual, there was something in her tone that made me look at her more closely.

"What's in Florida?" I asked.

Sheila lifted her shoulders vaguely, and I decided not to push.

After the past week, I should probably let some secrets of rush consultants remain that way.

"What about you? What do you have planned for this semester?"

I paused but decided that I could be honest with Sheila. We'd gone through a lot together this week. "I am resigning my position here at Sutton." The statement sounded completely reasonable to my ear though my gut tightened at the thought. Still, what else could I do? Any advisor who gets her chapter thrown out of rush was honor-bound to fall on her sword.

Sheila stared at me for a moment, then said, "I doubt that. But if you do ever leave, give me a call. I might have something for you." Then she turned and started walking off.

"In Florida?" I shouted at her back.

She turned and gave me a mysterious smile, then returned to the Tri Moo bid-day celebration, where I'm sure they were very happy about their perfectly adequate new pledges. I gave myself fifteen more minutes to enjoy the party; then I had a very difficult phone call to make to the Delta Beta president.

Chapter Forty-one

"ROBERT PLANT?" CASEY asked in a wondrous tone as we slid into a booth at Joey's Diner, right under a vintage eighties poster of the legendary singer himself. He picked up a sticky laminated menu from behind the ketchup bottles, and I stopped him with my hand.

"Trust me," I said after I waved the waitress over and ordered two double cheeseburgers, extracrispy fries, and vanilla-espresso milk shakes.

Casey sighed. "I don't know if I can afford the calories," and rubbed a self-conscious hand over his flat-as-ever abs. Please.

As for me, all my clothes were loose, and skeletal wasn't a good look on me. I could probably make a bajillion dollars marketing the Delta Beta Rush Diet of extra-shot lattes and twenty-four/ seven manic activity, but it wasn't sustainable or healthy. Which is what I was telling Casey when he got a strange look on his face.

"Don't start," I told him. "I have enough stress in my life, trying to figure out what I can possibly do to get the Sutton chapter back where it needs to be."

"Mabel didn't accept your resignation?" Casey guessed.

"Not only that, she gave me a raise," I said mournfully. Mabel had kept me on the phone for over an hour, begging me to stay on as chapter advisor. She praised my leadership, ethics, and personalized sentiments in the birthday cards I sent to everyone at headquarters, but I couldn't understand where she was coming from. I had let everything get out of control over the last week, barely pulling quota out of the mess that was Sutton rush. But Mabel was insistent. Quota was quota. We had our next generation of Delta Betas, everything else was gravy.

For her.

For me? Well, I wasn't so sure I was cut out to be a permanent chapter advisor. The stress, the drama, the constant threat of police intervention. When I expressed my feelings to Mabel, she said she understood; we agreed that I would finish out the spring semester, then talk over the summer about my future in the Delta Beta organization.

Casey looked relieved when I related that last part. Or maybe it was the waitress sliding a small side salad onto the table that made him relax a little. We started chowing down on our dinner, and Casey agreed that vanilla milk shakes with two shots of espresso might be a sign that Jesus loved us. After he finished most of his cheeseburger and sucked up the last of his shake, he wiped his hands with a couple of paper napkins and folded them together. It was a very official gesture.

"Remember that talk we had? Before I went deep undercover? About how worried I was about the chapter's reputation?"

I nodded, since my mouth was full of extracrispy French fries.

"And you said you believed in me and my mad PR skills to bring everyone back around?"

"Yes?"

Casey paused for a second. "You were wrong."

What? He pushed on, past my pretty obvious shocked expression, I'm sure. "I can't do it, Margot. It's been two semesters, back-to-back, of nonstop illegal activity."

"But the girls didn't even do any of it!"

"The phone-sex line, the murders last semester, more murders this semester . . ."

"Mostly committed by alumnae," I protested.

Casey lifted his hands a little. "Delta Betas just the same."

Ugh. How I wished that wasn't true. I'd never wanted to uninitiate a sister until I'd returned to Sutton College.

"So that's it?" I asked him. "You're just giving up? Throwing in the towel? Writing us off as a lost cause?"

"Well . . . no . . ."

I slammed my hand on the Formica tabletop. "What about the women we just pledged? How do you think they'd feel, knowing you didn't have any confidence in them?"

"They don't really know me, but that's not—"

"Leticia and Mary Gerald would not accept this. When they were told they couldn't live together, they didn't accept 'no' as an answer."

"You're right."

"And I'm not going to accept it either!" I glared at him. No one told me "no." It was a personality trait of mine.

Casey bit his lip, pausing as if he was afraid I was going to interrupt him.

"I think—" he started to say, but I finished his sentence for him.

"We need to shift the paradigm."

"The what?"

"If we can't redeem the Sutton Debs' reputation, we flip the script."

A look of dawning comprehension fell over Casey's movie-star-handsome face. "We change the parameters."

"Like Leticia and Mary Gerald in 1879," I affirmed. "The world had never seen a sisterhood like theirs until they invented it."

"Maybe there is something . . ." Casey reached into his man bag, unfolded a paper, and spread it out on the Formica tabletop. I read it once, then twice, then looked back into Casey's gorgeous baby blues. "What are you suggesting?" I asked, wanting to make sure I understood before I got too excited.

"We can't rescue the reputation of the Sutton Delta Betas. But we can build a new one."

I put my finger on the paper and read it aloud. "Win an all-expenses-paid spring break in Myrtle Beach. Bad girls only. Good girls need not apply."

"It's a contest," Casey gushed unnecessarily. "For the naughti-est sorority chapter. It's sponsored by this record company, and I think the Sutton Debs are a shoo-in. It's not even fair for the other contestants."

"Because their chapter advisor and S&M director have both been arrested for murder?" I asked dryly, the bitter truth stinging the back of my throat. This was nothing that I'd ever imagined for my chapter. When I'd arrived at my alma mater four months ago, I was proud of the ladies' high standards, our spotless reputation, and our dedication to ladylike decorum.

But not two minutes ago, I had made an impassioned plea to shift the paradigm. Change the rules of the game. Was this what would save us?

An all-expenses-paid spring break on the coast with . . . . I referred back to the flyer and the list of superstar music acts that would be performing that week. If we won, the girls would be granted all-access backstage passes and be guests of honor at the resort. Other prizes included makeovers, vacation wardrobes, and the use of convertibles during spring break.

It sounded like . . . good PR.

When I raised my head and saw Casey's eyes gleaming, I knew we were on the right track.

"If you can't beat them, have a damn good time anyway."

"Living well is the best revenge?" I mused.

"Exactly." Casey grinned.

The more I thought about it, the better it sounded, as Casey's ideas always did. Sure, it would sting a little to put together a video highlighting our bad rep and not trying to ignore it didn't exist, but if we won . . . The list of prizes, the fun of hanging out with A-list possibly illuminati pop stars, and glamour would bring us if not respect, then envy. And that was almost the same thing.

"I'll have to put it up for a vote," I said slowly.

"They'll do whatever you tell them to do."

"Should they?" I made a face. Like I had told Mabel, maybe my leadership capabilities weren't what they once were.

Casey reached across the table and enclosed both my hands in his. "Mabel believes in you. I believe in you. Even if you leave at the end of the summer, this will be your legacy."

Wow. My legacy.

I had never thought of that before.

Was this the legacy I would leave to Delta Beta? To the world?

As we drove back to the Delta Beta house, Casey and I were silent, probably both wondering whether we were bikini ready for a bad-girl spring break, and I kept coming back to the legacy of

Mary Gerald and Leticia. One of the things that I had always admired them for was that they were leaders in a time when women weren't expected to take charge of their college careers, let alone their lives. They created something new, something they believed in, and made other people's lives better, even when everyone around them was telling them they shouldn't. Or they couldn't.

By the time we had returned to the Delta Beta house, I was as determined as I had ever been.

Following the example that our founders had shown us, I would recommend to the chapter that they embrace their bad-girl reputations and start a new era of Delta Beta sisterhood.

Maybe it meant we would all be wearing bikini bottoms with BAD GIRLZ emblazoned across the rear and leading a twerking competition in front of twenty thousand spring-break attendees. It probably meant I'd be drinking heavily from my Delta Beta flask.

But we'd be taking charge of our lives, doing it together, stronger than we'd ever been. Which was sort of the point of everything that Delta Beta stood for.

About the Author

LINDSAY EMORY is a native Texan and recovering sorority girl. She is also the author of the contemporary romance *Know When to Hold Him*.

@Lindsay_Emory
facebook.com/Lindsayemorywrites

Discover great authors, exclusive offers, and more at hc.com.